CHILDREN
OF A LESSER
GOTHAM

D1524333

CHILDREN OF A LESSER GOTHAM

CHRIS KUBIAK

Rendered into English by Marian Polak-Chlabicz

PENUMBRA BOOKERY
NEW YORK

English rendition by Marian Polak-Chlabicz

Copyeditng by Chris Gelardi

Book design by MPC Graphic Studio

First edition: May 2021

Published by Penumbra Bookery
New York

ISBN 9798509045011

10 9 8 7 6 5 4 3 2 1

PRINTED IN THE UNITED STATES OF AMERICA

To the Homeless

CHAPTER ONE

"O my God, I am heartily sorry for having offended you. I detest all of my sins because I dread the loss of Heaven and the pains of Hell, but most of all because they offend you, my God, who are all good and deserving of all my love. I firmly resolve, with the help of your grace, to do penance, to sin no more, and to avoid whatever leads me to sin. Amen."

"Son, in my long ministry, I haven't met with such wicked and villainous behavior! Your sins are egregious. If I had to express them in words describing weight, I would say they are as heavy as well-fattened hogs (of course, with curly tails). And you have not even blushed with embarrassment."

"I assure you, Father, my soul is heavy. It's hurting as if it was covered with burning wounds, as if it was just taken off a gridiron, and hence my body is ailing."

"Your soul is burning and your body is ailing. What did you expect? And what about them? I know what you want to say: it was not your fault—they were to blame. You think that your behavior was just innocent fun. You do not even realize how many pairs of eyes follow each of your strides, how many pens record your life, how many cameras capture your life. In the future, someday, everything will be replayed, read out squarely and judged fairly. Do you recall, at least, how numerous were they?"

"I am ashamed to admit, Father, but I haven't counted. There were too many of them."

"That is bad. That is too bad. You are acting like a braggart, and only one place is appropriate for such persons!"

"Is it really bad, Father? Are you suggesting my place is in an infernal cauldron?"

"I am in doubt, but it looks bad. I do not really know what you are facing tomorrow: furnaces or Ferris wheels or vats, and for what sins an evildoer can land there. No one knows that. I can say only one thing—which is universally known—that there are four major hells on earth and under its surface: Jewish hell, Muslim hell, Hindu hell, and our Christian hell, this very familiar one. All of them are full to the edge, guarded by hell's best sentinels, albeit when someone asks insistently for an accommodation, it always be given immediately to them. However, where exactly the devil's abode is, we just do not know it yet, we do not know the road."

"So, there is a vague outline of this matter. Has this information been thoroughly verified? Frankly, Your Excellency, you've sown the seeds of fear in my mind."

"There are no direct leaks, but there are some indirect disclosures; however, they are difficult to decipher. Let us hope we will soon unravel these eternal mysteries. We will disperse the mist that enshrouds them tightly. We shall get to know the forces prevailing throughout the devil's abode. We shall break the wings of the griffins safeguarding keenly the code."

"Are the matters under proper supervision, in the right hands, ignored by no one? Won't this unknown and unbridled force slip out of the darkness and rule the world? It would be a bleak thing if this fallen fellowship found a tunnel and set out on a journey to our land."

"Do not worry about that. The most prominent representatives of physical and natural sciences deal with the subject of strange signs, keeping their guards. They have labs at their disposal, which no one has ever dreamed of. After all, there are more things in heaven and earth than are dreamt of in your philosophy. Royal domains in the lead with phenomenal engineering and meticulous mechanics are kept on polymaths' tight leash. Backward evolution is just behind their backs. Moreover, there are only hermetic, sophisticated arts, and, in them, a series of smart tricks, having nothing to do with cards. And there is nothing ordinary in them. The compressing of the cosmos is extremely easy for them, as is the stretching of water. The scholars will use all of them in this uneven fight. They will never approve superstitions and lies."

"It's elevating, Father, what you're saying, but hasn't science been successful in this respect for centuries and constantly on the offensive? Isn't it written in the old books what it looks like 'there'?"

"The books were written rather vaguely a long time ago and predominantly drew on legends. Their parables are contradictory. To tell you the truth, a sage's magnifying glass and eye are inadequate here. What is necessary is a drastic provocation in order to bring out that which is out of sight, in the darkness, and access the contents hidden there."

"What would it consist in? Could you unveil the secret a little bit? I'm very curious."

"The subject matter is not simple, but exponible. Appealing. The point at issue would be to find those willing among the host of sinners—defendants, those still without a sentence—and to send them on a journey to the edge of life, leave them there and bring them back after a year. There would be a chance that some dark matter would come out of hiding, showing its shape to those unfortunate people. Then they would tell us what they saw from the very edge. Or, what else in our wildest dreams appears here: it would be possible to employ a stratagem to lure out the force, and behead it—if it enfleshed itself. Or to burn it in public—if it had more heads than one and resisted. Everything filled with cheers of crowds, dances of joy— to an accompaniment of cymbals. We owe this to the people, after all, they are brave, tax-paying, exceptionally simple citizens. Until then, such a thing happened that God gave the devil sinners into captivity, losing His control upon their fate. There is a certain antinomy here, because, if God is omnipotent, how can you explain this fiendish power right under his nose? When hell's abyss disappears once and for all, our eternal damnation will take on a different form. We will free the sinful continents from fear, destroy the whipping posts erected for the people. The joy of amnesty will prevail forever and all bastards, scoundrels and other faex populi will return to favor. Everyone will cry out: 'Hully gee, let's party, there is no hell!' until the walls are shaken, the bridges are broken, and the earth comes out of its frames. He will go straight there—as if to be burned at the stake for the instance which he does not understand, a laughing, happy and simple man, with wind in his hair and songs on his lips. And if anyone did oppose, stay behind, or hesitate, it would mean he was a man of the fewest words, he betrayed, he was a virtuous oaf. So, one has to find volunteers, for time is running out, and the matter is urgent and grave, lest the unleashed prodigal should mix up his way, lest he should go back to hell, but sail straight to Heaven—where, alas, the sun will be no more."

"Father, why have you glanced at me as if something occurred to you. I'm listening humbly to your discourse and drawing conclusions. What's more, I have fear of heights and my eyesight is somewhat failing. I'm still young and have other cares of the day in the main. Maybe, instead of me, those unfaithful women go up in flames?"

"I shall not breath a word whether women are unfaithful or men are lewd. I am not to judge. I am under the seal of secrecy, and I will pass it over in silence. However, if you wanted to send so many persons, you would need a long train or a huge bus. Now, returning to you, my prodigal son, such an idea has dawned in my head here that you could be the first volunteer to know the truth because you are so skillful and young. You could also earn a slice of bread."

"I'm not short of money, as I've already mentioned. Neither am I John Glenn nor Yuri Gagarin. I don't want a blessed vessel with me inside to plunge into fire."

"Someone, son, has to take on this challenge. Maybe, listening to my discourse, you will not adhere to your stubborn opinion anymore. Science should not go backwards, but forwards, and all your talking is to no avail here. You furtively laugh, hiding your joy in the cuff. However, we agree on one thing: life is too serious not to mock it; therefore, we repine at seriousness with pleasure. And, since so serious is life, imagine what death must be like! Because it hides so many secrets, get ready for the journey, it's time to win this fight."

"Oh no, Father! There are better disciplines of sin than me—those on pedestals. I have a little plinth under myself. I can listen, but I'm not going to change my mind. And this is why I will show them a gesture of incompliance, as a sign of my strong will. And, to say the least, overstated are my sins."

"You are bantering with me like a seventh-grade schoolboy, even though you graduated from the best universities. Maybe it is fate that has chosen you as the protector of the human race and shown you the way to me, predestining you to fight the sinister force, shoulder to shoulder with God. From the Creator, for this deed, you will receive some prize when you appear on the fateful day, as a defendant with the downcast eyes, before the court of the saints. And do not let your flightiness prevail, because you can crush the walls of hell's fortress only with faith and sense."

"What's gonna happen if I don't return from that journey?"

"Then you will render service to the cause and the others."

"Before I had come here, I tossed a coin, and it turned out I didn't need a human word to prove the existence of God. The coin pointed out that one didn't go to Heaven for being highly articulate, but for modesty, honesty and praiseworthy acts. Dear Father, isn't that apparent?"

"So, where did a barbed wire on your biceps, a cobweb on your elbow, and a dragon around your legs come from? So, where is your modesty in the name of the Father and of the Son and of the Holy Spirit? Why have you thus chosen? For what reason?"

"Father, that's where my penance comes from. The body is covered with the mistakes of youth. People have their five minutes of folly in life, when they live large, have not too many duties to carry out and not much work to do. That's how it sometimes happens. But I see nothing can be kept secret from you."

"People will report anything on anybody—out of boredom and out of envy. This is how their right prevails. They have no mercy for the rich in money and mind. Did the coin come down heads or tails?"

"It landed vertically, on its rim, ignoring the Earth's gravitational force. It stopped my decision, and, furthermore, confused me to the core. I was going to get drunk—though I fight shy of honky-tonks, and I'm not a bibulous guy—but last night I dreamed about a sinner-faced clown, who whipped me to a church. And he flogged everyone—the old and the young, the hale and the frail, popes, bishops, servants and kings. He drove all of us to the church's confines. That dwarfish guy of the deepest dye under the sky in which the moon didn't shine for a long time, that sinful gargoyle presented an extremely repellent appearance. He refused even slice of bread to a starving man and berated even small children and women. As a further matter, he used to laugh scoffingly, even scurrilously. I've squandered good money my whole life, but starting from today, I will always stand by the bride of Christ because, in my dream, I've received the hints straight from God. That's why I stood in a long line to confess my sins."

"You are so much of a mediator and seasoned trader, but defeating all the ignoramuses and Hydra is in our best interest. The controlling of people's minds is a common thing. Therefore, we need a good reform, not a hypocritical one. Before you came here, we knew your case from other penitents, complainers rolled into one. Maybe, if you firmly resolve to behave better, not a hair of your head shall be touched. For now, you can sleep well—our investigation committee is fighting a different war. However, it does not mean that the sufferings of sufferers will never be avenged. When you are up to no good again, the judgments that have not been made will be reinstated. Rethink your irresolution. Let me send you to the edge of life before something unpleasant happens to you. Perhaps it looks scary and sends shivers down your spine, but a temporary inhumation is straightforward, just like any magic. We will measure your body with a volume meter. Over it, we will conduct a few secret rites. We shall incense the limbs, we shall swathe it in a shroud—and until you descend, and then awake—we shall set a guard so that your flesh should not decay."

"Father, sated with doubts, I'm asking you once more: what will happen when I don't come back from that journey?"

"I am repeating this refrain as I see you only want to pose and pose questions: only then you can render service to the cause and other persons."

"Your Excellency, I have to defend my own honor, not the remaining dorks. I am not afraid of the Highest Court, and as I am kneeling before you, and not standing, I swear I always reach my hand just for what's mine on my own land. And I do vouch for my righteousness. Even if it was a harmless hypnosis or incensing with a secret thurible, whose results could be neither experienced nor augured. I want to go neither through the dark tunnel nor the light corridor. Last night I dreamed about a sneering jester, and it's a bad sign. Holding a bullwhip behind his back, he asked, 'Will you die on behalf of your brother?' I said, 'I will,' seeing he was very sad. 'And try not to die!' he crossly replied, 'Cruel fate and anger shall befall you.' That's how that smart haranguer threatened me. But I'm not gonna budge an inch from my views."

"Frankly, for all intents and purposes, you don't have much of a choice here. When the die is cast, they will claim their rights to you, and they will not ask."

"How come? Without my permission?"

"I see that you underestimate our abilities. We can send anyone on this distant journey when we receive the order. We can put the screws in you: it's an extremely simple procedure. The tax machinery is more effective than the heaviest flogging. We want to encourage you with a good word, not with a scourge of control or a merciless anathema, which means that a different turn will take place when the tax shepherds knock on your gate. Faith has not yet perished while we are alive. What Satan has taken away from us, we shall take back without delay."

"Father, we don't live in the Middle Ages. People fly to space, to the boundaries of the Solar System, and even farther. And you're telling me stories about plagues and excommunications. Who hit up on the idea of provoking God along with Nature?"

"This lofty idea was conceived during the Great Symposium. Scholars reached a conclusion that it was high time to break the monopoly on the sacred and unanimously adopted resolutions on that matter. The most talented speakers, supported by connections, delegates from different departments, obtained engagements—and they wrote reports and petitions in Greek, Latin, and Morse code. The Congress lasted two days; however, under the authority of the Supreme Committee and at the instigation of the Holy Office, they drastically truncated that text. They also expurgated debates that elucidated nothing, and then, they discarded unimportant conclusions and fake news. Next they submitted the document to the Supreme Council, which, in turn dispatched it according to the protocol, via the most official and special diplomatic channels (not via grapevine) with unforgeable seals and the most-favored nation clause, directly to the higher authority. The protocol adviser together with his chief clinched the matter, and after their detailed analysis, forwarded it via diplomatic mail with a classified memo. In that way, the written decree of the positive sciences report reached a straight, albeit very pot-holed road leading to the oak desk of the Capital Monsignor, who previously was a minor inspector in the Major Inspectorate, and who now titularly is an august faith ambassador. The Most Secret Chancellery approved the report (including all the resolutions), re-encrypted everything and, slightly tardily, deigned to dispatch it to the world—to all its four cardinal points. Then they announced the news to all and sundry, and trumpeted the triumph through the mammoth megaphones of their mass media friends."

"Couldn't they send that secret letter by e-mail, postal mail or a homing dove? It would cost less than enough."

"The authorities do not tighten the purse strings when it comes to sciences—provided that they prove what the members expect. But I see you have a big mouth, standing up for homing doves. You strike the same notes as our critics, questioning the existence of the holy capital and facts from the distant past. We know who is inimical to us and what the title of their anthem is. This is neither 'The Song of Roland' nor the holy psalms, but the vibrant 'Ode to Joy.' And did the apostles have their own capital city—the seat of their government? This, for obvious reasons, cannot be determined. However, we shall also determine this if the need arises. I shall share some secret with you, which was revealed to me in confidence, with honesty by a repentant penitent just after he had confessed on the last Sunday: He was fired from a respectable post office and exposed to foreign post offices by the whim's anointed, serving 'His Wicked Majesty.' And although it is hard to make head or tail of all this convolution, he gave me a clear account of what had happened, not insisting, however, that I kept these arcana only to myself and put them in a drawer. That is to say, for some time secret service, not trusting couriers or messengers, trained homing pigeons. Feeding them only on odd days, they broke them up with hunger, and from dawn to dusk, they bewildered them to the wide. And when one of them rebelled and took flight, they painted its wings in démodé radiant red, and then such a dove became inconvenient for the rest of the flock, was destined to be pecked to death. And if it did not help, they clipped its wings and put it in the coop without door handles, with the inscription 'BEWARE OF DANGER!' And they locked the bird up. That painted bird was a proof that the trainers always found a way to avert the shortage of birds. They still had sparrows in reserve. And although they are less clever and are garrulous by nature, they can live on bread and water. After all, mind is not indispensable. And sparrows are more reliable. Even a clerk who disgraced himself by commissioning this roguery forgot everything and became a shining example of abiding by law and order. As long as he was in the spotlight beaming with its refulgence, we could be sure that nothing bad happened to the national lawfulness. Chaplains, rabbis, journalists, and the proletariat can sleep peacefully. For silence, favorable disposition, and peans, the authorities will generously bestow their love and honors upon you. But like any power, when put into a hypnotic state, its representatives will make a sluggish cross sign in the air, lying in a mortal pose, supine, afraid that they will be thrown into the dustbin of history ahead of time. He spoke his mind in these words: 'In the name of power, honors, and the commander-in-chief, who holds all the strings in his hands—we will go into battle as national pride demands as long as the commander-in-chef leads us playing the pilgrim of peace. We do not care about the fate of the Nation nor the reason for privation, and even if an ape ruled and undoubtedly drove us to war, we would give him our mandate of trust anyway. We will leave in time, when the country is drenched in their gore. Yes to heroism, but only if displayed by others, otherwise it is folly, my brother countryman. Let the people fight, bleed, and daydream. And though he feeds us on fragrant hay, we, ungrateful, will take the people for a ride, singing aloud for the leader: Glory! Glory! Halleluiah!'"

"Father, the world is freaking unfair."

"Go on, son. Do not abandon your pearls of wisdom. Let some of them be mine."

"When I was in disguise and asked for aid to the people, attentive to injustice, lost in thought, unrecognizable in solitude and among the multitude, but still fleeing from the crowd, heading for the gates of manors and inns, asking for food and support—I heard only a clang of reloaded guns, a clatter of unlocked cages with dogs, and terrible yawps. I told them then: 'I am a barefoot heir, humbly asking for a bowl of food and lodging for the poor.' At that time a curse came out of angry mouths, and it tasted of moldy bread. Also, I tasted that bread on which the poor are fed. When they found out who I was, the wrought-iron gate opened up before me. They no longer needed the army to guard the estate, even though they knew what a dictator I was in my trade. They bowed very low, knocking their heads against the floor. The curses became joyful arias and were no longer the same ire. Dogs readily ate from my hand, and servants (not so long ago shaking their fists) all of a sudden paid, so to speak, their devoir. Father, can you believe it?"

"People have only themselves to blame. When you show them respect, they are so nimble that in a moment you have them breathing down your neck. They jump on the back like a goat on a fallen oak. And to add to misfortune—all those never-ending countrywide spats."

"I know it's abysmally musty in the country. Because of the surface of our mortal shell, we should breathe in clean breeze, not suffocate ourselves and be continuously sad. It's so stuffy here in every place. Even on the green hillside that is covered with woods and is close to the skies. There is no clean air even in the City of Angels. These poor souls choke on human ignorance even after death. But, can we talk about all those noble investments that are to illuminate the darkness with a wonderful shaft of light? It is your words that the outstanding figures of all cultures have been attempting to enlighten humankind without a satisfactory outcome for twenty-five hundred years. I'm also afraid that it will share the fate of the philosopher's stone and will get stuck in the department of troublesome affairs and events for longer time, just like Noah's Ark on Mount Ararat, and the alliances there make no sense."

"Yes, these are my words, I do not deny them. I shall say more: The observations and conclusions contained in them are stunning to a great extent, but not surprising, and they are even expected. However, I shall defend the signed concordat and avoid any precedent. There will come such time when they will speak to a dormant mind, ignoring the laments and protests of thousands, and not asking, but forcing them to make concessions. If it were otherwise, the consequences would be fraught with trepidation. We already lost the only Son of God because of the unenlightened people. It looks as though there is going to be another loss of the next one who may come again—really soon. Malefactors always have more respect in the crowd than the saints. However, in order to give minimum justice to the other side, it is necessary to mention how recondite it is to renounce temptations and resist Mammon, especially by those who live off sin and human credulousness. It is in their best interest to petrify the dogma and keep Satan alive, as well as keeping people in constant disbelief. Therefore, we are building celestial telescopes without mirrors inside in order to look into the scenes of life and see what germinates. Guided by the newspaperish national viewpoint, combining the old views with the one of late—recently so popular and up to date, but so uneasy in our circles. We try to make soft circumstantial evidence hard; at the same time, not desiring to adulate the crowds nor make their minds turbid like muddy water, and not to give them hope that there is no hell. It is, however, in constant transformation, and it will soon take on the form that none of us ever has expected. Time is running out, and we are up against the wall. According to my knowledge and as felt in my priestly bones, the Supreme Justice is not so fell. It is true that the wall is now a sky-high barricade; however, the infernal torments are jejune rodomontade. Therefore, it is necessary to make the monad a more complex structure—a living organism strongly anchored in God, respecting Nature, able to perceive without mirrors its sinful face as well as lost time. Therefore, it is necessary to change blindness into omnipotent knowledge— for the reason that only knowledge saves the world from losing its collective mind and puts an end to inherited poverty. You know what I mean?"

"I'm doing my best, Your Excellency, but I must admit that your discourse is convoluted. It embroils me in politics and deprives me of emotions. It whirls through the canons ground to powder, making my head spin from hearing all this blather."

"Let me tell you something, young man: In all the bestiaries, annals, and journals by Hubertus, which are known to me, you can read that when you kick a dog, step on a frog, whip a horse, the Lord will give you the same suffering. And I can assure you that all wastrels will experience it if they like to see fear in our little brothers' eyes. When you do not like something in your life, you have to look into the eyes of the stronger and not bother the weaker. This is the courage and strength given by God. Animals cannot defend themselves and take shelter from the tormentor. They are defenseless and innocent like infants. Enchanted in this is all wisdom in order to examine who is a miscreant and who is a child of God. Those who will oppose it and call in the guns will be swept by God's fist from the face of the earth, and then they will be transformed into worms trodden on by humankind. This is how the Lord will pay them back. As for our illustrious figures, do they have any plan of action for the next century? I do not know, and I think that even the capital does not know that. Apparently, they play with our team, but they probably try to break loose from the chain. It will soon become clear whether they are doing it out of conviction or they are trying to deceive all of us. I only know that the budget is seriously undermined and our annates are running out. Do not tighten the purse strings if need be. Let your generosity render service to the studying of the beyond."

"Father, perhaps a different word was supposed to get out of your mouth. Or, maybe I've misheard, though I tried to grasp the sound of each word of yours."

"What I wanted to say and what came out is another story. My thought contained wishful thinking—but in it, there was also a concern for the future. Sometimes I have the right to commit a lapsus linguae when a wolf is kneeling before me, instead of a sheep of God's. It is not easy to turn a wolf into a sheep like it is not easy to turn abundance into generosity. But I promise that I will do my best."

"Your Excellency, you're judging my statements one by one

without mercy. It can't be disguised that this despicable wolf didn't sneak up to the sheepfold, but before the lion and was seeking love, though he could've remained with the servants in his warm home."

"Since you have come here uninvited to philosophize, try to find a sponsorship. I shall gladly listen to your advice."

"One piece of advice will come from my daring lips: Scroungers should be fired; expenses should be bridled. In such uncertain times, to be generous and live big is unbecoming, to say the least. No one should pay too much for a piece of junk."

"It is true that expenses are enormous. Bureaucracy is bloated. Erroneous decisions, for which you have to pay, are made at every level, not only at the top. All commissions have their subcommissions, and these in turn have their subsidiaries. Every commissioner settles another commissioner's hash. Moreover, on top of it all, consider their secretaries as their foot rests—who, by the way, are also quite well off. The secretaries are followed by clerks who carry folders full of files, putting a good face on a bad business. This is how the human chain—patiently and politely standing in line for money—sets the direction for science by choosing the longest route, not standing up to any criticism. The supervising authorities cannot deal with this matter because they do the same. Fortunately, the post of decision liquidator has not yet been filled. I do not know who will take the office, although it was previously established with me that the tribune must come from the people because someone has to comply with their will, taking care not to do any harm to the officials. I was offered a post in the Supreme Tribunal, as a reward for my service, virtues and other details. I have lived a peaceful life so far, although it is not easy to listen, from dawn to dusk, about iniquities and offenses I have never dreamed about before. I give advice both in the confessional and from the pulpit."

"Father, can researchers of Positive Sciences be trusted? Can you trust the results of their research and their assurances that they're going to make it on time? After all, it's the matter of more supreme importance than affairs of state."

"They are selected from an army of the best university experts. Comparative works have already been off like a shot, because time is running out. More and more sinners are coming, and the capital is pushing. They even prepare a delegation. Therefore, we have to hurry up and get ready for the soon-to-come discoveries, reconcile with whom you need and wait patiently. The new chronicles have been already prepared. The pens are waiting, and the hand that is supposed to fill them with not-yet-discovered knowledge is ready to do so. We are still waiting only for the 'supreme' official's signature. Nothing can be done without it."

"Is it going to change anything, Father? It's an old-established fact that white is black and black will always be white. It would be good to change something in human minds."

"That will have its turn, too. For now, with the new beginning, new law has to be created and new books have to be written. But it is not our concern anymore. We have scholars, by the way, of the highest honor, who deal with these matters. We will soon solve the riddle of all riddles. Recently, one of them, who, while kneeling before me as you, told me in the utmost secrecy that superstitions take a heavy toll among people. In order not to make assertions without substance, he gave me an example of the thirteenth floor—or, to be more precise, its non-existence. Because of this inadequacy, the residents had to climb a ladder from the twelfth to fourteenth floor. They are scared stiff of the number thirteen as the devil is scared of holy water, and yet the number thirteen is not unlucky. As a proof, he showed me his worn-out shoes in size 13, which he wore luckily for many years. His whole life was a streak of success. Although I must admit that when he rose from his knees and headed towards the gate, a vicar's black cat stood in his way. And what did the scholar do? He turned on his heel as if performing a pirouette, and, turning his back, he made his way towards the altar across the kitty's path. Moreover, he spat over his shoulder. Struggling with the spell, and to add power, he hit the vicar's hand and the offertory basket. After all, we have scholars, right?! They are going to take appropriate measures in the near future. They will compress any inaccuracies, put up theses, and then theorems. In the meantime, they will examine thoroughly all these phenomena, processes, and analyze them scrupulously, waiting for further instructions from their superiors. Their latest reports indicate that they have noticed in the phenomena and fauna a certain off-dimensional signal directed to our gray matter with the sharpest end. Here, I am going, son, to use a small cheat sheet, because there is a great deal of that, and my memory fails me when I am hungry. You will need this knowledge, although if I were in your place, I would not hurry too diligently to find myself 'there' to serve the sentence."

"I'm not in a hurry, Father, to enter Hell's abyss, and I'll gladly listen to what is going on in Heaven."

"Take the first example to come to mind: Only yesterday, we could see flashes of lightning in the sky. They took various shapes, for some reason, contrary to logic. Each of them jagged as a sprig of spruce—pricking the clouds with its needles—and each of them carried a message. The air was clean after them, even if they hit in the dirt on the ground. Their thunder was worthy of God, never squeaky. In my humble opinion—if I may refer to this phenomenon as long as God rules this world—a thunder will always be a thunder, even if a storm is weak. It will never be a swansong. Here, once more my digression: It should be the same as far as people are concerned. The Creator gave proud voice to humans. And what do they do when poverty and disappointment in love look into their eyes and push them down to the ground with a boot? They squeak like mongrels instead of biting on a leg as once did a Cossack to a Mongol when he clutched his noddle! Let us follow the trail of signs: a dance of the sun in the sky. Many saw the miracles occur, and crowds on their knees there. Did you not sneeze when you looked at the sharp beam without permission? How do you explain it, if not with an admonition?! An innumerable multitude of phenomena is manifesting itself to us here and riveting the attention of re-spectable scholars. Let us take another example here: an owl's hoot, which hides itself in a spruce. Do you think it produces the sound of the bassoon just by itself? Always after such hoot-ing, a funeral procession arrives at the cemetery. And a sparrow. Have you ever seen its beak trilling awry when it is hungry? It will follow you everywhere as a faithful mutt. You have to do no more than to throw a handful of grains to the ground and force it to fight, and it is exactly like people. Although there is plenty of food around, it pecks up a bite from the others' beaks. Let us think in a similar vein further: crabs. When we throw them into a bucket, they climb to its rim vying with each other. And do you know why none of them will reach the rim?! I will answer immediately because, as I see, you are slightly confused. As soon as one of them reaches the rim, the one just behind it, grabs its abdomen and pulls it to the very bottom of the bucket, slowly until the poor thing, losing the edge, flattens its face. Are not these also human flaws?!"

"I see, Father, you like to talk, and I get it. A confession without a discourse is boring and jejune! And with those hells, is it a serious matter?"

"Moderately serious. There are usually very mitigating circumstances. If, let us say, God would have to throw you into one of them for your offences, which of those hells would you choose to serve your sentence?"

"If I had a choice, I'd probably choose ours, the familiar one. Maybe I'd meet a fellow national. The more the merrier."

I see that you do not realize how serious the situation is. You think that the Supreme Judge will send you on vacation. However, if I am to judge your assumption, I think that your fellow nationals would have the entire city at their disposal, at least three long avenues."

"What about those other hells? Won't their administrators harbor a grudge against me for choosing 'ours?'"

"Do not worry, they have their own compatriots in a plentiful supply. And a human soul accommodates itself to a place, hence the administrators have a considerable problem to solve. They have been deliberating over this for a long time, in the hope that they will find a new eternal vexation, and that they will discourage people. This is not easy due to the nuances of faith. They will probably reach an agreement. After all, what choice do they have?"

"From what you say, Father, I assume that they don't have much experience in managing such a complicated Moloch of justice. Every now and then you can hear one of the devils escape from hell and prowl the earth. Hence people suffer such a great deal of injustice. The supervision is definitely insufficient there. I would organize it otherwise and even apply something from our earthly solutions."

"I see, son, that you are on good terms with earthly vicissitudes. Maybe you are right, maybe not, but with your ingenuity, you could help the Lord in hell's casemates."

"Oh, Father, I'm just considering, theorizing. I'm not in a hurry. By the way, I heard, when I was waiting in line for a confession ticket, people complaining about life, which is one mammoth machine for wiping sweat from their foreheads. You have to use enormous strength to turn the crank to set these huge cogs, gears, and shafts in motion, at the end of which a rag flutters and wipes sweat from the foreheads. One of them even said that once it had been much easier to have a place to live in and have food to eat. Does this rag symbolize nonsense?"

"Stupid is the man who shirks work. Were it not for that crank turned throughout their lives, they would know no ethos, but only mediocrity, and they would be condemned to passivity. And wanting to live life to the fullest and dream of prosperity, you have to go to work like a cart horse and turn the crank till the day you die. If I did not turn it, I would not be who I am."

"Fools should be ruled by fools, Your Excellency, the wise by the wise. Only then it would be fair."

"We do not need enclaves. Fools need to be enlightened, otherwise we will become like them ourselves. Besides, what can you know about living among the lower classes of society and managing the masses? One has to reign over them, because if they break loose, they will again bring misfortunes on humankind."

"Father, people have to get rich and enjoy life, and, just in case, when they have a moment of reflection, and when they mature enough—as I did—to share good with the right person, even give away everything."

"This wad hidden in the boot top and a silver coin under the heel? The bridegroom of fortune has just spoken in a human voice! Until now, you have lurched and plotted, and now, all of a sudden, the springs have spurted."

"This is not my credo, Father."

"You believe that?"

"People have to believe in something. Metaphorically speaking, Fortune had proposed to me before I met her. But now I want everything to be different."

"You have gotten cold feet. The feet of a prophet. Someone has foretold you something."

"People have their own familiar fears. I'm not afraid of mine. I don't get rid of them, just in case, not to attract the new ones, the unknown ones."

"Get serious, son."

"Father, I stopped being serious only yesterday. I went to sleep with very serious thoughts, and I woke up as a coxcomb with the matching coxcombic face. That's why, I've grasped the opportunity, and now I'm bothering you."

"Nice are your words. They sound nice, but they have no meaning."

"Your Excellency, in contrast to your words. Your voice is soft, but I can hear a scream in it. It discomfits me and clips my wings. It doesn't allow to—"

"I am not going to debunk this truth, neither will I confirm it, but it begins to rile me. You are bothering my soul and I cannot let you do that. So, kneel down and swim with the flow, otherwise you will never reach the destination. Since you are here, swim!"

"Your Excellency, you were swimming, and you swam up to the shore, but now you don't allow others to reach it."

"You do not have any right to gain authority, but you are philosophizing and giving me cheek. Through what hoops have you jumped so far?"

"I was struck by a moral leaning. I had an internal imperative to do harm. On top of it all, this continuous mood swinging, and then some. bulls, and bears, and indexes."

"If another opportunity arose, would you take advantage of it?"

"What are you talking about, Father?"

"If somehow you had a choice, would you rather be a cherub or seraph?"

"I don't care. I just want to be close to God, and that's it."

"I shall do my best to realize your dream, but be patient."

"God bless you, Father. Let every day be friendly to you and let your heart never bleed."

"Those social ties that have not trammeled you are still waiting for you. In this day and age, it is not worth being a recluse."

"For a long time, the general public's matters have been unimportant to me."

"Envy was—and maybe still is—your cardinal evil."

"You're too stern, Father. What else do you know about me, which I don't know about myself?"

"Who would not know your tricks, young man? You throw away pennies from your wallet and your worries along with them. He who stoops to pick up the coins becomes a new proprietor of your worries. You have concocted a really cunning plan."

"This is an old superstition, Father, but thanks to it, everything is as if by enchantment. For my worries, I gladly add a silver coin."

"You have already exhausted the limit of vain words. Taking a shortcut, most frequently, turns out to be going around and around without any goal. Get rid of that crafty scorpion from the boot before it kills you."

"There is no spike or word that could hurt me. Life has made me immune to all venoms."

"Hmm . . . it is quite the opposite than in my case."

"Father, auditors are always treasured and welcome, and others jaw away into their ears, compulsively and without restraint. They have no respect for sacred places. They palaver and palaver for the sake of palavering. They confess for the sake of confession, even sins that are not theirs. Just stop, cut, and barge in. The ears aren't of wood, and they get red-hot quickly."

"Maybe so, but it would not be appropriate."

"Your Excellency, if this piece of wood had teeth, it would bite each of them. They cook up stories just to be heard. It tastes so good Sunday purity! They come here like to a municipal bathhouse. The one who is really dirty will come in disguise and ask for clean, icy water. I know it from my own experience."

"It is easy for you to say so, son, because you do not understand. There comes a stage in life that you absorb all these impurities. Whether you like it or not, you absorb them. You drown in this slime instead of fawning as a dog licking its paw in peace. Hence nocturnal fears, blood pressure spikes, and photophobia. They will not wash by hand, but they will come with armfuls and stick them into the ears like a ramrod into the gun barrel. And you have to sit quietly and listen because if you do not, they will complain, suspend, remove. Afterwards, they will stand for hours and fix their wolfish gazes in the hope of some divine sign that their sins will be absolved. But the bells are silent, the storm goes away, and the sun hides faster than usual. Nobody wants to have anything to do with them. They wait for someone to do the laundry for them, starch the washing and, what's more, clothe them. But how much burden can I carry on my back? They do not care. They throw their worst sins onto the impious pile of iniquities, even if the faults are false— instead of changing for the better and starting a new day with joyful thoughts, and doing a favor to at least one fellow citizen. Little pleasures are also important. Even so, I do love them. Yes, I really do. You have not misheard. I have noticed that a word is taking shape on your lips."

"Before people like you, Father, let kings kneel down as if in front of a sacrificial altar. Let the party princes, who've never done any good to anyone, pay tribute."

"We have beautiful temples built of stones and bricks, and the same hearts. It would be sufficient if they do not pass by indifferently and stop to think of their homeland and all its children because they should. And eventually, they have to reach a higher level of morality. It is not cirrhosis of the liver that will kill them, not a scorpion, but their own impurity. Those who were foretold of their imminent death, those playboys, survived all the others. And they ignored temptations and luxury most. Those who listened patiently went wild. Also, I am fighting a losing battle; therefore, I do my best to defend myself against savages. Such barbarians always look at you as prey, not otherwise. Therefore, I feel better in the vineyard. I am listening also to you, not interrupting you, although I am itching when I hear that it is the fault of fate. The piece of wood will not bite you, either. However, it definitely wants to take you by the scruff of your neck."

"Me, that's different, Father. Nothing can bite me anymore— neither in my boot nor in my conscience. False friends are the only thing that chafes me. They're like wolfberry and ivy."

"The situation in which you have found yourself, son, is unenviable, and it demands of you to be aware of its gravity. And, if I may say so, if time has some highness, it is now the highest time you sat down against the wall—which you have separated from the world—and start crying. Perhaps your sincere tears will soften it rather than it burst under the pressure of your stubborn head. Let it be your personal Wailing Wall. And do not wait until things turn out well, circumstances happily coincide, and events accidentally entwine, because they will not save you from the ultimate responsibility."

"Your Excellency, I stopped believing in myself some time ago. I even don't like my handwriting anymore. Maybe because things are different. Once to the left, once to the right, and even up and down. It is not always as I intend. It isn't easy to trundle the wheel of fortune on the fields of the poor, either. It can fall apart like a horse's fart. There are too many who want to jump away from poverty to a safe distance."

"The nature of your thoughts, son, is too convoluted. There are too many contradictions in them."

"Because I don't care about the world's micro problems? I was created for the bigger ones."

"Hold your tongue. It is by those like you—in the fields where the poor found shelter and contempt along with disregard and pitched their camps. People who are silent should not be silent, but they are because of people like you—bribed in their dreams. But soon anger, hatred, and contempt will collapse as Rome once did. And their disseminators will parish along with them. This is God's idea. Do not avoid honest life because it will take from you exactly that which it wants to take. Even if it happens with your last breath, with your last honest stare of deceitful eyes. Now it is time to give orders."

"Father, to whom?"

"To yourself, and absolutely carry them out. People wake up too late, in the middle of their lives, or in the evening, when it is time to die, when it isn't within their reach. They think that they still have time to have a black oak coffin made, with spacious drawers into which they will put everything departing to the other world. People like you do not like people. They are parsimonious. In fear, they look around with worried eyes throughout their lives."

"Is it written all over my face?"

"In every gesture you make. You are immersed in glaring

consumerism. You are quite a fat lynx, fattened on other people's suffering. But remember, it is easier to excoriate such creature."

"Your Excellency, do you know that people like only fat lynxes? They hate those that are thin or those that can be ridiculed and mocked, without any consequences. Why should I share this with them? I prefer those who have squandered their wealth—frittered and drank it away. Those fallen and fortunate again. And, meanwhile, the poor despise the poor."

"Let us call a spade a spade—people like those who are more stupid than they are or equally stupid. All the rest pose a threat to them. The same may be coming to you when you believe too much in your lucky star."

"Father, I just try to keep the rhythm and hit the right sounds. And, so far, I've been good at this. I don't play out of tune, and I wield the baton like a knight—his sword. My orchestra plays a wild march, and, if necessary, it slows down and plays the waltz in three quarters and intones an angelic song. That's why, the notes I write change into gold."

"And others? What about the others?"

"Like I said, Father: Micro-problems are for micro-people. I'm not interested in pettiness. I wash the feet of those who are great."

"It is hard to fathom you, son. Increase the brightness of your lamp, because it is dark under it like hell, and I would love to see you knock on the gates of Heaven."

"Poverty has various faces, Father. Some are innocent, some are born out of confusion and laziness. Many have made art out of their work: the art of loafing around. And they are absolute artists in this—the last to work, the first to grub. There is too much artificial light in them. When they're out of power, they sit down and pity themselves. Their legs and minds rebel, and they quickly get used to comfort."

"What the family has spoilt, son, no school will unspoil."

"Your Excellency, I've graduated from many educational establishments, but I will tell you this: If we had teachers educated by Socrates, Plato, Leonardo, Frida—"

"Oh no, son, you have exaggerated here a little."

"Let me finish—Nietzsche, Goethe, Skłodowska-Curie, and the whole rest of the pantheon, we would've been a nation of their caliber. Anyway . . . you see for yourself who walks the earth."

"Stop talking about all those ideologies. It is not worth your trouble. Take what life gives you and do not complain."

"I also have a proposal for the Creator: I will send as many as I can to these fields. If He deigns to help me grow my capital, Your Excellency, I will remember what you've done for me."

"You are imposing conditions? Do you want to bribe me? You have only just gotten rid of your not-so-little hoglings, and you have lapsed into delirium again. You have gotten worse. The difference between us is that you, son, value highly material goods, and I value spirituality. Everybody boasts benevolence because it is in vogue, but nobody will go to live under the bridge in sympathy with others, even for two days, bearing in mind that there is neither hot water there nor servants . Hey, why have you become sad and hung your head?"

"You're reproving me, Father, but how do you explain I was standing for a confession ticket for two hours? By what right is a human being so humiliated like that?"

"I am a legislator here, and it is nobody's business. The most important is that it delivers desirable results. Who once stood in line was never heard of hereupon. In general, be happy that you have received the ticket. If it were not for the printing of a few dozens, you still would have stood in the queue stock-still like a fence post. Albeit I was informed that you bribed several money-grubbing slowpokes, and you reduced to some extent the waiting time for your turn."

"It's true, Father, I bribed, but only those dozed off, looking rich, and eagerly holding out their hands. I didn't want to offend others. They were decent people. I know those too well."

"Human interests are divergent. That which is the floor for some, for others is the ceiling. Therefore, you have to walk carefully enough not to rouse anyone from sleep. Like a cat hunting a mouse. But remember that not every cat is fat, though they sneak in the same way. A fat cat never bites the hand that feeds it, whereas an emaciated cat, familiar with nature's manners, a creature of honor, often scratches the hand, and catches it in its teeth. Therefore, it is still a sack of bones."

"Yes, Father, you've mentioned it. Which is worse: a rich man's wealth, or a poor man's poorness? A poverty-stricken guy who is envious, or, maybe, a man of means who makes generous donations?"

"Before I answer your question, I also would like to ask you something and to avail myself of the opportunity to ask for help."

"Go ahead, Father. Ask."

"Whenever you turn to me, you address me as 'Your Excellency.' I understand this—it is a universally accepted religious title. However, that is not why I have been turning the crank all my life, with the utmost effort so that a person like you addresses me as if you address your aunt and uncle at the Sunday table. Be more careful when you address people."

"Of course, Fath . . . Your Excellency, although I consider this relation rather to be a filial one. What do you want to ask about?"

"I am extremely curious about how you have prepared yourself for today's confession."

"Perfectly . . . without major problems, but with a small exception."

"Have you assimilated God's Commandments?"

"This is what I'm talking about! This is the exception."

"I am waiting. Show off your knowledge."

"Your Excellency, do I have to list all nine of them? It will be tough."

"List those that you know. It would do no harm to exercise algebra."

"Remember to keep holy the Sabbath day, Your Excellency; honor thy Father and mother, Your Excellency; thou shalt not steal, Your Excel—"

"Enough, enough!"

"Thou shalt not covet— "

"Enough, I said! I see that you have studied your lesson. Only preserve the prescribed order. It is important!"

"I promise, Your Excellency."

You can address me as 'Father,' or 'Reverend Father' or even 'Brother,'—just as you like. I think thus things will get better."

"As you wish, Father, Your Highest Excellency. I apologize to you for my levity. By the way, what about my question? I'd like to remind, Your Most Reverend Excellency, that it is about the tickets, for which people had to stand in line so long. I haven't received a satisfactory and comprehensive answer."

"You are really importunate. Let your curiosity be rewarded. I will tell you what I think about your world, although tomorrow I can think quite differently, because deleterious advertising exerts an evil influence on me, as well. I succumb to temptations as everyone. The one I recently yielded to was 'Spike Force H.' Can you believe it? Sometimes I am one of you."

"I don't know Spike, Father. I prefer modern craft. And I have passion for games."

"You can learn a lot from young people. In exchange for indulgence, they will reveal all tricks and techniques. My nick on the net is Joker. They say I have a knack for it. In this day and age, logic is unimportant. Quick reflexes are important."

"I've heard a thing or two—almost only good things, Your Excellency, but I would've never thought that Joker is you."

"What other than the good ones have appeared there?"

"They aren't worth mentioning, Father."

"Do not complicate, son. Go ahead."

"They uploaded photos from the casino. Those who lost money to you. No, I don't mean you're responsible for spinning the wheel, but at the opening, when you blessed that surrogate who was there, by sprinkling holy water with a silver aspergillum."

"You see how you have to be careful about everything. This is a classic example of a ram in wolf's clothing. The Internet is also a sabbath for the frustrated and the fearful."

"Returning to our passion, Father, also I'd like to fight fiercely. Preferably, to find myself in the middle of this cyberspace and see what it looks like on the other side. It would be an unforgettable adventure."

"Be careful, son, not to make wishes in evil hour because they may come true."

"Like I've already mentioned, I got rid of all threats. I'd go the whole way and shoot on a range or somewhere in caves. And you, Father, do you play in a band?"

"Well! I need to know what our striplings are preparing for the future."

"Striplings, weaklings...it's hard to foresee where all this will lead us?"

"So far, the rates are inexorably adverse: more and more games, fewer priestly vocations. These people bear bad testimonies. They fabricate all sorts of slanders. This is an enormous problem of the present time."

"It's no wonder, Your Excellency. You need to modernize the current machinery and allow more."

"Every new, valuable enterprise is ridiculed, derided and flouted by the hoi polloi. They prefer everything old, tested, and fossilized, and, although they have taken some hard knocks in their lives, they do not want anything other than that. A widespread mechanism has wrecked too much havoc in their minds. It will be hard to undo it. But when, in the end, worse days come, when a pack of wolves chases them, they will abandon everything and follow the shepherds. However, there will be no shepherds because they themselves have driven them away from this green meadow. Although we may also be guilty of bringing it on ourselves. Maybe in our flock there is no pluralistic counterpoint. Maybe the surrogates have ruled too long. I have already done my minima, and now it is high time you did your maxima."

"Come to the point, Your Excellency, and tell me what you think about our world. I'm beginning to fall into a slumberous trance when the emphasis in your orations dwindles to a trickle."

"On more than one occasion your ears will vibrate when I bash them with my words. So listen attentively to me and try to remember at least two of them in the last sentence. The world has gone to the dogs. All nations have mongrelized themselves. Everything is in poor taste and is for sale. Philosophical thought is less and less desired today, and we know what will happen to humankind when desire disappears. Humankind itself will vanish as well. After all, this thought, the mother of all thoughts, is so needed for human beings, especially now, when the unreal dimension steals so much time from us, distracting our attention from seminal matters. Nothing can make up for lost time. This thought has expanded and developed over the centuries like a beautiful plant. It has bloomed and bore fruit. Today, it is being unplanted and replaced by a delusion, an alien program, by someone else's not always healthy imagination—fed on empty words. People want to replace it with artificial intelligence. Woe betides us if this happens. And all the signs in heaven and on earth are that this will eventuate. Only divine intervention can prevent it. And this is what I shall pray for."

"Says who? This famous Joker? I am of the opposite opinion, Your Excellency. What we need is a stimulus—not only a material, progressive one, but also a spiritual one."

"Joker, Schmoker—all the same, son. Higher morality will always be in the first place. Today, profit is a major player—a huckster and a purchaser, a purchaser and a huckster. You can no longer distinguish who is who. Hucksters buy from hucksters and become purchasers. The wheel has turned full circle. The turbine of kitsch drives the machine of profit. Greed is fuel. Those who reject kitsch, wanting to shine with their own light, fade away and die, and along with them the last isles of wisdom. They disperse in billions of dust specks that suffocate and suppress natural light. Today, those who pay more are right and win. And those who sell more pay more. In order to sell more, you have to offer goods in low prices. And cheap is only what is simple, of low quality, that which reaches undemanding mind. And the outcome? Defiance and revenge. These are so well-known mechanics. We have to take into account the worst. Therefore, you have to be prepared for everything—even for death. We need to build a new ark. However, teak trees are expensive, and there are fewer and fewer forests. Our annates are also running out. Sinners sin excessively. They have become sin-addicts, ready to pay for it. So let them pay as you pay. If a penitent wants to confess to having wet dreams entirely gratis, I shall not refuse my ministrations, and I shall not give that person a reprimand. I constantly call up people to mend their ways, to come to their senses, but they have become accustomed to this like to the rainy weather in autumn. Thus, they continue to sin. They think that because they pay, they are entitled to buy Paradise. Poor beings. Nature the Great Tamer cannot cope with all of you; however, this day will come."

"Praise them for this, Father."

"I have a malediction on the tip of my tongue, but I will respect the majesty of this place."

"Don't be a pessimist, Father. Pessimism isn't a sacred thing. It's a profane thing. It wasn't him who made you eminent. Those who continually complain and complain, always have their place in the flea-filled tail, and thus they miss all honors. Sometimes you have to catch a bull by the horns and even by the—"

"Control yourself, son. You are not in a tavern. You have gone too far. Though, I have to admit that you are partially right. When I went to Wall Street, I saw human crowds standing in line to see the bull. They humped with joy and glee. I couldn't stop marveling each time I saw them stroke and grope that bronze bull on the head and on the rump."

"I apologize to you, Father, I've got a bit carried away. I didn't mean the bull's privates but an oar's blade."

"You do not have to apologize. Sometimes you need to call a spade a spade. A bull is a bull, not the Liberty Bell. Patriotism should be instilled in the new generation—not greed, not frailty."

"One has to pull hard on the oar batting the rapids with its blade, often sailing upstream. And those who patiently turn water back maybe will evade poverty. Believe in the prime mover of motivation and the nature of money."

"And when you run out of money? Who will stand by your bed when you ask for the last sacrament? Do not delude yourself. You will not receive the friendly hand that will give you a glass of water. It is better to have joy in your heart of justice, which is done in life, than to catch up in afterlife. If you want the world to regard you as a righteous man, reject egoism. It is the ballast that sinks boats in the depths of solitude, even the sturdiest ones."

"That's why I humble myself before you and God. I want to experience this joy that I haven't experienced so far. Make me a just person, please."

"You have chosen our Christian abyss. Let us hope that the Lord will take this into account, and I will do my best to help you. What must be done, must be done."

"Your Excellency, I haven't said I will do it of my own free will. I've only expressed my view. I daresay in my humble opinion that in order to punish someone, you don't have to send them unavoidably into hell's abyss."

"I see, my son, you have the gift of gab and retort, but keep in mind that the Lord can point at you at any time. A few more such wacky antics and your cell is a dead cert! By the way, a revolving one. And in Jewish or Muslim hell, they will take a tough line with you, and get ready to forget about performances by angelic choirs."

"Okay, Father. In that case, let me go to our hell—while the place is still vacant, and as a volunteer. For the public good. You've convinced me."

"Wait, do not be in such a haste. You are not as bad as it seems. Give me a chance to do something for your case. What afflicts your body?"

"I'm gonna turn a deaf ear to that, Father, though I must honestly say it robs me of my sleep and torments me at night. The reason I came to you is not to complain and lament over myself, but I badly need a conversation with God."

"Pangs of conscience trouble you and do not let you sleep at night. And it means that a spark of humanity is still flickering in you and all is not lost. However, you must still wait for the conversation with God. Now it is time to make amends. Do you want to say anything else?"

"Your Excellency, I'm ready to make amends to the people I hurt, though I have to add—as my excuse—I haven't foreseen such drastic consequences."

"Do not excuse yourself. It only aggravates your situation. God does not like when people try to justify unbridled pride."

"You are right, Father. I'm ashamed of that and I'm waiting for you to give me penance."

"Wait until I knock on the wood three times. Let us pray. [Only whispers can be heard.] Our Father, who art in heaven, hallowed be thy name, thy kingdom come, thy will be ... forgive him ... he did not know ... made mistakes ... he regrets ... or maybe not, but at least he says so. [Still in a whisper:] Lord, I have a hard nut to crack, and I would say, it is an enormous stone—a very real granite rock. After what I have heard here, I would preferably sentence him to exile, heavy flogging, or deglutition of hemlock. But it is not me to replace you, Lord, and pass such severe sentences. I shall only fulfill your will, for I can hear your voice in myself, and I know what bothers you in people.

And if he lies to us that he regrets and comes here again in disguise, under an assumed name, I will prepare a surprise for him, the one he will deserve. I never thought that I would like to see the day when such an insolent lucky blighter would wipe the floor with his knees. So give me strength for delivering this difficult judgment because, God forbid, a comrade of his may cross our threshold with a similar litany and put my patience to the test. Let the pain that I have settled in my head, Lord, be soothed with a sip of wine, because, today, another ship is delivering such a large load of sins to our port. My forehead is blazing, and sweat is running down my spine. Bless you. Forever and ever. Amen."

"Father, I've been waiting so long. Can you speak to me?"

"Patience, my son! Can you not see how important a conversation I am having right now on behalf of you? Mollycoddled by your nanny's nipples, are you always so impatient? Stress-free upbringing has borne fruit here! You do not know the weight of your father's hand or schoolmarmish reprimands. New, progressive times influenced your personality traits and behavior. Here you will feel the scourge of God on your back. I already feel it. Your suffering has also fallen to me. They are coming, I can hear their footsteps. Soon you will receive what you have asked for."

"Whose footsteps are these? Who are you talking about?"

"Very soon you will see. I can hear them more and more clearly."

"I'm not urging you, Father, but let's get to the point. I'd like to have it behind me as soon as possible."

"You want to be the first to get everything right away, off the reel; however, starting from today, it is over. The gravity of your sin is massive, like a cannonball with which you have made holes in the sky. Now you have to patch it up. Starting from today, you will be the last in this line, and if someone wanted to push you out of it and promised shortcuts, do not be enticed! Remember one thing: Only the last will be the first, and the first will be the last. You will turn your cheek as God has commanded, and only you will hear His voice. And you will hear this voice only from the 'Last' lips."

"Father, I cannot make anything of what you have just said!

Your Excellency, could you please speak to me more clearly?"
"Do I have to explain what cannot be more lucid? How is it possible that such an ignoramus and sybarite has survived?"
"Forgive me, Father. I don't want to make you angry—I'm only asking for penance.

"I shall say it as clearly as I can: If someone comes here and bangs on the door, do not open it until you look in his eyes and hear his voice. The stranger certainly will use a ruse in order to enter your place, but don't let him in. Otherwise, this stranger will burn you like a piglet on a spit, pinch your skin with tongs, and make you imbibe a pint of good liquor to burn your entrails and enjoy your pain."

"I am not an ignoramus, Father. It's not fair what you've said. It's not easy to coax me and make me drunk on booze. So let me try this wine. Let me prove."

"Do not forget that I am judging here what is fair and what is not."

"Father, I hope you're not the one who deliberately puts liquor under the nose, tempts and entices with the noble idea of freedom. After all, you've said that evil trickles into people by using tricks. Sometimes being nested in a good word, it strokes vanity while causing us to relax our vigilance. And that it smuggles a bacterium clad in the uniform of a liberator, which multiplies forever, joining the ranks of weakness."

"That is too bad, son. Instead of a savior, you see a tempting serpent in me. Let us make a covenant. You will trust me and you shall dance to my tune, and I shall intercede for you wherever need be. Let us make a deal: For one day, I shall take advantage of this service of getting you back on the straight and narrow. Frankly, I also have many reasons to apologize to the Lord."

"So be it, Father, it's a deal. I rely on your experience and I hope I'll enjoy God's confidence. Pour it to the full so that we'll feel dizzy. Another sin won't make a difference, and, besides, it's our national virtue to fraternize in misery. When everything passes and returns to normal, we'll again sit on both sides of the round table, of our eternal barricade where it's so tough to find out who is saint and who is ordained."

"Here you are, son. Try this liquor. Do not be too afraid. I shall intercede for you as I have promised. Just do not nudge the goblet and do not spill the wine. Hold out your hand carefully and take the chalice in three fingers. The rug is clean and heavily starched for this occasion. It is much harder to remove wine stains than those on reputation. However, just in case, if someone comes, run away."

"Okay, only this once, only this time, only to be your drinking companion and for the sake of decency. Here is to you. Oh, Father, what power is in this wine? My head's instantly begun to spin."

"You see, son, it is autosuggestion that has occurred here. It is just pure water, with the difference that it is blessed by me."

"How come, Father? Everything here is suspicious now. These portraits and those dogs barking in front of the church."

"The beasts are hungry. They have sensed your blood. They are beasts too, only worse. You cannot trust them. Never. Remember, blood attracts blood. Now they are doing justice, not me."

"Are they dangerous? Can they hurt me?"

"There is no perfect crime. They do it because they are scared, because there is such fear in them that no one can describe it. This fear is everywhere. Everywhere and always. By day and at night, when one wakes up, it is always there. Always inside each human being. They are coming here. Be quiet. Put your finger on your lips and stop talking! This will help. And extinguish the fire coming out of your mouth. Hush . . . When we are speaking in whispers, we can hear them more clearly. Can you hear? They are conferring. They always lie, they pretend. If you say that you have no money, they will cut down a tree to cross the river and get what they want, and then they will deny, they will say that they were not home."

"Please stop talking, Father. We have to listen. Can you hear? The dogs stopped barking."

"Maybe they are sniffing at the door, maybe they lost the spoor. Try to crouch lower and start counting shots. . . but only those fired as a salute. I am more of a drinker, and the shots do not bother me at all. I am a seasoned fighter. By the way, where have you come from? Have you also run away?"

"But why?"

"Well, I do not know. Maybe they were throwing stones. Yes, they certainly were. They have no scruples, no sins. Do you have more sins except those you have confessed?"

"Like everyone, but not too many. Only as many as needed. And only the very venial ones."

"Because of your curl-tailed hogs, we almost have reached the bottom of the bottle. I have never thrown stones . . . however? Once, at a neighbor's dog, just for laughs when it did not want to bark. But these, now, near the church, are not common dogs. Are they tracking you?"

"No, I did not always have wounds. Not always. I never leave my tracks."

"Oh, is that so? What are they like? I saw them a moment ago. Everything was fine with them."

"No, those couldn't be my wounds. The dogs would definitely sense them!"

"Yes, I saw them throw stones many times! Therefore, I'm so severely scarred."

"Father, please, not so loud, or someone can hear us. Oh, can you hear the shed's door slammed. They're looking for someone. Can I take my finger off my lips?"

"Not yet. Do not forget that also we shall hide in the shed one day. And there, it is not always safe. For the time being, we are not in danger as long as we are in the church. They will not dare to enter this place. However, we cannot stay here forever, in this suspense."

"Father, I think they've already gone, as I can hear music."

"No, it is not music. Someone is snoring in the pew. Go, son, it is dawning now. You have accomplished your task."

"I will stay here a bit longer, Father. I have something to do."

"But it is not a court."

"It doesn't matter. Anyway, I don't have a lawyer and nothing to say to justify my behavior. But I have a stone as a proof."

"Courts are now busy with other matters, and the stones have justified as the end justifies the means. It will not be easy to find justice. However, I believe in human nobility, although God is silent on these matters through His servants. Look into the well afterwards. I have heard laughing and a splash at night. Maybe a stone fell into it. You need to pick it out. It will be useful for your defense and as supporting evidence in the future. But wait, I have forgotten, water is not there either. The drought has become more and more of a burden for a year or so."

"Maybe, Father, the one who was running away from the crowd was laughing?"

"No, they caught that one and hanged him—just a two-day hanging, as a warning. Tomorrow, they will feed him and let him go."

"What religion did he practice?"

"He was a human being like everyone. A hanged person does not care—God is one. Only those who dragged him onto the bough have forgotten about it. However, they also will be hanged. People are stupid thinking only two thoughts forward and one backward. And when they encounter the bough, they regret everything being in deadly fear, but it is already too late. Kick the stool here. Do not sweat anymore, poor fellow."

"Father, do you have a family?"

"No, I make only rounds of house calls on my parishioners and for other people's absolution. I am scared of my circle. Tomorrow I shall continue my journey. And you? Do not you intend to escape?"

"I have nowhere to go. My family forgot how I looked like. They are all dead. Father, are you a servant?"

"Yes, I have been serving for a long time, but I do not know for whom yet. Sometimes I have a moment of doubt, but blessed are those who believe without seeing. It is better to know the prayers to anyone than to hide in a haystack. It is not always safe there. If you ever erred, do not use fire. It is dangerous, it is only good for the moon."

"Yes, I know, Father. I try not to grope in the dark, as I have done until now."

"Where are you going, son?"

"I have to go here and there, and somewhere else. Wherever I go, troubles always find me."

"Why do you embroil yourself? Follow a straight path, build friendships, and be merciless to your enemies. Only then you can be respected."

"May I take my finger off my lips and blow out the candle? It's dazzling my eyes and there is no air here."

"Not now. You need to see them, just in case, and know what they think. I know—I have heard it more than once. After each salvo, they come to confession. It has become a habit with them."

"Your eyes are big, Your Excellency. They're glistening in the candlelight, and they can betray us. Get rid of fears or narrow them considerably."

"No, I cannot close them, I shall not be allowed to tie them up. It is out of question—only hands can be considered. I want to look them in the eyes when they cock a gun!"   "Father, you can go out and negotiate. Maybe it'll be possible to placate them, and they will go away."

"No! They will always be here. They come unaware and allure with promises, and then they laugh sneeringly. You must be guilty of something, since you do not go to confession on a regular basis. That is why, the investigators are watching you. Oh, can you hear that? They are laughing at someone and smoking cigarettes. Go! It is dawn now."

"We haven't finished yet, Father. And what will happen when I realize that I've forgotten the rest of my sins, leaving this place?"

"Then join them. There is one amongst them who once confessed. I know all of them, from the stack and the well—they are all the same. They were also hiding from someone. These days they write denouncing letters. And you? Who are you really?"

"I am innocent. I'm the son of my father. I used to be a bookbinder. I know that the book of books is not yet written."

"Aha, hence comes this rush. Everything for the sake of science. If you are dragged to the stake, say that you like vodka and tell them not to kindle fire, and tell them that these black books are as rare as white ravens. The people are always hungry."

"Hungry for what?"

"Being a witness to someone's downfall. Cursed be the one who strikes a spark that kindles the people."

"I don't condemn the people, though I don't want to fraternize with them. I've already suffered too much injustice. Now my countenance is ordinary. I've got rid of the problem."

"Did you suffer? Did you feel rejected?"

"Yes, but I'm not so brusque as you think."

"Brusqueness and suaveness. Austerity and leniency. Profundity and shallowness. Ups and downs. Praise and disgrace. Servility and pride. A freak and a human. A balance. Divine imperative. Without it, there would be no sense and fascination with life. There are people who serve and those who are served. An overlooked and forgotten paragraph of the ancient book of justice. Dynasties and lieges. A monkey and a mirror. Human inventions appealing to vanity. The First Cause of all wrongs and injustices. However, servility and service are two different things. Frills and whims. The sulks. Unjustified tragedy. Anger. This incomprehension of other human beings. Evil intentions at the service of good ones. Like looking reciprocally in the eyes. Each pair of eyes sees something different. Do not avoid someone looking you in the eye. Do not treat the glances as an assault but as an expression of admiration. Then you will have a better night's sleep. If everything has its opposites—day and night, and all that which I have mentioned earlier—there must be a better life and a better world. God will not leave us at the mercy of our own fate."

"Father, I know you have to talk to people. But how do you do it when everyone who listens and nods in understanding doesn't remember the first words of the last sentence. I bear no grudges against people, but against the system that handed over the helms to mediocrities."

"You cannot break through the walls. You can neither hop over the fence, nor can you jump through hoops. Many of the noble and righteous could not break the walls with their heads. You are not the first, not the last. You need to use a different force here—shrewdness. It is a blessing in disguise that reason does not always go hand in hand with beauty, just as monstrosity—with stupidity. God thought it up well. Ugliness is a human invention, not God's. If the appearance is not only a key but also a gateway to success, nothing will save the people. Sometimes the fist clenches itself on a whip. Ugly people clear the way for the beautiful, as do the hunchbacked for those standing up straight, the short for the tall, the sick for physicians, the wise for fools, dervishes for ayatollahs, and so on, and so forth. No such rules should prevail in this world. There is only one exception:

A blind man will never make way for a sighted one. We, too, should follow these tracks."

"Father, have you ever seen a bear stay out of a wolf's way? Such is the law of nature and no one should change it. The strong always dominate the weak."

"A wolf is a wolf and will always be a wolf. What is more, it will even assault a bear, standing up for its rights, even if it may lose its life in that skirmish. And people? Is it not true that a man is a wolf to another man? Many of them whip the weak, although they are weak themselves. Such people always have to take their anger out on someone else and they always look for victims."

"Your Excellency, would you stoke up my stake too? I have people at my beck and call, but they aren't servile."

"If you were a madman who wanted to rule the world, I would say 'yes.' However, you are different. Although your life is sinful, I see magnanimity and strength in your eyes. Do not tuck your tail between your legs, when you must bare your fangs. Be yourself. Do not change your appearance. You can adjust, but have the area where only you have access. Shake your fist when your family is in danger and do not beg for mercy. Pity and compassion are the bane of this the world. When you show them, they will hang such a load on your back that you will not be able to stand on your feet. Do not make trouble out of rudeness when there is no friendly word around. Draw strength from it. Use it as a weapon in the kingdom of bad words. Ward off pity and compassion before they beset you for good. Providence takes care only of the strong. And remember, the one who fights with a brittle sword dies from a hard sword. You can buy peace with submissiveness, but not in the long run. When you buy it, you will have to pay higher and higher price for it. When you see a flower, go carefully in its vicinity and delight in its beauty. And when the creepers surround you, make your way through with the sword. Let's drink some more water, just as an evocation of its taste. Cheers! Oh! How strong! I am confident that it will work on the devils! Lord, forgive . . ."

"Although I know it is only water—admittedly holy water —I will refuse, Your Excellency. Sometimes I drive like a tired chauffeur."

"I am in a better situation. Carriers lug my portable sedan chair-confessional. They shoulder it towards inaccessible places as well as towards turmoil—I call them 'shoulderers.' The highest of them, by height and rank, is the one who holds the right handle, and he represents the front guard. He is uncompromising and knows everything better. He gives orders when I'm indulging in a nap. Well-mannered, he does not wake me up unnecessarily. He is lame, but serves faithfully. The second one is deaf, but eagle-eyed. He watches the left flank. The third one is blind but with absolute pitch. He keeps the rear guard. And the fourth one, a signaler, is the smallest of them all, but he is the strongest. He holds up the right handle on his right shoulder while he gives signals with a flag in his left hand and indicates the direction. Nevertheless, everybody sings nicely, and it is very important on the march. Oh, why not have a fiddler on the roof to play for dancing? I have my eye on a young one. He plays so beautifully that my heart fills with bliss. And how he sings! He studied to be a cantor."

"Father, is that right to exploit the disabled?"

"Thus spake who? I would say: Why beholdest thou the mote that is in thy brother's eye, but considerest not the beam that is in thine own eye? I do not ridicule other people's fate. They are not disabled persons. They pretend. They just care about jobs, so they lie to me. As in the old adage: They take with the left hand what is given to them with the right hand. When I wanted to expose this bluff, I felt sorry for them, although I cannot stand pity, and I turned a blind eye to that. They have been playing this comedy for almost ten years, and I have gotten used to this so much that I sing this song with them going to this service in step with them. When they are in need, I will not leave them alone. I will hear their confessions and cheer them up. When the sun rises over these roofs and spires, we will keep going through sands and quagmires. Nowadays there is a shortage of confessors. There are no volunteers for service. Times change. Everyone chases after an easy life. Therefore, even 'Your Excellencies' are following this path."

"And Father, that lad on the ladder, struggling with a candle and scratching his head, who is he?"

"He is called Candlekindler, although usually he trims wicks.

Sometimes he puts myrrh in the censers, sometimes he does his apprenticeship and applies for permanent employment. You see for yourself the candle smoke—he just has no flair. But he has an uncle who holds an important office in the capital. Maybe he will contrive something. The boy will not stay long on the lowest roost pole. When he gets a command from his uncle, I will have to place him somewhere in the administrative office or in the garden. And if he fails there, his uncle will send him to be an envoy or attaché. With the coming of the new season, there are more job vacancies. For the time being, I am going to give him the keys. Many keys. He likes to carry keys. Let him enjoy this."

"Someone is coming here. I can hear footsteps. Father, don't put out the lights—this will fool them."

"Yes, I can hear them clearly too. These are well-shod footsteps. Beware of shod footsteps. But there is no light here, not even torch-light. Only candelabras are looming in the distance."

"I can't hear them anymore, Father. I think they have gone somewhere farther away."

"No, they just pretend to be afraid of them. Liars, they are liars. They are deluding us shrewdly so that people will be afraid of them. Oh, have you heard? Something has moved. Keep your eyes peeled. I will say a quick prayer."

"Yes, it's a good idea. Perhaps a sincere prayer will drive them away. As soon as they come, I'll tell them it is not us."

"They will not believe. They have their informers and spies. I know their tricks inside and out. They cover their heads with hoods, use codenames, and communicate with light. Oil lamps and torches. Flashes and murmurs are their specialty."

"Father, what stinks like that?"

"It is carbide or sulfur."

"Your Highest Excellency, where are we? I feel strange. And your fiery eyes, like tongues of fire. Who are you, really?"

"It is just water. It makes miracles. Would you like me to be him . . . but it is only your reflection. Take a closer look!"

"Is it my face looking at itself in your face? It's scrutinizing me carefully with its eyes, and, at the same time, knitting its brows as if it wanted to devour me."

"Yes, it is you all over. It has been only warning you, at least so far. You see, you have asked for a conversation and you have received a picture. Mysterious are resolutions. It is better to see oneself in someone else's face than to believe the mirrors. Mirrors lie. If it were not for mirrors, people would not hate each other. They would not feel so old or envious of others. Every reflection is a lie or an illusion. Only water mirrors treat people favorably. They reflect what really is in us. In them you cannot see your imperfections or bad moods. Those who look at themselves in water never spit on it. You cannot trust mirrors. They lie as a desert mirage. Let us drink a little more of this holy water to refresh our souls."

"Father, I keep asking myself this question: What is the smallest size of a water particle that can be called a droplet?"

"I do not know. I always shed a tear in this pre-eternal life, and, out of regret and longing, I sought for a safe place on earth. I will not return to the land of happiness. Too strong winds blow there, and there is too much noise in the ears, in forests, and in glades. The fewer roads lead to me, the better. My house was burnt here, and gusty weather is still there. All the time I am looking for my place on earth, and I listen to what people have to say. And they do not always have something to say. That is why, I still have to bend my head and dust it with ashes. I will not return to my homeland until the shadowy graves bother me with lights. For the time being, I mislead them doing my best and vice versa. As long as you applaud them, they applaud you, but when you pay no attention and fall into a reverie, they will trample you and hurl insults at you. However, you have to talk to them, seek an agreement. But remember, you must not succumb to the persuasion of your friends, because it is an instigation of envy. The helm of your ship rests in your hands. Have you found the answer to your question?"

"Father, are angels big?"

"Well, they are not small, because who would like to get out of the way? Do not say that—"

"Yes, mine was really large. He could reach the ceiling with his head. My Guardian Angel."

"You have fallen into a dreamy mood, kiddo. But tell me whether he had the wings."

"No, not like in the paintings. They didn't grow from his shoulders. It was dark when I was waiting for sleep, all alone.

First, a few gray streaks slipped by in the dark as if announcing someone. When I looked hard, the streaks and lines disappeared. I couldn't see clearly but well enough that I recognized. He stood seven or eight steps away. He was not flesh and blood, that's for sure. Rather, like a thick gray-brown cloud, like a hologram. He was very large, broad-shouldered. His wings— if I can call them so—were joined together with his shoulders as if he was covered with a wing-like cloak. He held them on his chest. His face was half hidden in them as if he was cold. He looked at me through the curtain of darkness, and I looked at him. His skin was also different than human—sort of similar, but not like the skin I know. He wasn't white either, but he had human eyes. I didn't feel fear, but rather something opposite. I never had siblings, and I felt like a little boy whose elder brother came to protect and take care of me. I'll tell one more thing: Even though his figure looked young—maybe twenty-plus years old—you could feel he had already lived for thousands of years. I was seized with serenity and a tremendous sense of security, which I had never felt before. It lasted for a quarter hour or more. When I fell asleep, all of a sudden, a bout of apnea expelled me from sleep. I looked at the clock—it was two hours later. I felt very bad. I couldn't catch a breath, my legs rebelled, and the wind raged in my head. Everything passed after a while, like a violent storm followed by silence."

"Perhaps it was not Guardian Angel who visited you . . . With that one, you can feel safe too. He may have warned you, admonished you for turning your back on people."

"I know what people want to hear, but I don't always tell them this. I don't want to win my friends in this way. Why do I have to be on good terms with the world? After all, the world is not serious. It's so hard to put on these masks every day, to take them from the cabinet and to put them back there. Each for a different occasion."

"People hear what they want to hear. Each of them is a different country, kingdom, republic, not excepting dictatorship; guarded borders, not excepting open ones. However, there is too much no-man's land in them and empty words to which too many claim the right. Today you are in alliances, tomorrow they will declare war on you. Only evil makes people better. A hunter and game. The eternal law of everything. You always told them what they wanted to hear; that is why they loved you. However, they will persecute you for not paying attention (even if only for a split second), for forgetting something, for not being yourself—your own conscience—for this mistake. They will not forgive you for that. But it is not the way to live your life. It is killing. They are constantly demanding this from you, as if by virtue of a decree—'The Decree on Non-Refusal and Flattery.' When you reject them, leave them, they will join the ranks of your enemies. And believe me this army is mighty, with enormous power. This little particle, the droplet you were asking about, eroded your rock in which you felt safe, but when you renounce them, it will hit like a waterfall against the stony bottom. When you want to walk dry-shod across the ocean of lies in order to save friendships, keep your distance. Overfamiliarity destroys every relationship. It will bestride you quickly. It will make a donkey of you. Ahead of you, there are only heroic deeds, and you will need a strong steed on whose back you will hang yucca-fiber nets. You will bring your riches into the world, for decent people. This is what intuition is telling me. Let's drink some more drops—each of us a deciliter. Let's drink. Confusion to the devil."

"Father, let's polish our throats as shoemakers polish their boots. Let's rest a little. It calmed down outside. Maybe they stopped eavesdropping on us."

"It will take a long time before they are wide awake. They are just waiting for your mistake and your purse. They keep narrowing the circle as hyenas—patient, watchful, hungry. Keep your ears and eyes open, even in sleep. The boors have received carte blanche for their lives. They can imbue it with whatever they want, including yours. Beware of those whose minds are effete, whose minds cannot control their animal nature. The world only then will be better, when it will have one common constitution. For the time being, there is not even a single punctuation mark. That's where we are. Oh well, let us hope we make it on time."

"Father, I apologize to you for my audacity, but don't you think stinginess and squandering wear the same pants? I mean each in a different trouser leg!"

"I will pretend that I have not heard it. A storm is coming up. It is about to rain."

"Father, let's polish our throats as shoemakers polish their boots. Let's rest a little. It calmed down outside. Maybe they stopped eavesdropping on us."

"It will take a long time before they are wide awake. They are just waiting for your mistake and your purse. They keep narrowing the circle as hyenas—patient, watchful, hungry. Keep your ears and eyes open, even in sleep. The boors have received carte blanche for their lives. They can imbue it with whatever they want, including yours. Beware of those whose minds are effete, whose minds cannot control their animal nature. The world only then will be better, when it will have one common constitution. For the time being, there is not even a single punctuation mark. That's where we are. Oh well, let us hope we make it on time."

"Father, I feel better. Let's go back to my misdeeds. I've just remembered something, though I don't know if it is an offense."

"Father, let's polish our throats as shoemakers polish their boots. Let's rest a little. It calmed down outside. Maybe they stopped eavesdropping on us."

"It will take a long time before they are wide awake. They are just waiting for your mistake and your purse. They keep narrowing the circle as hyenas—patient, watchful, hungry. Keep your ears and eyes open, even in sleep. The boors have received carte blanche for their lives. They can imbue it with whatever they want, including yours. Beware of those whose minds are effete, whose minds cannot control their animal nature. The world only then will be better, when it will have one common constitution. For the time being, there is not even a single punctuation mark. That's where we are. Oh well, let us hope we make it on time."

"I have a headache and, to make things worse, this damn whining! They must have caught someone in a net. The dogs are processing him and fighting for a better bite. They are going to catch all decent people. What mischief have you been up to now when I have been deep in thought?"

"Father, let's polish our throats as shoemakers polish their boots. Let's rest a little. It calmed down outside. Maybe they stopped eavesdropping on us."

"It will take a long time before they are wide awake. They are just waiting for your mistake and your purse. They keep narrowing the circle as hyenas—patient, watchful, hungry. Keep your ears and eyes open, even in sleep. The boors have received carte blanche for their lives. They can imbue it with whatever they want, including yours. Beware of those whose minds are effete, whose minds cannot control their animal nature. The world only then will be better, when it will have one common constitution. For the time being, there is not even a single punctuation mark. That's where we are. Oh well, let us hope we make it on time."

"An event from the recent past has made me realize what kind of rogue I am . . . Oh, the dogs stopped barking. Maybe they've finally gone."

"Father, let's polish our throats as shoemakers polish their boots. Let's rest a little. It calmed down outside. Maybe they stopped eavesdropping on us."

"It will take a long time before they are wide awake. They are just waiting for your mistake and your purse. They keep narrowing the circle as hyenas—patient, watchful, hungry. Keep your ears and eyes open, even in sleep. The boors have received carte blanche for their lives. They can imbue it with whatever they want, including yours. Beware of those whose minds are effete, whose minds cannot control their animal nature. The world only then will be better, when it will have one common constitution. For the time being, there is not even a single punctuation mark. That's where we are. Oh well, let us hope we make it on time."

"Father, let's polish our throats as shoemakers polish their boots. Let's rest a little. It calmed down outside. Maybe they stopped eavesdropping on us."

"It will take a long time before they are wide awake. They are just waiting for your mistake and your purse. They keep narrowing the circle as hyenas—patient, watchful, hungry. Keep your ears and eyes open, even in sleep. The boors have received carte blanche for their lives. They can imbue it with whatever they want, including yours. Beware of those whose minds are effete, whose minds cannot control their animal nature. The world only then will be better, when it will have one common constitution.

For the time being, there is not even a single punctuation mark. That's where we are. Oh well, let us hope we make it on time."

"Father, let's polish our throats as shoemakers polish their boots. Let's rest a little. It calmed down outside. Maybe they stopped eavesdropping on us."

"It will take a long time before they are wide awake. They are just waiting for your mistake and your purse. They keep narrowing the circle as hyenas—patient, watchful, hungry. Keep your ears and eyes open, even in sleep. The boors have received carte blanche for their lives. They can imbue it with whatever they want, including yours. Beware of those whose minds are effete, whose minds cannot control their animal nature. The world only then will be better, when it will have one common constitution. For the time being, there is not even a single punctuation mark. That's where we are. Oh well, let us hope we make it on time."

"Father, let's polish our throats as shoemakers polish their boots. Let's rest a little. It calmed down outside. Maybe they stopped eavesdropping on us."

"It will take a long time before they are wide awake. They are just waiting for your mistake and your purse. They keep narrowing the circle as hyenas—patient, watchful, hungry. Keep your ears and eyes open, even in sleep. The boors have received carte blanche for their lives. They can imbue it with whatever they want, including yours. Beware of those whose minds are effete, whose minds cannot control their animal nature. The world only then will be better, when it will have one common constitution. For the time being, there is not even a single punctuation mark. That's where we are. Oh well, let us hope we make it on time."

"Father, let's polish our throats as shoemakers polish their boots. Let's rest a little. It calmed down outside. Maybe they stopped eavesdropping on us."

"It will take a long time before they are wide awake. They are just waiting for your mistake and your purse. They keep narrowing the circle as hyenas—patient, watchful, hungry. Keep your ears and eyes open, even in sleep. The boors have received carte blanche for their lives. They can imbue it with whatever they want, including yours.

Beware of those whose minds are effete, whose minds cannot control their animal nature. The world only then will be better, when it will have one common constitution. For the time being, there is not even a single punctuation mark. That's where we are. Oh well, let us hope we make it on time."

"No, they are still here. I can hear the supervisor praise them. You say that your heart is heavy. I will give you good advice: Pour out a bucket of hot water on the soap castles in which you have set up your abode. Do not shun a woman, even if she was wise, but do not judge her by your own standards, because the sun's rays cannot be counted or grasped. Avoid aqua vitae like the plague. It would lead you astray by trickery. Before you know it, you will live on the streets."

"I don't drink, Father. If anything, once in a blue moon—just as I'm drinking now with you."

"Where is this smell, lingering over the confessional, coming from?"

"I don't know. After all, we only have drunk water. Maybe the sexton is drowning his sorrows as some kind of insects. I saw several beetles in the aspersorium."

"It is difficult to go through life when sober, when there are so many iniquities and base acts around. I know something about it. And who has to hear all this? Well, who?! You need to have understood for the priest in his strenuous service. But you, young man, would rather worry more about your suspensorium, which you carry under your lower back! Take care not to drop the jewels from it, and then they would roll under the confessional!"

"How do you know, Father, that my sword suffers?"

"I have seen many swords in my life. I know also the melody hidden in a voice. Shy eyes are like a seal at the bottom of a letter. I told you that I cured infertility with herbs."

"You didn't mention it, or it escaped my attention as a warning you gave me, but it is a fact, in recent years, after I lost 'something beloved,' I suffered terribly. Temperance is my tormentor. And that's why I know that money is not the most important thing in life. And if not money, then what? This is why I wanted to talk about to God. I'm full of grim forebodings."

"Teetotalism torments many people, but you can get used to it. Its sibling is routine. What boredom, being predictable. I think, eventually, ennui is better than cold loneliness. So how do you call the state in which you are now?"

"I don't know the name I would call it. Loneliness, the cruelest of all tortures, the saddest child of Mother Nature. It's unclear whose revenge and what it is for. It tortures me every day, burning me with a searing sharp blade. It cuts my skin piece by piece, and, in the end, when day gives way to night, it keeps my thoughts so tight that I can't escape from it and hide—even in the haven of sleep. I persistently drive the thoughts away, but they come back and circle like a bird trapped under the cathedral dome. And when, in the end, from tiredness, my breathing calms down, my pulse slows down, it wakes me up with the morning silence. Loneliness has no children. After it, everything ends. Perhaps it would be better if it was never born."

"Do not let such a thought haunt you. You need to look for new roads. Determination—let it fill your life with itself. Your eyes are saying that something else disturbs your sleep."

"I must admit I haven't said everything."

"Have you withheld something?"

"No, Father. I'm just not sure if it's worthy of condemnation."

"Let me judge it. How long ago did it happen, and what exactly happened? You have told me nothing about this fact."

"Six months ago, it struck like a thunderbolt."

"And only now you are coming to me with this? Tell me what occurred! Maybe it could be remedied!"

"Father, I wouldn't like to expose my feelings completely, from first to last."

"You can be absolutely anonymous. I am going to respect your privacy."

"Oh yes, now when I'm incognito, I feel safer. When I walked along 72nd Street near Central Park, I saw a beautiful girl sitting on a bench. Dressed modestly, with good taste, she was waiting for a bus. The girl had that something . . . something fascinating, some kind of indescribable charm. Talking on the cell phone, she confided her problems to somebody."

"You were eavesdropping?"

"But of course not. I wouldn't dare. It was by pure chance."

"What turn things take is not determined by chance."

"I heard in passing that she was given a compulsory leave so that she could rethink everything. She also said she had no money for food, and no place to spend the night. People who stood nearby began to look on her with suspicion. My conscience slapped me hard on the back, and when she finished the conversation, I offered her a small loan. Naturally, without a receipt."

"How much?"

"How much what, Father?"

"How much time had it taken before you stopped eavesdropping on her?"

"Not more than one minute. I swear."

"You do not have to swear. I take your word at face value. So, how much . . . I mean, how did it end up? And you see that you made haste again. You wanted to bring all glory to yourself. You could not be a confessor, son. Oh, you could not. Come on, speak out! I am listening."

"I wrote a check in as little time as possible."

"How much?"

"Two grand."

"Oh, Chri . . . forgive me, Lord! I have not meant the amount of money, but how much time did it take to—"

"Fifteen, maybe twenty seconds."

"Why do you not write checks in such an impetuously generous manner for other causes? And what happened to that check afterwards?"

"She looked at the number, then at me and . . . I'm embarrassed to tell you . . . but you—"

"Why have you quit? Continue your story."

"She slapped my face."

"Hmm . . . Was she discontented?"

"I guess it was not what she expected from me."

"Well, and the check . . . what happened to it?"

"She tore it to shreds and scattered in the air . . . like confetti."

"Attagirl. But she did not act too wisely. Did she reveal the reason behind this ill-considered action?"

"She said honor and faith were more important to her than money.

She dedicated this apothegm also to me. Finally, she told me to write another check so she could gladly give it to a homeless man, who was sitting nearby on the stairs."

"And how did you behave? Like a gentleman?"

"It was the last check I had."

"Oh, you young people, who can understand you? So, how did your meeting end?"

"She ran her eye over me, got on the bus, and it was the last moment I saw her. On parting, she smiled at me and made the sign of the cross in the air in my direction."

"What did she wear? Which hand did she use to make the sign of the cross? From the left to the right or from the right to the left?"

"I seem to remember that she walked around in a circle as if she found herself in a small maze. And she was so sad. Before getting on the bus, she stood in the middle of the street and looked for something. Cars were floating around her like a river current floating around a stone. Only people jostled her, just as weeds and dirt in the rapids get in the way of a holm. But I'm sure she didn't take anything."

"Ah, yes! Now everything is clear. The maze, cross, islet, isolation. Love and curiosity, not compulsion, steer her way through life. As you see, she did not take, yet she did take."

"I don't know myself anymore if she took or not . . . No, she certainly didn't. As I said, Father, she tore it to shreds."

"She did not accept the money, but she took you into her heart. She took the bait like a carp."

"I don't even know what her name is and where she lives."

"Put your rust in Providence. It will direct everything. It is not going to rain—the clouds have dispersed."

"Thank you, Father, for understanding. What about my penance?"

"I believe that your repentance is not a deceptive token for which you want to buy an indulgence."

"I've been walking various paths so far, but I know that I'm close to the goal. The sky over me is full of signposts, a maze of thoughts and unspoken words. I don't know why the road I'm going now is full of boulders. Father, show me the right one that leads to God. I can't stand any longer at crossroads—there're too many outcrops here. I'm going to obey your orders to reach the perfect creeks."

"Where did you learn this? Did you play in a school theater?"

"When the Guardian visited me, my thoughts went crazy, Father."

"Remove the outcrops from your path first, even if you had to lose your diamonds. Do not look enviously at the towering summits conquered easily by others. And when you see blood on your hands from this effort, it will be the sacred stigma of the Annunciation."

"Father, it will be hard to separate the noble from the common, and then to throw the chaff into the abyss behind us. We'll create new foundations from the boulders that stood in our way. We'll mark out new routes. We'll feed the hungry on precious stones."

"So be it, son. Listen carefully, for I am not going to say this twice, and, as if out of spite, other penitents are still waiting just when I am on duty. The moment you hear the last clang of the bell, rise from your knees and go into the world among people, poor people. Your master will be a homeless man, and you will be his servant. You will leave a tithe of what you possess, and you will spend the rest on the needy so that they can feel happy at least for a while."

"But it's a huge fortune, Father. Three generations have worked for it."

"Do not waste words, for it is an egregious misdeed. Your banks have ruined people's lives and souls, and you do not want to give away the devil's lucre? Be glad that God has let you keep some."

"Maybe two tithes at least, Father?"

"Go away before the Lord is angry!"

"So be it. I will gladly share the tithes. The cow has gone, let the calf go."

"What have you said, son?"

"If anything happens, Father, don't tell anyone about this.

"I, the doctor of two laws, master of sacred theology, professor of all the Slavonic languages, absolve you of the sins that you have committed, and that you, here lying, have confessed. The mercy of God is unfathomable. Since you have wanted to become convinced, you have reached the aim.

I hope those sins do not turn out to be prophetic. Go back where you came from."

"Thank you, Father. As you've said, I will do so. Praise be to your wisdom. And one more thing: What does the word 'novitiate' mean?"

"God forbid. Go away. Now. Good riddance . . . Next, please!" Harameus rose from his knees and headed for the gates of the church. The sound of his heavy steps carried around, reflecting off the temple's vault, returning with higher intensity. A few people engrossed in prayers muttered quickly under their breaths, as if they were in a hurry and were afraid that God would give them a momentary chance to confess all the evil deeds they had committed, and in fear that the enormity of their sins would not fit within the assigned time. They talked faster and faster, more and more indistinctly, until finally they went quiet. Then great relief prevailed in their hearts. They certainly forgot many of their sins, but they felt liberated, justified, and happy. At last he found himself at the temple gate, behind which the white stairs led to the courtyard. He went past a ragged, bearded beggar without a leg, who sat on the marble floor. Seeing Harameus, he put up his thin hand, trembling from the cold, and shook a small wooden mug, hoping for a widow's mite. The mug was almost empty and did not give out a loud sound at all. There were only two coins in it, but it was enough to get someone's attention.

Harameus stopped for a moment, looked at the hobo, then ran down the stairs, reaching the white fountain behind which stood a car waiting for him. He could smell the overpowering reek of unwashed body, unwashed clothes, hearing at the same time a muffed begging:

"Mister, have mercy on me, a poor man. Give me at least one coin or anything to eat. I am hungry, I don't have a family or a roof over my head. Please!" Having heard these words, doubtful in his mind, pushed by his old habit, always shunning poverty, Harameus stopped, moved by the hobo's words. Without looking at Harameus, he spoke again in a voice stripped of any hope, "I know I smell like a dog drenched in rain, but at least give me a good word! Mister, come up to me at the distance of the stick, at least." Harameus turned away slowly, and at a leisurely pace, headed in the direction of the beggar, stopped by him at a distance of half a pace away, and, looking him straight in the eye, he asked, "Would you, wayfarer, forgive me my faults?" His voice trailed off into trembling.

"I don't know you or your faults, mister, but you have a kind look in your eyes and you seem to be a decent man. Yes, I would forgive you, no matter what they were. In Harameus' downcast eyes appeared tears: first one, then the second, and then his eyes glazed, as if he had traveled a long way upwind. A few tears fell on the beggar's hands, marking them as the first drops of rain falling on the sun-cracked soil. The hobo, being dubious about what he saw, raised his hands to see them more closely. After all, he was still young and his eyes could not fail him.

"No one's ever shed tears in my presence." Totally taken aback, he looked in disbelief at Harameus, who took a handkerchief out of his pocket, wiped his wet eyes, and put dark glasses on them.

"Why are you crying, mister? Did I make you sad? I apologize to you for that. I didn't want to say anything inappropriate. If you don't have money, it's all right. I know how hard it is to make it. I have some bucks in a small bundle for a rainy day. I can share them with you." The hobo reached into the pocket of his pants, belted with a string, and took out of it a cloth pouch.

"Thank you, I'm not short of money. I've lost something much more valuable."

"I'm sorry, mister. I hope you'll find what you are looking for."

"I hope so, too. Do you often come here?"

"To this church, mister?"

"Yes," Harameus replied and added after a moment, "you don't have to address me as 'mister'."

"As you wish, mister. I'm here for the first time. The church is beautiful, but I haven't gotten too many handouts. I know people are having a hard time themselves. But tomorrow, I'm going on a journey. To Paradise. Maybe you'd like to go with me?"

"You're saying to Paradise . . . Do you know the way to it?"

"I know not only the way but also Paradise itself," said the beggar, looking at Harameus and giving him an idyllic smile.

"So tell me, if it isn't a secret, how can you get there? I'm trying to find this way, too."

"Time will come for everything, mister. Be patient and listen raptly to other people's hearts! But let me tell you one thing: Paradise is closer to you than you think. And the way? . . . You just entered it." The beggar touched Harameus' hand, grabbed it and said, "I'm going to Charleston. After all, maybe you'd like to go with me?"

"Ah, this is your Paradise. I've heard it is a nice city, but, unfortunately, I can't go with you."

"It's a pity, mister. It's much warmer there than in New York. A lodging will be no problem—there are parks and good people around."

"I have no money on me, wayfarer, but I can give this to you." Harameus reached into the inner pocket of his jacket and took out of it a brown leather wallet. There was an impressed round image of two fish between which four Chinese characters were squeezed. To the wallet, between its inner wings was clipped a fountain pen glittering with gold. Attempting to take it out, he knocked a loose insert, out of which credit cards and colorful business cards slipped and scattered all over the stairs. He knelt down on his knee, trying to quickly pick them up.

"Let me help you, mister. There're really a lot of these." The beggar held on his crutch, lifted his hip and with a few flings, he moved onto the first stair step. With a trembling hand, he began to gather up the scattered cards, looking at them with curiosity."

"Don't worry, mister, I can't read anyway. At school, I wasn't a very diligent student, but I must admit they're pretty." Harameus picked up the pen and put it in the mug.

"Don't lose it. It's worth a lot money and brings good luck."

"You got it as a gift from your wife?" said the beggar, grinning and showing the full mouth of incredibly white teeth.

"No, it's a graduation gift from my father. My wife is dead. My father, too." Harameus shook dust off his knees and put his wallet in his pocket. The hobo, holding the pen carefully, turned it over several times. Then he scrutinized the engraved small letters, slowly uncapped it, and gently ran the gold nib across his dirty hand. The beggar's dark big eyes were alight with delight. He picked up the last business card and doodled something on the reverse. "It is wonderful and writes so nicely

and smoothly, he said, spellbound, and gave a white and chartreuse card to Harameus.

"I'm glad you like it. What's your name, wayfarer?" Sweeping
back the bushy bangs hanging over his eyes, the beggar
scratched his forehead, and then, somewhat troubled, answered, "I am an eternal wanderer, Your Lordship. I don't remember my name. I come from Louisiana . . . and . . . you know,
I once remembered it." He turned his eyes away from his benefactor and fixed them on the crowns of trees growing behind the
fence. "Yes, I know it's strange, but I really don't remember,"
he said once again, worried, and his thoughts drifted somewhere else. Harameus, seeing that the poor man was trembling
in the cold, hastily took off his jacket and covered the shoulders
of the hobo, whose face suddenly brightened up with joy making
him again beautiful and happy. It reflected on the faces of
people, well-disposed towards him, as a sail reflects on the surface of a lake. Friendly sailors who went home after the Mass
expressed cordiality and admiration in their glances. They
greeted the wanderer waving to him, and then disappearing behind the mass of the church, while others, mainly latecomers
and stragglers, were stupefied by his adroitness and finesse,
which aroused envy in them, locked in their sinister glimpses.
All of them wanted to wear this sartorial masterpiece on their
backs. It was adorned with a pocket at the top from which shimmered a satin mokadour with a white stripe. Envy and contempt
emerged from the eyes of the stragglers and pierced him
through. He noticed this and, just to spite them, stuck the
golden fountain pen in the breast pocket, making the 'penrest'
of the satin pocket square. Stiffened to attention, like a string
tightened to its ultimate strength, in front of the pages, he sa-
luted with his hand laid on his heart and the pocket with the
pen, receiving honors from the creeps incarnate. He followed
with his eyes—one by one—those covetous souls who, even from
afar, continued imprecating dozens of curses upon his head
under their breaths. Then, hiding behind a corner, they jumped
on top of each other, furtively peeping at the lucky man. His as-
sets were quite abundant at that moment. The beggar's treas-
ures got enriched with pride, and the money box full of cash
failed to close completely. When the row of no-hopers raked aside,

he assumed again a casual pose, in which he felt at ease. Tickled in the nostrils with a pleasant scent, he pulled the sleeve closer to his face and sniffed. He repeated this action several times until he felt pleasantly dizzy. Just as a dog scrubs its back against the grass, he began to rub his body with the sleeve. First the neck, then the chest, finally the face and hair. And it was not clear whether he wanted to leave his scent marks on the sleeve or if he wanted to impregnate the dog's skin with the scent of flowers. Overwhelmed by the magic of the new fragrance, as if exhausted by a severe winter, yearning for spring, picturing a bush that makes it all of a sudden, he let out these words from his chest filled with joy:

"It seems to me jasmine blended with lilac." Intoxicated by the aroma, he looked again at the gray tree. Only a bird's singing is missing here. But my soul rejoices anyway. This is what I needed at this tough moment. I'm glad, mister, for this generous gesture and friendly words," he said with gratitude, and breathed in the air deeply once more, giving it back with reluctance."

"It is barberry blossom, my dear friend, stronger in its fragrance, more effective in the fight against bad moods! I don't use it very often, but it's true it has something in itself. Ever since I've discovered it, I can see much more around myself."

"What do you mean by 'much more,' mister, that you can see owing to the herb?" he asked and slid his fingers into the pockets of sartorial masterpiece going through their narrowest corners. He finally caught himself committing this obvious gaucherie as he was caught by his benefactor's eyes. He suddenly froze, showing an innocent face, and said succinctly, "Empty!" and shrugged, squinting one of his eyes at the benefactor's face. The latter was excluded by the sun, closed tightly also because of shame; it was waiting for the matter to come to a halt. He narrowed even more the former, half-open, when the sunshine dazzled it falling between his eyebrows along with a light curl. With a blow on the curl, he tried to chase it out of the eye, but it was as if the sun did not want to give in.

"Forgive me, mister. I just wanted to make sure I didn't borrow anything for keeps.

"That's kind of you," said Harameus, "that you've made honesty, this noble virtue, your spouse."

"Oh, fair-minded master, you are filling my heart with pride and hope. Your words are at least of equal value to that of gold. Though I must honestly say that if you offered me ducats, I wouldn't say 'no,' and wouldn't withdraw my hand. Not for myself, mister, but for my brothers." The hobo, whispering, began to count something on the fingers of both hands, then raised his head and said, "Do you know, mister, that if you gather together all beggars and tramps and those who feel unhappy, put them all on a big ship—of course, if it could be built—and send them on a sea journey, then the Earth would be deserted, leaving on its back only a few lucky people. The seas and the oceans would break all their banks. So, the fate of those few also would be sealed! If nothing changes," he said, preoccupied, pulling out a rumpled scrap of paper, which he started to smooth on the palm of his left hand. Peeking at the scrap, he continued, "If nothing changes in the distribution of funds and only royalties play first fiddle in this idea, such Brobdingnagian water will come that it will plunge everything into its depths. And us, and you, and even our little brothers, land animals. But you, mister, are different, and even though you wouldn't have to climb aboard the ship, you would be the first to come and help others, although many of them are scoundrels, scalawags, who aren't worth a damn! Tell me what is the power that pushes you to reach out to the poor."

"For some time now, I've been seeing people glow. I haven't seen this before. Also, their scents have misled me in judging them so far. Now it's quite different."

The hobo rested his chin on the chest, pulled his linen shirt with two fingers, carefully sniffed it, and said, "If I were in your place, mister, and smelled such odors from you, I'd avoid you like the plague, like a huge puddle!" His chapped lips released a smile, unveiling white, even ice blocks on which polar bears were basking in the sun.

"Thank you for your sincere words, but I have already made up my mind that I won't change my way! You never know who will be in whose place! Today, this barberry shrub smells of me, tomorrow it may smell of you! I used to hold my breath when I scented out poverty. Today, my taste has changed: I don't turn away my nose. That's the way things are."

"Maybe it's not the smell that sets you the path, maybe the shrub of your soul fruited at last?! And the fruit was not poisonous as it seemed. Perhaps the person who planted the shrub took it out of the greenhouse, where the seasons can't be distinguished! Now it is enjoying the rain, and the sun, and it will survive even a harsh winter, when it can jolly up human eyes.

"I don't know, wise gardener, what your name is, but you know more about the sun and rain than I do."

"I've been growing on this barren soil for a long time, and I know the whims of climate very well. I can't fruit myself, as I am not predestined for this. However, when I see it next to me, my heart rejoices and is filled with pride. My eyes draw in this view and rise towards Heaven to announce the good news that all is not lost."

"Wayfarer, your words are wise. You should watch the gates of churches, and turn the teachings into action."

"That's what I'm doing, mister." The beggar raised his head, closed his eyes, measuring with them the brightest point on the horizon.

"May I address you as Altus?" The hobo smiled and looked at him again.

"Oh, yeah, that's a nice name. I like it. Does it mean something?"

"Yes. In Latin it means tall."

"Do you think I am tall? Seriously?" he asked, happy and encouraged by this news. Later on, with a glance he swept his left leg, and stopped it on the stump that ended just below the right knee. If his legs were siblings—let's say, two sisters—one of them would be tall but excessively thin, with a straight waist, the other swollen, chunky, broad-shouldered, with a short neck; hardly fitting in the trouser leg, it reached her waist. They are entirely unlike each other, as if they were not begat by the same father. Despite this difference, he loved them both dearly and felt equally. It was the healthy one on whose shoulders' hardships of his life rested. It endured walking and cold weather, climbing and rain, and once in a while, it had to drive away a dog. The smaller one, constantly swollen, with a never-healed wound, was only helpful with sitting. Sometimes it served as a table on which a piece of bread was lying along with pleasant memories.

"But what else could it do? Just to watch and wait for another cut when the disease was in remission. I haven't noticed before that I'm tall, probably because I always sit in front of the doors of churches, as far as remember," he said, cheered up. "Ah, how good it is to be tall." With these words, he caressed his misery, making the day that was gray bright and merry. He took a clasp knife out of the pocket, and, out of the cloth bag, he took a gift apple and cut it into small figures of eight. He stuck one of them on the tip of the knife and ate it piece by piece, relishing the sweetness of each atom of the apple. At the same time, he smiled, having an inner conversation with his soul.

"Wayfarer, can I ask you something before I leave? Although I must admit that there is some kind of resistance in me. I do realize you can consider this as nosiness and hold a low opinion of me."

"You address me like no one has ever done. You respect me, and on the whole, this is a rare trait of persons who decide to talk to a beggar. You talk to me as the king with the king. Ask me questions, mister. I will gladly satisfy your curiosity."

"Is your leg stricken by a disease or there is another cause of the injury?"

"I once met evil people on my way. It happened suddenly. I remember this vaguely. I still hear that noise in my ears, and the wind whistling in my head. I don't even have dreams. The last dream I remember was about a flash mixed with a bang. Doctors cut me down piece by piece and keep me alive until there was nothing left."

"I have to go, Altus. I promise we'll meet again."

"No doubt, mister," the hobo answered mysteriously, nibbling the apple.

Harameus went down the stairs, going straight to the car waiting for him.

"I wish you luck, Harameus. Find what you have lost."

"Thank you!" he shouted back and suddenly stopped as if struck by lightning. "But you can't read!" He turned back sharply; however, on the stairs, the beggar was no more.

"Sir, are we going to the castle?" asked the driver.

"No, Walter, to the bank" he answered indecisively.

"Have you seen where that hobo has gone?"

"He entered, or rather dragged himself to the church, sir. As if someone called him."

"Do something for me, Walter. Go and see where he is. I'd like to talk to him."

"I saw him walking towards the altar, but I'll check it out right now." A few minutes passed as Walter reappeared.

"He is not in the church, sir. He must've gone through the sacristy. I don't see any other way."

Harameus slid the window open to get some fresh air. He lounged comfortably on the leather couch and fell into a pensive mood. A breeze coming in through the window brushed his hair and face. It was obvious that the earlier confession and conversation with the priest, and afterwards with the beggar, soothed and comforted him. The car slowly started. Harameus always thought that money did not make people free, but it was only that moment he really felt so.

"Sir—"

"Yes, Walter, go on."

"You see, sir, when I entered the church—," Walter said in a faltering voice, "I saw the priest who had his hands folded in prayer and . . . looked towards Heaven, so to speak."

"What's strange about that? This is the way, priests often pray."

"Yes, but somehow I felt strange. Everything around seemed so beautiful. These images and statues of the saints looked as if they were speaking to me. There was such positive energy emanating from them, and somehow a soft light fell. I've never experienced this before, and yet I am a believer and I attend Mass every Sunday."

"Such mood prevails, Walter, in many temples of different religions."

"And one more thing—next to the priest, on the fence separating the altar, there was a mug with coins, and at the side of it, a crutch was resting."

Harameus looked into a narrow strip of the mirror, in which he also saw Walter's eyes. They both looked at each other without saying a single word. The car purred along an almost empty road, finally reaching a large gray edifice, at the top of which, huge, golden letters announced to the world: "e-Invest Haram Bank. Your New Home. Your New Life!"

"Thank you, Walter, take a day off tomorrow and rest a little. The day after tomorrow we'll fly to Charleston."

CHAPTER TWO

The sun was high in the sky, and the day had just entered its second half. In the radiance, the churches shimmered with marble whiteness, taking bright color—even if they were built of gray limestone. Having slept poorly through the night, Harameus approached slowly the last church of over a dozen other churches that he had visited for two days. His face was tired and his body moved sluggishly as if he carried a heavy burden on his shoulders. He came up to a large column, which upheld the portico of the cathedral, to sit down and rest for a while. Suddenly, he heard silent words coming neither from close up nor from the distance. They paraded in a marching rhythm:

Marines, O marines
Exit your canteens
Pray before the fight
Not all will survive.

He stopped momentarily to listen more attentively, but the sounds instantly fell silent. He thought that the heat was playing tricks on him. He sat down in the shadow of the column, took a bottle of water out of a bag and started to drink. From behind came a coarse voice, "May I have a sip of water, good man?" A woman, with a face cut with wrinkles, dressed in worn-out jeans and an old army blouse, sat on the other side of the column. Her long hair fell to her shoulders, partially covering her face. Nearby lay a large black bundle that contained all her belongings.

A thin blanket and a small pillow stuck out from it, accompanied by plenty of squashed aluminum cans. In the other smaller transparent bag, one could see a hair brush, a compact vanity case, and several summer dresses.

"Drink it, please. It's so hot no one can walk in the open sun," he said, taken aback, and gave the bottle to the woman.

"Ha ha, sizzlers will soon come, young man. It's only April," she said merrily, taking a few small sips. Harameus glanced at a white damp label, which was marked by her slightly soiled hand.

"If you have no place to refresh yourself, you can use my bathroom in the hotel. It's not far away from here by the old city hall," he said bashfully.

"In the Monte Carlo? No kidding! Before I crossed the threshold, they'd set dogs on me," she said. "For me the Celestial Peace would be more suitable. It is on the other side of the park. They wash such persons as me at the city's expense. But, God forbid, far be it from me!" Harameus looked at her, not fully comprehending what she meant.

"I know what I'm talking about. I worked there for some time, when recession and banks got people into troubles. No doubt, I'd keep on dressing stiffs if that unlucky night had never happened. Phooey!" she spat over her shoulder.

"Do you believe in ghosts?" Harameus asked ironically.

"It doesn't matter. I ran away from that place faster than from an explosion in a war battle. But I'm not going to bother you with my troubles." She spread out his hands in a resigned gesture.

"Go on, it's very interesting," he said, stretching out on the marble floor more comfortably and resting his back against the column.

"Are you sure you wanna listen to this? I warn you it isn't a tale for milksops." She turned her head aside, eyeing him, from the polished shoes to the designer dark glasses rested on the top of his head.

"I'm not moved by such tales," he replied.

The woman lifted her hand and shoved her frosted hair over her right shoulder. In the cladding of the dazzling light, Harameus discerned a dark face, as if created of roasted coffee grains, proud, world-weary. The profile, which he saw was on one line with the sun, made him realize that human life goes by before you know it, and that everything in the human body inevitably deteriorates and fades away, except one thing—pride. He could compare the face only to the face of an Indian warrior, who was both indomitable and unenslavable in every inch of his existence. A subtly curved nose, nice, thick, still dark eyebrows, as were her eyes. The uncovered tattoo, featuring an eagle holding a rifle in its claws, brought a smile to Harameus's lips.

"Tell me your story, warrior-woman. I'm dying of curiosity," he said. The woman took a pouch with tobacco out of her pocket and hand-rolled a cigarette.

"Maybe at one time I was a warrior, but now I want only to be with my yoke-fellows." Harameus took over a matchstick and lit her cigarette.

"You're a well-bred man, and you know how to behave in the presence of a lady," she said favorably and inhaled deeply. "It happened a long time ago, but I remember as it was yesterday. I almost finished dressing a woman, sent to meet her Maker by her jealous husband, when someone started to bang at the door, and the doorbell was buzzing like crazy. Even though I had a few drinks to soothe my nerves, I still felt anxious."

Harameus unconsciously put his right forefinger on his lips and started to chew his nail.

"When I opened the door, I saw, just on the threshold, the Reverend Dominique in his pajamas, trembling with the cold, and pale."

"Was he sleepwalking?"

"Why, no! I thought to myself he must've drunk too much sacramental wine and confused the addresses. But it wasn't what surprised me the most. At the very thought of this story my shoulders shudder. Don't you have something in your breast pocket, sweetheart?"

"I'm sorry," Harameus said without any regret and helplessly spread his arms.

"Do you know Latin?" she asked all of a sudden, "Every classy man should know Latin at least a little, and you look like the one who does." The woman again looked at his appearance and his fairly neat clothes, hardly combed hair but not ruffled, a shirt tucked smoothly into his pants; only his shiny shoes were slightly covered with dust, for which he found a remedy—immediately after he had noticed her scrutinizing gaze— rubbing their tips on the trouser legs. The only thing to which one could have a slight objection was a small coffee stain on his pants, as well as ketchup and turmeric mustard spots on the top of his shirt—a kind of stamp from the nearby fast food restaurant. However, it did not affect the first impression he made on her, and it is known to be of fundamental importance. Judging by the gleam in her eyes, it was quite favorable. And that essential question that had been just asked, to which Harameus was already forming an answer. "I know Latin quite well."

The woman took a drag on her cigarette and let out a thick trail of smoke. "That's what Father Dominique looked like that night," she said, looking at the white cloud. Harameus coughed and chased the smoke away with his hand.

"Sorry, I rarely have visitors." She smothered the cigarette ember with her fingers. "The Reverend told me I had to wash him, shave him, and change his clothes, because he would be meeting Bishop Garcia soon and he had to look elegant. In this sudden commotion, I forgot that the bishop had died long ago, and when I wanted to serve the Reverend with my arm, he violently protested, stopping me halfway, showing the Stop sign with his hand. Father Dominique began his ministry many years ago under the wings of his Excellency, who I hope has already joined the winged group in the heavens. Am I boring you?" she asked when she saw Harameus putting up his hand to hide his yawn.

"Of course not, it's a very interesting story," he replied, "I'd love to hear all of it. Better to listen than to talk nonsense—it doesn't tire that much."

"Forgive me my talkativeness, my inconspicuous friend, but I haven't talked to anyone for weeks. Fate brought you here, so suffer a little."

"I'm not so inconspicuous," he said with some denial in his voice.

"No? Then look," she said, struggling to get up from the stairs, and straightening her back. It was evident that her arms, legs, and neck had become numb, because she made several vigorous turns of her head—once to the left, then to the right—then she spun her arms holding her hands on her shoulders. Finally, she carefully rolled her hips. Moments later, when she had already stretched, she made a movement as if she were drawing a bowstring. She repeated this action several times, alternately changing hands, aiming at an extremely well-groomed fop with an arrogant, even predatory face, just getting out of the service car. He was a clerk-like man with a scar on his right cheek, in a well-cut suit, with a thick gold chain and a massive cross slung around his short neck. The man was clutching a roll of shiny scarlet fabric under his left arm and a roll of hand-painted silk under his right. He might have been a wealthy mercer with many social connections, or a tailor in the services of the curia— after all, not just anyone was invited to today's ceremony. The woman aimed at him just as he said something rudely to the driver by the name Silvester, who was opening the door. The driver's face was elongated and thin, with protruding cheekbones, and weak dark hair falling over his forehead. On his honest face were old traces of someone's anger, possibly a dandy. Silvester, regrettably due to sheer carelessness—and it is almost certain, because who would like to tease the boss with such a good job—hit his hip against a piece of fabric, causing her to rub against the dusted side of the car. The dandy caught with the corner of his eye the woman pointing at him and instinctively covered himself with a quarter of a head shorter with Silvester, who had nearly fallen for it. As soon as he realized the comic side of the situation, he gave the woman a nonchalant smile and stepped forward with his head held up high on the broad steps of the temple, going straight towards the thick wooden door, where the canon priest in a beautiful crimson or raspberry inlaid chasuble (shadows of palm trees waited and greeted him personally' palm trees and aloe vera in pots mixed with the sun's rays, deceived the eyes, making it difficult to read the colors correctly). As they caught each other's eyes, their faces gleamed with joy, as if they were about to cut the cake and cut the ribbon. The dandy gave Sylvester some last orders by gestures, and when the latter, after deciphering his gestures, started polishing the car, he handed both rolls of fabric to a churchman and placed two fleeting, unvoluptuous and dispassionate kisses on the canon's cheeks, taking him by the hand with familiarity, with which, judging by the priest's face, he earned his even greater grace.

The merchant led him into the depths of the basilica. Shortly later, the organ began to squeal. Ascending and descending cadences of songs flowed from the choir. Then followed the organist's baritone solo. He must have had strong lungs because he was singing incredibly loud without using a microphone. The people rose from the benches and formed a chain of raised hands, swaying like meadow grasses. Although the organist (the jokers called him 'toad,' or 'pipechoker') initially did not fit well into the key of the tablature, he sang the final notes, despite the hard accent, almost perfectly. After that effort, the beautiful organ fugue sounded. A lamplighter, who was hanging around outside the chapter house, with a snuffer in his hand—that is, a long stick ending with a metal cone, used to extinguish altar candles and fire clocks—dragged on his cigarette with a few short inhales, and also went inside the temple captivated by the music. Additionally, today it was supposed to grace a prominent apparatchik, commonly known as 'Bull terrier' from the chief's circle with the sacrament of marriage. He himself was still unmarried without having experienced a serious love life; however, when the opportunity arose, he happily fixed his eyes on the bride and her bridesmaids, daydreaming about something no one knew at all. His facial expression showed that now, too, he was overwhelmed by the most vivid thoughts. He was still young (barely turning thirty) and not entirely morally formed. The lamplighter was also followed by Ms. Casimira (whose marriage dilemma concerned no longer), called here by everyone Ms. Cassie—a name once extremely popular in the south—known for her careful care for all temple plants. She especially liked the poinsettias, thick aloes and fuchsia trees outside (she could look at these for hours, when the birds nibbled on the berries), and the wild hops growing in the rubble behind the engine house. Ms. Cassie was a cheerful woman endowed with a polite reverence for almost everyone. Quite recently, she had to endure another affront by the canon priest, which she felt very acutely (the priest often exposed her to such tests, for the slightest motive). In a fit of anger with all the service employees present, he called her a "scattered hair with provocative carmine lips" (which was not true, because Ms. Cassie always wore carefully tanned Pre-Raphaelite curls and her makeup was never flashy) when she insisted that she could go up the main winding stairs, not narrow kitchens, like the rest of the servants, and that they could also eat butter and country eggs donated by generous parishioners—previously reserved only for clergy—instead of margarine and egg powder, from which they often got perleche. As a result of that arrogance, Ms. Cassie almost fainted. What can one say, the priest was a difficult man to live with; he had a neurasthenic disposition and frequent bouts of anger. When she recovered consciousness and digested this disrespect, she did not find the courage and did not allow herself to repay the priest with the same coin, although, as God knows, it was undoubtedly due to him. The image of his approach to employees was not uniform here. The clergy liked some employees more than others. Ms. Cassie came somewhere in the middle, and the lamplighter-mockster (behind whom, until recently, his mother carried his briefcase to school, despite the fact that he was over his age, not yet well acquainted with savoir-faire and thanks to his sharp tongue) came a few positions lower. Ms. Cassie led a peaceful and happy life. The children were already brought up, and the husband had long been six feet under. Some accused her of being garrulous, that she was constantly talking, that she had a weakness for gossip and her tongue was long to her knees; she could not address the objections and charges because they were leveled behind her back, but no one doubted that she was good-natured and pious woman. Petite and seemingly weak, she in fact had inexhaustible bodily strength and demonstrated an exemplary conduit. When the sexton pointed at the nosy young man standing in the threshold, Ms. Cassie sent him a meaningful look and vigorously shifted the young man with her arm, pushing him outside the temple, slamming the gate behind herself. The latch rattled. The youthful curiosity prevailed, however, because the boy climbed the scaffolding by the wall and peered inside the temple through the missing piece of stained glass in the rosette window. He stood on the plank for a while longer, but, called by a friend's whistling, who was waiting on the other side of the square, he jumped down in two leaps along the metal pipes onto the stone ground and ran towards him. Moments later, they both disappeared into some cold metal gate. The decibels have fallen.

The song was a little softer, but still sounded beautiful. After the sounds had ceased, the official masquerade began. First, there was an exchange of courtesies and greetings between the officials and the clergy, then, when they had already bowed down left and right (before more important to dignitaries and figures) and sluggish nods of their heads (towards those meaningless), the fuss went aside since the chief himself was about to visit the cathedral any minute now, who probably deliberately was late. He rushed hastily in the company of a few party courtiers, like an illuminating flare at an instant becoming a cynosure of all eyes of the celebrants. The saber blades held in front of the face by two representative officers at the entrance flashed. The chief was amazed when he saw that the front row of pews by the presbytery was occupied. Without revealing himself to anyone, he made a secret gesture to his vanguard to prepare a seat for him, and then, he moved on in small steps to give time to execute the command, slightly limping misleadingly, he moved towards the altar. The envoys obediently did what the chief's petty hand dictated, asking a few lower-rank clergymen in altembassic attire, who came here from other parishes, to take their places in the other part of the basilica (only a familiar exorcist was allowed to stay), to which, in a gesture of solidarity, three almsmen— one lay postulator, one orionist, and a monastery gardener— went with them, sitting on the hard benches without support in the aisle.

"They don't sow, they don't plow, but they live," said one of them with displeasure, looking at the dignitaries, quoting the beautiful words of Saint Francis. The vacated seats were swiftly taken by a member of local camarilla, who was passionate about speeches, never refrained from speaking, had the status of an eternal vassal, but also having access to the treasury. Moments later, when the chief's tired derriere found the desired rest on the bench, the party apparatchiks were given the green light to deliver their speeches. Priority, as always, was given to the prettiest and most handsome of them (you know, the first impression was supposed to be electrifying), but with a tendency to less effort in the intellectual domain. This favoritism caused frustration in the less successful colleagues, but the more skillful in speech. They secretly cursed such criteria, which had such a profound effect on the chronology of speeches. What was the content of the first speech, after a while no one remembered. Then, for almost a quarter of an hour, the new bishop, fresh from the ingress, sermonized from the pulpit. It was not an oratorial masterpiece, but it was one of the few that found its place in fragmentary memory. He tried to speak to consciences and common sense using the simplest of words, especially when he spoke at the end in a hoarse voice, strained tongue. Everyone listened to these words with bated breath. Then the bishop added, "Love should be a light hug, not an overwhelming Nelson hold." Then he lowered his head, closed his eyes, was silent for a moment and said, "Father, I am beginning the ministry in your name. Let old prejudices and old demons leave us. Let us get rid of pride and selfishness. Please do not send your archangels to the asteroid belt" Then he cast the nets more widely, saying, "By God's will, I declare: For the sake of posterity and contemporaries, I renounce God's immunity. I will challenge any judgments of the courts that will ever condemn any book to be burned, and a dissent to stoning." He ended the whole thing with these words: "The belligerent church is the abode of the Antichrist. Humility kills the soul and homelessness is a scourge of human life. Each and every one of them is capable of state life and our calling is the state of humanity. Prosperity is a goal for all of us, and being single is good, but only in the pit. The world is not arranged in the way the bishop used to talk in the pulpit so far." Saying this, he slid his glasses down a little on the weir of his nose and looked swiftly over the participants, silently but attentively listening to him. Here and there one could hear the faint cathedral echo of hawks and muffled coughs. Probably most of the audience gathered here wondered if these were his own words, or it was a higher authority speaking through him. After a while, His Eminence added quite to the point: "If someone throws a stone at you, throw a loaf of bread to him." From under the choir, where young party activists knelt piously, ran a rumble of discontent. There were also words that could not be printed. The cathedral filled up with whispers. Consternation and expectation hung in the air. The silence dragged on, but when the chief clapped his hands, the rest followed him. Unexpectedly, a long applause was given to His Excellency, until he did not stop wondering. Immediately afterwards, the bishop's ear caught also a hostile opinion somewhere on the edge of the right side: "Damn! Big deal, a great luminary of morality is here." Another well-fed gentleman chimed in: "What a morality play, just empty nuts." Nearby, an old lady raised her tone in delight: "Bravo! Bravo! Bravo!" In opposition to her, the young boy entering the breaking of his voice said, "What a fake!" The bishop left the pulpit. His tired legs carried him towards the throne. He walked slowly, taking small steps under his long russet coat. He almost fell over, wanting to avoid the pool of wax on the floor, which flowed from the crooked candle on the candelabrum.

"Send me an altar boy here," he said to the Latin American deacon accompanying him. Then the bishop looked at the chief. He tried to communicate something to him with a gesture of his hand and facial expressions, not wanting to harass him personally, but the chief read his intention and quickly turned around, pretending that he did not notice this and that he was curious about what was happening in the choir. His Excellency, undaunted by this ignorance, made an extra effort and took a dozen good steps, thus moving away from the throne and bending down, covering his mouth with his hand, offered a long, silent plea to the chief's turned ear. Judging by the curious glances of his closest viewers, he did this to some extent effectively when it comes to keeping the content secret, but despite this precaution, some of the words got out, as the party assistants sitting closest to him cocked their ears at the highest possible attention, nodding their heads involuntarily, which confirmed that quite a few words reached the boat-shaped hand clung to the ear. His Excellency was advanced in his age, so he might not have realized that his hearing was worn out and not as sensitive as it used to be, and what he thought was a whisper was not a whisper at all. Under the cover of his hand, he pleaded with the chief to share his worldly intuitions with the celebrants, and also to delivered a speech on behalf of the nation across the ether, who went from the cathedral on that day (there was even one television station befriended by him), a nation caught up in such a cruel world, entangled into such hard life, trapped in such cruel world and times.

But the chief was quite fastidious about it. Some idiosyncrasy shook his body. He felt under no obligation to speak on behalf of anyone, and certainly not on behalf of the philistines whom he considered the poor and the half-poor. Besides, since childhood, he struggled with shyness, so why would he force himself now. He would not get any benefit from it. Perhaps, if he could slander the world a little from the pulpit, blame the people, who were critical to his actions, for his errors, the matter would take a different turn. However, the message would have gone into the ether, and he, by no means, could not afford it. Also, the overtone of such a speech could have been too much political and left its deep mark on him. Twice as much, he preferred to sit in the meadow and to daydream. The conciliatory bishop still endeavored in an endearing way to persuade him to do some noble deed, which he could promise here, and which might become an icon of his reign, but he waited in vain. The chief was adamant, and even he did not try to lie his way out of doing so. Expressing his dissatisfaction, he waved his hand, cutting it off in advance. The citizens' problems that occupied him so much in the past lay today beyond his world, with which he was still tied with cold relations. Devoid of empathy, he loved only one individual—himself. It was hard to tell looking at his face what his current mood was—just a mask-man. A phalanx of officials stormed the pulpit, peering at the chief. The college of prominent jugglers pressed. Duty clerics, who were keeping the order and the organization of the ceremony, were pushed to the second stair step. They confronted a dilemma whether to push the others away or give way. They could not let them all in at once because the pulpit was wooden and it was in danger of collapsing. The chief, however, quickly came to their aid, looking at his wolves with a fierce, overbearing gaze. Under the weight of this gaze, they quickly scattered and blended into the crowd. With his right hand, he dictated who was to get up from the front row of pews and go to the pulpit. Finally, he took into account the intellectual rank of the speakers, those who had some linguistic reserve. At the third stage was the man with the curls on the ears, who went by the nickname "Coral", though no one knew why (unfortunately, the urgent issues of women, which were to be discussed here by themselves, as well as the decarbonization of the air, were not included on the agenda due to lack of time). However, also here there appeared glitches, because this little charming gentleman, famous for his expert speeches at a lavishly set table, liked specially to discourse at great length about the invention of a new gunpowder; his tongue sped up then. Today he once again brought from the bedroom heavily dark circles under his eyes and sunken cheeks (he rarely ate and slept very little, he lived to serve the chief), which could not be easily masked with powder and passionate subsequent veneration. However, when he received the speech text, he spoke for almost five minutes praising the footprints the chief had left on the ground. It was said secretly that Coral had been recommended by the chief himself to inherit his armor, that beloved and longed-for prey he dreamed of and intended to lay for regardless of the recommendation. Many argued for him, betting all on one card that might turn out to be a losing one while the chief still blinked his eyes and the end date of his life was still an astrological dark number. Coral was ready to compete, like Ajax the Great with Odysseus for the armor of Achilles. Soon, in an indefinite number of years, the final decision was to be made. For the time being, the chief had made Coral temporal party quartermaster, for which the latter was extremely grateful. It was a payment for ten round years of faithful service. At the end of the speech, he also lied that the leader did not avoid intensive contacts with the people and was ready to follow him into the fire. The rank of these lies was, of course, unimaginably high—even the chief, hearing it, raised the corner of his mouth cynically. All the following speeches were synonymous and of the same boring tone. Honey dribbled from the mouths, which was understandable, because everyone wanted to stay in the chief's golden-haired zone, where they could easily go from zero to hero. Nobody wanted to die in poverty, go astray, or lead a wandering life. Each of them wanted to get as many profits as possible for themselves. Material benefits obscured everything. It was just a typical human calculation. They were courageous only in the crowd, cowardly when dispersed. They often got involved in machinations and schemes, especially against themselves. With every bite they acquired, they aroused mutual envy. It happened that in many important matters, about which they were disputing among one another, they asked for the chief's intervention. They complained about one another, slandered and tripped one another. However, they had one thing in common—the opportunity to get rich quickly attracted them as much as a she-wolf in heat lures male wolves, or the smell of a chamois lures Billy goats. They fought for each and every bite like devils. They did not think that they would commit any infamy. They always left behind a dug-up waste land. There was as much use of those speeches as the outcome of a wise guy milking a bull, or another who tried to grind water, as ancient adages used to express. However, despite this, in order to please the rallies, they proclaimed a national republic of prosperity and well-being every now and then, under a pompous name, which is not worth recalling here, demolishing palaces of justice, hanging a blacksmith instead of a shoemaker. They pinned medals for actions that had not yet happened to one another's jackets. The central figure of the ceremony put his signature on everything, put the stamp of final validity, sanctioning this scandalous pathology.

The Oracle, an absolute Zarathustra, the source of all wisdom, to whom the most outstanding character traits were attributed, a great resident of a guarded, green metropolitan district, an honorary citizen of ten cities, smacked his tongue with delight, especially when his subordinate read the dithyramb from a threadbare page, whose words were arranged almost in chant: "Our greatest one in all the world, leader, most wonderful being, guiding star. You did not become big in body, but you became a great man. All the languages of the world will praise you as long as there exists human," which in his own language meant, "I will eat with a spoon often, and not much until we will have as much moolah as we need. Let us not delude ourselves that the boom will last for a long time, the chief's love and favors as well."

At the end, other pages, also married to good jobs and perks, read the proscription list of their opponents—after all, the chief could not live without an enemy. It did not matter whether it was a good enemy or a bad enemy. There were also no compromises with him, and he never complied with the contracts he had made. At the end, a few more frantic shouts to cheer on, which the rest of the camarillas eagerly picked up on. Then they

chantingly summoned the magical powers to the taint of the opposition, which was also not holy, often drinking vodka with
them under the table. Moments later they chanted the verse that
the chief's might will never be broken. The number of throats
was incalculable. The chief did not treat everyone with the same
care, especially the minister of public enlightenment and the
minister of social order. He rarely allowed them to kiss the ring
of power. Moments later the name of the chief was chanted five
and a half times. Despite the fact that he was greedy for such applause, he quickly put them out with a gesture of both hands, not
allowing the sixth cheer to finish. The noise was reduced to a
minimum, but, as they descended from the pulpit, they were
seen off by a standing ovation directed at the chief. They clapped
their hands like crazy. They did what the little hand dictated. Orders were taken with complete rigorism. Every time he looked
at one of the pages, he made him bow. Every time he looked at
any of them, he forced them to humble themselves. Venerations
flowed again from the wide-open mouths. The swollen noses of
the young bulls caught the chief's pheromones. There was no
chance that today, on this beautiful mustard festival, these
minds existed on their own. The knowledge read over many
years from the books evaporated. Only the chief did not rise from
the bench as the applause roared, as he did not have to. Some of
them were able to cry tears out of emotion or sadness, which was
an extremely difficult art and at the same time troubling the
leader. It even angered him. The leitmotif of each of the speeches
was that the greatest miracle of civilization was the birth of the
chief, an unquestionable prophet of the centuries (anthropola-
tria in the full sense). Indeed, the chief's power seemed unbreak-
able. As long as the treasury was full of cash, it was basically a
doomed thing. But self-destruction was already just around the
corner. In the dark, clouds flashed menacingly and ominous
murmurs sounded. The gigantic storm of the crisis was looming
inexorably. Ever since the chief had entered great fame, no
matter which road he walked, all the bells rang glory, torches
burned, and the course of his great period of life was measured
by the invar weights of ebony clocks. By the cathedral wall, next
to the hermetic plinths, a huge dolomite raw stone waited under
a tarpaulin covering. He expected a sculptor who would have the

courage to pit themself against it—use a hammer and a chisel to sculpt the horse in the levada, fastened by the chief's golden spurs. The family's pride, however, did not allow the chief to protest; he had already seen himself on these steeds and pedestals. Several wax models were approved—as for one—the quartermaster and the artist had a word about the payment, but the chief did not like any of the designs. (He insisted on the habergeon with head chain armor, although the artist made his remark in a veiled manner, not wanting to cause the chief suffering that this was just a model, and that his oval is too chubby, which, of course, he did not say directly, and the head armor would not suit him, suggesting that he would be more dignified with a horse-tail ensign.) Having heard those remarks, the chief made a concerned face. Annoying the chief was not the artist's intention; that is why he counted on the help of the quartermaster in a soft explanation of the matter. In vain. He did not want to risk it; therefore, he was neutral in silence. The chief did not want to fall into oblivion, so he was still patiently waiting for a model that would amaze him. He himself was not sure yet what horse he would mount—a Friesian black stallion, the white one, or maybe a charming chestnut mare and what words he would put on the shield. Until then, it was only the wheel of time that held him on the horse's back. It rolled downhill after the fourth twenty years of life, which was an obvious reason for his undoubted concern. The until recently beautiful wrinkles on his face deepened by worry, and sadness entered the eyes.

The newlyweds waited patiently for the chief to give a sign for commencement of the nuptials. The bride was indescribably beautiful, a woman as a vision, but a bull terrier was an antonym of beauty. One could say that with this large, round feline head and chubby face, he did not fit in with beauty. Well, God connected even more extreme opposites. Colored and retouched on the wedding portrait, he will probably look much better.

"This music is a balm for the soul," thought Harameus, looking in admiration at the taut figure of a woman, holding an illusory bow in her hands. "Wow! How much is it?" he asked, amazed.

"A whole six feet," she replied, straightening herself even more.

"Not every bow can take it. There is no escape from the world
of the living or return to it. Are you slouching at the table?"

"It happens," replied Harameus, "especially when I have
smaller and smaller letters to read in the contracts."

"Bank hyenas have found a way for old eyes!" she said bitterly.
"The only thing missing is what virus they created against old
people! All of this, I tell you, will someday be properly judged.
Even if they summoned all the saints for help, none of them
lifted a finger in their defense. Greed, that son of a bitch, is the
same thing as pride, and hubris, that bitch, is synonymous with
decay and demise." Harameus had a sudden thought. She understood him as wrongly as possible.

"What do the scriptures say about it? No hidden usury. None,"
she added, indignant. Harameus ignored it with silence. He could
have given her a lengthy explanation, avoiding the fire of explain-
ing something difficult with something even more difficult, and
not entangling even more the already tangled fabric, but he was
not sure if the knowledge he would share with her would fall on
the fertile ground and she would understand him properly. He did
not want to impose his arguments by verbal force, and if he
wanted to reach her, he would have to use an advanced prestidig-
itation, petty juggling, turn and twist the point of view, present
such explanations that would be transparent and understandable
to her—such a proverbial red ironbark climbed by a grazing goat.
He meant nothing offensive, because he himself felt profane in
many sciences and was not surprised by her passionate and ex-
pressive words. The more so because the case concerned such a
boggy ground, and, unfortunately, often wicked ones. And if, out
of perversity, she did not want to understand it and started behav-
ing unsteadily? Such doubts also appeared. In the end, he gave
up all explication and did not bring his knowledge into the air,
which allowed the woman's agitation to cool down and air out.
And that eagle tattooed on her neck, holding a sniper rifle in its
claws—t intrigued him very much, and he could not stop thinking
about it. Especially the tiny stars below the rifle. Lots of stars. He did
not underestimate it. On top of that, he was aware that he had ven-
tured into some other territory, so he had to be vigilant and apply
the principle of limited trust. Not because he was fearful, because
he wasn't, but out of foresight. Harameus had a strong spine,

not of some plasticine or putty. He was always an independent character and temperament, mentally mature early. He was wise by nature. His perspicacious mind proved its power when he was a boy, a little unruly drum, a spritely bumming top, who knew much and had quick-witted eyes and a smile like that. Oh, what brightness and wisdom were in the eyes of that cherub. Nimble from birth. By the time he was five, he could jump on trees and write simple sentences, make a bonfire without anyone's help, run his hand over the mossy nettle leaves painlessly, and catch wasps and bumblebees into a matchbox, wondering how many devils could fit in that box. Always a quick-witted crafty scalawag. Soon afterwards, his courage also manifested itself. One crisp morning, when the day caught its first breath, when the cows were watered, the ponies fed, and the poultry released into the yard, out of curiosity, he climbed, by some miracle, over the rye straw sheaves, up to the very roof of his grandmother's Dutch house (adapted in the harvest season as a barn) wanting to look at the rural landscape through the roof hatch. Climbing a tall tree in a cherry or pear orchard, or a walnut growing in the garden, was also not any obstacle for him. Clinging to the highest branches, he jumped to the ground, absorbing the impact of his fall, landing on his bent legs. He was laughing very loudly when his grandmother and mother lamented and said prayers under the tree. Spending his summer vacation in the countryside, he acquired fitness skills, love of nature and tenacity. Only once did he experience an unpleasant situation when his village mates conspired against him and threw him in a duck pool so that he could learn to swim. He entered pre-adulthood with similar traits of character. The parish vicar quickly became convinced of the boy's strength, who conducted religion lessons in the church's catechetical room, where his mother and grandmother sent him once a week, despite the protests of his father's family. One week, when a painful stie formed and grew on Harameus's eyelid (it was swollen despite being rubbed with a fly and a golden ring), on a stormy, windy evening during religion lessons, the priest, seeing Harameus's torment, summoned him to his presence in order to look closely at the annoying ailments. And as he twisted his teenage head, held in his hands, he spat at Harameus in the eye out of nowhere. The enormous contraction that followed nearly damaged that fragile almond window to the world. Stunned by this highly degrading and incomprehensible act, he carefully opened one eye, the healthy one, then barely raised the eyelid of the other. Then he saw, instead of the chubby face of the vicar, a sudden and baleful darkness—the darkest and blackest imaginable, which he had never had the opportunity to experience before. It made him panic, but as soon as his ear caught the laughter of his peers, and when he noticed sparks in the nearby space between the match and the edge of the box, being struck by the vicar over the candle, his fear suddenly left him. There was an overwhelming urge to retaliate. Then he moved his half-blurred eyesight around the room, and after a while he looked again at the vicar. First did he look at the vicar, then at the classmates, then at the vicar again, then at the class again. The teeth of his peers were flashing with whiteness of the mocking giggles, in the gleaming pupils of a satisfied priest, and the candle flame was reflected in the eyes of the classmates sitting closer. Moments later, the bulbs resurrected again. The power plant turned on electricity gain. The humiliated Harameus almost collapsed underground from shame he felt then. He quickly remembered the grandmother's life motto she had coined, when she was deceived in a restaurant being given bream instead of zander and ice water, for which she had not asked before, as well as when once she was offered horse tartare steak with gherkin to mollify and appease her. Then she said to the waiter, "There will be no waiter spitting in our face, shortening the horse's life, and seating guests in a windowless room, by restrooms, at unset tables."

Harameus, encouraged by this memory, immediately repaid tit for tat to the vicar thus blocking his way to the upcoming confirmation. And although the stie quickly receded as a result, Harameus still has a grudge against the clergy to this day. And when meetings have taken place, he has kept a safe distance. Although there was a separation of several years in the meeting of Harameus and the vicar (he did not hide his grudge), he did not fail to send him birthday cards with wishes. It can be safely said that he was, however, the antonym of a beautiful young man, despite the fact that he came from a well-mannered family. He was not a pretty, charming teenager, but with time his features grew noble and his temper weakened. He preserved his cheerfulness and proclivity to jokes on a decent level. For the first money he earned at the fruit market-place, he bought a bacon slicer, giving it to a herring trader who constantly complained about adversities of life, who lived next door, and who had just entered an independent business. As it soon turned out, it was a turning point for his whole life as he soon became a regional tycoon in the meat industry, quickly acquiring two new stores on the street front. Harameus had a lucky hand in business. Whatever he touched, he turned it into a precious metal. But he disposed of cash prudently. He was not wasting money. At the time when he was brought up without a father, he was cared for by a somewhat strict mother who held home rulership. For that reason, he had some of her personality traits that made him grow into an old-fashioned boss who made employees stand to attention and stuck to the walls as he walked down the bank corridor. It was said about him in the city that he was a bastard, that his tourist combination of spoon and fork, apart from a straw for drinking blood, that during lunch he made himself constantly entertained with conversation; that he would not be able to try soup until he was bored by the humorous stories and jokes that were told to him; that he hated any opposition, and even as a child he must have been a stubborn, mouthy tyrant. Just a born predator. These were quite risky and harmful theses and terrible aspersions, because no one, so far, had managed to prove it. As it really was, there is no way to know. Today's pseudomonographers who create these anti-legends, belonging to coteries and teams that they created themselves, show-offs without talents, harmlessly mediocre, wool-producing rams, sitting in bars, spending time gossiping about other people's asses, where after returning home they grooved each other's asses, these people knew better than Harameus himself what he was like in his heart and what kind of human being he was. They filtered all the information they heard and read about him by passing them through their small minds, which resulted in a distorted satire, macabre, and marvellation. The desire of knowledge was so big and vain that they did not hesitate to question Harameus's closest associates about financial results and other sensitive data. Despite his vices, no one breathed a word, even then—apart

from a few timid protests—when he introduced an order so that
a dollar must be thrown into a large jar, located in the welcome
hall, every other hall, and by the fountain outside, for each
swearword uttered. This applied to both employees and customers visiting the bank. This self-punishment was voluntary,
and as Harameus assumed, no one shirked responsibility by
honoring their weaknesses. The jars, as it soon turned out, had
to be turned into ten-gallon barrels, but after the peak of the
sixth week of that regulation, the expected values came close to
zero. The times before the Tower of Babel had returned, when
only a proper and polite language was valid. The tightening after
the spring quarter was suspended. After less than a year, it was
completely abolished. In spite of the steep course he took on the
indecent word, the bank staff remained loyal, even more than
before. Therefore, for curious philosophasters, financial results
and other banking secrets were still unknown, always dark
numbers. Jealousy—that grudge that was borne by them—did
not give them peace. They would happily stand over the ruins of
his company should there be any economic disaster or hostile
takeover. Still, the world did not scare him. He did not consider
worst-case scenarios. Even if he did, he would get down with zest
to any new idea that came to mind. For him, the world did not
end with banking. He was even ready to become a bell craftsman
(when he was a child, he often watched their work) and cast
bells—after all, he knew metals quite well. The same applies to
the art of jewelry, whose arcana were introduced to him by his
cousin. In this case, he was distracted by the ever-black fingertips from polishing compounds, soldering and using a file. But
he would have gotten used to even to it if he had to. In the bell-
foundry, his heart ached and became broken, because, in one
summer month, an undefined year, when he witnessed how the
bells that were cut up into pieces, brought from impoverished
cathedral were sold and delivered there to be melt into canons.
He admired the hard character of the bell founders. He saw them
struggle with their conscience as they packed the pieces of the
bells into casting vats. Too many of them (these bells) had gone
to slaughter this century. For want of anything better, Harameus
could also find happiness in the Texas oil companies or some
turquoise-managed company. He was not afraid of any work and

could lie down next to each one, as one of his former employees joked. It was true that Harameus was neither sentimental nor effusive—much less willing to open up. It was extremely difficult to gain access to his heart. He did not reciprocate politeness to his interlocutor very eagerly because he knew perfectly well how it usually ended. When he extended a finger, he had to keep his hand stiffly leaning against the table. Besides, such courtesies only limited the honesty of statements. At his bank, not all employees were honored generously, but the payment was always adequate and on time. The employees did not have to sign any receipt—he trusted them to the fullest. Only once did he put his signature on a blank check out of carelessness, which cost him a large overpayment, but it was a time of youth and he was not devastated by this experience. He was the employer as he was, but he was always decent and honest about matters. He had moments of breakdown when the state of cash flow became alarming, yet he never made a single rumble, no boo at all that there were holdups and bottlenecks, that costs and jobs had to be cut. When the recession began and the circle of problems narrowed, they all took hitch in their belts equally and mobilized each other to toil. Nobody complained then that he had to work overtime, and he did not demand to be paid for his overtimes. And the fact that he implemented and used the Prussian discipline, not tolerating any excuses or idling—as he himself characterized by diligence and subtle distinction—actually, this was good for everyone. He did not jealously keep his secrets, and he willingly shared his knowledge, thanks to which many were initiated. His thorough knowledge of economics made him a repository of knowledge. Harameus also did not use any quackery or jugglery in doing business with his customers, as well as he did not practice fraud. He did not manipulate unaware people. And since the contracts had a lot of content, they had to be put on vellum somehow. Hence the print was the size of poppy seeds. The real miracle of banking, which he had dreamed of for years, would be the universal acceptance of people who were forever penniless, impecunious, financially bleeding out, under the yoke of the thick cares and woes of life. To allow them to suppers and to lavish breakfasts. This is what he wanted with all his heart. To give a chance and an opportunity to start creating a small business—step by step, through the trot to the gallop, from begged bread to their own bakery. However, he realized the industry would never forgive him. For the fact that he wanted to betray his social stratum, that he could use his mind to make people happier; that is why he has made many confirmed enemies. He even heard that he was commissioned to be killed.

"Some drill would be useful to you," the woman said with her eyes down on him. Harameus glanced at her with simultaneously tired and surprised eyes. He ignored the peculiar offer and began silently cleaning his pants with a damp handkerchief.

"To be a subordinate of a woman isn't disgrace at all," she continued

"The big tomato plant processes small tomatoes," he replied impatiently.

"Come on, don't be shy."

"The king of Judea was overthrown by the grace of Rome."

However, seeing that the woman did not give up, reluctantly, he rose up from the stairs. With a telling gesture she showed him a place on the paved square in front of the temple. He reluctantly followed her order. As he stood at the focal point, he looked around in some vague fear. Seeing that there was no living soul in the square and its vicinity, apart from Silvester pollinating the car, he straightened up and threw out his own chest. The sun dazzled his eyes. From a cast-iron balcony under a two-arched arcade, the chief's bodyguard watched him, and from the nearby gate turret, on which a city flag fluttered in the air, a scarecrow (to scare off pigeons) was looking at him. In the sky, hawks, carried by a warm current, were circling. The space was relatively clean and serene. The sparse clouds on the high layer were flowing slowly. A papal pennant was fluttering gently on the mast by the square.

"Attention!" she commanded, "Boat-shaped hands against your thighs! Head up!" Harameus tightened up like a string. He seemed to have heard the sound of a cavalry trumpet, and then the battle trumpet sounded. Instinctively, he looked at the towering campanile. The woman, seeing that Harameus narrowed his eyes and blew his bangs, shouted, "Turn left!" He obediently turned on the heel of his right leg and toes of his left.

"Forward march!" He started moving vigorously. Meanwhile,

the sounds of Wagner's "Ride of the Valkyries" came from inside the temple. The organ boomed with full force. The bellows and pipes were working at full speed. The organist's feet pressed against the pedals. Harameus, picking up the pace, marched around the square. On the second straight he lost his hand swing and step a bit. He also missed the beat, but he quickly corrected these shortcomings and continued marching along with the note. After a while, the "Valkyries," which probably escaped from the organist by some small mistake, or a mess in the tablature, which probably no one but him caught on, were replaced with the proper wedding march. But before this happened, the organist angrily punched at the wood side of the keyboard—and what is surprising here is it did not cause any scandal among the celebrants—and then shouted a scolding at full strength of his lungs in a hard Prussian accent and not very fluent English in the direction of the lamplighter, perhaps as innocent as a lamb:

"Me like ze German order, not ze pigsty!" He did not stop there and after a while he shouted even louder, when he discovered that the box standing on the chest with the tabs was empty. "Ver is my pork fat and kummel schnapps?" Indebted, being perhaps undeservedly scolded, the lamplighter shouted out what he had been planning for a long time, mocking the organist:

"Me don't like ze German pork fat, me don't like ze schnapps or Nutella! Me don't like ze Pipechoker! Me don't like toads! Me don't like ze BMW!" These words enraged the organist even more (strong emotions and anger emanated from his face, he turned purple, the blood was bursting on his temples) since he hurled an insult towards the lamplighter, who was on his way out, striking the wooden side of the organ with extraordinary force with a leather horsewhip:

"Trottel! No kindergarten here! Ze times are zo cruel." Then he added in German:

"Nichts und nichts!" Meanwhile, the lamplighter proudly marched to the exit taking a cage with a parrot, which he had earlier taken down from the storeroom closet for altar candles and fire clocks in the office for altar candles and fire clocks. The parrot was hitting the cage wires with its beak, and the lamplighter reacted quickly by pouring a handful of grains and crumbs of fermented wine yeast into the cage. The parrot was well trained, because when she sensed some trouble she shouted partly in German, partly in English:

"Long live the Kaiser! Long live Frau Kanzlerin! Long live the organist!" So that immediately after some kind of lamplighter's trick the bird would scream at top volume:

"Kaiser kaput! Pipechoker kaput! Toad kaput! Frau kanzelerin gut!"

The cries of the parrot echoed loudly off the walls. The organist, still heated with anger, shouted in the direction of the lamplighter:

"Halt! Halt! Kom back to verk!" However, he was happy, no longer burdened with any commitments and obligations to his superiors and holy walls, constantly robbed of his dignity (once he was even thrown into a marten without cause and bashed with a stick) whose robbery of dignity was brought about by the strict rule of the cathedral and the evil powers that sometimes there appeared. Now freed from everything, he got fresh air. He must have planned his escape before, because his legs were shod in travel shoes, and in his bosom was peppered bacon wrapped in cellulose wadding, which he now pulled from behind his belt. First, he sniffed it through the sticky paper, then carefully folded it in half and tugged at a bite with his side teeth. Luxuriating in the taste, he reluctantly spat the skin to the ground. He did a similar thing with the schnapps poured into the bottle, but not wasting a drop here. Then he put everything in a felted bag slung over his shoulder and, whistling, disappeared around the corner of the nearby prelate's place. A choral harpist with a myrtle wreath in her hair attempted to appease the situation, chanting a song pleasant to the ear, and tugging the golden threads of the harp with her slender fingers, but it was to no avail. Only the smell of cheap cologne stayed behind the lamplighter, and black peppercorns sprinkled on the stone floor, which the parrot swept with its wings out of the cage. The situation there was not a good situation at all; it was a complex, desperate, even borderline situation, and things did not go well, because the chief broke away from his nap, into which he was immersed by a minor fugue, and exclaimed, "divide et impera!" He wanted to scream something else, but as his eyesight blurred as he remembered where he was, his unspoken thought was hidden as classified. He then signaled through the chain of attorneys accompanying him, with whom he never parted, just in case, for the 'Toad-Pipechoker' to play something to lull him to sleep again, but the latter, still in an angry state, struck completely different tones, which he probably fell a bit on the lead, because he began to smack his tongue out of dissatisfaction. Wagner's wedding march, on which the organist got to work (he played from memory), sounded too fast. There was also an unintentional transposition, as he dropped the piece onto a higher octave, which Harameus did not mind at all, as he was marching on around the square.

The newlyweds approached the presbytery. As they knelt on the marble platform, laughter spread through the basilica, to which immediately the sexton, a stooping marantic guy, responded. With a clever move of his hand, he flew over the knobs of potentiometers, diming the lights of chandeliers, heavy from crystals, those glass spiders, and scattered wall lamps. Then he activated the window blinds and the rosette, which fell down at once. It seems that from under the dome lantern, a bat freed itself of the hold and glided down. Some people covered their hair with their hands fearfully. The Australian black fox twisted a few circles overhead and disappeared again somewhere. An owl followed it. The bird made a bit of a stir among the people as it made a few figure eights just under the chandeliers and then took off somewhere in the air as well. The basilica sank into darkness. The laughter subsided. All the people gathered in the temple held their breath, and when they got used to the darkness, the pupils of their eyes found some smoldering and flickering landmarks in space and on firm ground, they heaved sighs of relief. The 'Bull Terrier' did not mind the darkness, he always felt comfortable in cloudy waters. Dark red smoke detectors shone in the roof of the dome in the thickened air of myrrh, and below it, due to lack of oxygen, dimmed the almost dead flames of the altar candles. Only the deformed remnants dripping with solidifying wax, stayed on the fire clocks. Meanwhile, the soles of the BullTterrier glowed with phosphorescent paint. On the left, one of his witty servants wrote in a capital letter: 'HELP,' on the second 'ME!' thanks to which the Bull Terrier, involuntarily, briefly became the hero of the end of the ceremony. Until now, it was the Bull Terrier who made fun of the common people, today he was the one at whom laughed. Someone, in euphoria, threw a handful of heavy coins towards the bride and groom, which fell with a clink and rolled on the stone floor. Another hand added grains—a model example of human recklessness. The sexton did not mind the coins, but the grains set him in a foul mood. He lit the interior only when the Bull Terrier could feel the fence beside him by the presbytery and rose to his impending oath. Immediately afterwards, the just-put-in-motion blades of windmills hanging on the ropes chased away the smoke.

"Right hand, left leg, left hand, right leg! Not otherwise!" the woman shouted to Harameus. "Legs up, straight!" Harameus wiped his dewy forehead with his sleeve. There was also a slight frown on his face, most likely from the tapping of the thin soles of his shoes on the pavement. Perhaps his feet were burning. As the organist played the last bar, someone peeked out from behind the temple door. It seemed it was a sexton's assistant.

"Don't disturb!" the woman said, grasping the half-opened wing with her eye. Pretending to be brought outside by the creak of hinges, he maneuvered the door back and forth. When she gave him a stern look, the door quickly shut.

"Run, march!" she commanded.

Harameus took off. He did less than three rounds, when the woman, seeing that he was barely breathing, shouted again, "Cigarette break!"

"I don't smoke," he shouted back, barely panting.

"There are those who smoke," she replied in a formal tone.

Harameus returned to the fluted column. His shirt stuck to his body. They sat down.

"You have a knack, boy," she praised him. "You hit the beat. Were you a Scout?" Harameus just smiled. When his breathing became even, he said, "I was also a drummer, but these are the old days."

They sat in silence for some time, sipping water alternately.

"And what happened next with the Reverend and Excellency?" He asked curiously, after he had cooled down completely.

"Do you really want to hear this?" Harameus nodded.

"His Excellency was a person of the highest goodness and he

distributed favors fairly, although he also had his weaknesses."

"Who doesn't have them?" said Harameus. "Most people take what is given to them with the right hand with their left hand."

"Oh, now, it's like hearing Bishop Garcia. He was a real good man. He never refused help, and certainly a good word. And it's much drearier than money, when comfort comes from nowhere.

"Good words, if you look closely at them," Harameus said carefully, "often lose their value."

"Man, what are you talking about!" she huffed. "Maybe those coming from flatterers' mouths are, but not those coming straight from the sympathizing heart. Excellency was a man of ineffable kindness! Always close to people. Of course, he sometimes happened to have a lavish dinner with the town's rich and famous, but he also didn't shrink from honey vodka with spices, kugel and eggs Benedict. He was absolutely reluctant to eat using silverware. He neither cared about a red zucchetto nor show interest in hawking. High life just didn't attract him. He went to dinner parties and banquets without enthusiasm. After insincere friendships, he never bent down. Usually he snapped something small on the run, prompted by pastoral duty, and rushed to real people. Usually he only came back for dinner and sleep. It's just a pity that he died so prematurely. He was convinced he had sails for all kinds of winds, but as it turned out, his false lanterns were lit by those he trusted most, and eventually he smashed into the reefs. From regret, his heart could not hold out anymore."

"Gratitude is such an ephemeral flower," said Harameus.

"You are probably curious how I know all this."

"Not really."

"Well then, I'm gonna tell you. I often used to pick blueberries with Ms. Cassie in the woods. Silence tired her a lot." The woman smiled. "I envied her only one thing," she said, looking at her own flat belly. "Ms. Cassie ate a lot and had a sweet tooth, and sugar never went into her hips, though."

"And Father Dominique?"

"Oh, that one . . . He did like to eat and seldom did he speak a word, but when he eventually did, he cut to the quick."

"I mean the further progress of events of that night when he stood at the doorstep of the Celestial Peace."

"I told Father Dominique to sit down and wait. In the meantime, I went to the back room to bring something to warm him up, because he was freezing, but when I returned, he vanished into the blue. The banging at the door started again, but this time, it was much louder."

"How much did you drink before?" Harameus asked with some irony in his voice.

"I always told myself, as a consolation, that I worked in a theater dressing room, but a little bit colder, ha ha." Harameus glanced at her with compassion.

"I opened the door again, and, much to my surprise, I saw no one other than our young vicar with a pale face, I thought to myself that there were too many visitors for one night. I wanted to slam the door in his face, but he insisted on seeing the boss of the morgue as the Reverend Dominique just passed away and needed to be prepared for the funeral. This information was too heavy for my legs. I felt dizzy . . . and I remember nothing of what happened just afterwards. When I regained consciousness, the boss stood above me and poured water over me. Because I knew Father Dominique for many years, the vicar often asked me to prepare the deceased on his last journey. I had a kind of inner resistance because of what he had done to me a few years earlier, but the vicar was very generous with cash, so I gave in to him."

"Something very unpleasant?" Harameus inquired.

"I'm gonna tell you later. I'm out of sorts now."

"But why did you run away faster than from a battlefield?"

"It was only the beginning of the story. The fact that I saw the almost naked reverend at the doorstep of the Celestial Peace is nothing compared to what happened next. When Father Dominique was brought to the morgue and, when he was lying so calmly on a stone slab, I started to remove inch by inch of his hoary facial hair. When, like a mother, I stroked his head, and he, as if ashamed smiled at me slightly. I asked him if it was worth suspecting an honest woman of theft to all and sundry. When, in this anger of a sort, by accident, I cut him on the cheek with a straight razor, he hissed loudly through his teeth and opened his eyes. I only remember only my legs again becoming rubbery and soft and sinking to the floor for the second time. Luckily, the boss was nearby and heard the thud of my falling body.

When I came to my senses and saw the untouched face of the reverend, I sobered up at once, and, barefooted, stormed out without stopping to think, straight to the street. I will never again set foot in the Celestial Peace. I even didn't go there to pick up my paycheck. And this is how the recession and the reverend changed my life. But I blame nobody." Harameus lowered his eyes.

"Don't worry. It's not your fault. You look like a decent man," she said in a comforting voice. " A nice bottle. This water must be expensive."

"This is my favorite, Manhattan Spring. Have a sip. You look thirsty." He gave her the bottle.

"Since you have nothing other than this," she said, staring at his watch. Needles of the beams reflected off the bracelet dazzled her eyes, so she narrowed them and fixed them on the dial.

"I see it's not a knockoff," she said with admiration. "My husband wore the same watch as yours. Oh well, those were the days," she sighed.

Harameus pulled down the sleeve to cover the watch. Surprised, he looked at her, but he said no word.

"Good water. You always have good water in New York. Good water runs where people are good!" she said, "Drink some more. Heat dries the skin and slows down the senses, and this is highly unhealthy. I'm now satisfied."

"What is the reason of your satisfaction?" Harameus asked with unconcealed disbelief.

"The reason is I've met you today," she answered without a second thought. „At last, I can talk to someone wise."

"Don't exaggerate. Maybe once I was wise, but now . . . it has probably changed. God has decided so."

"Oh, if that's the case, God knew what he was doing. Maybe once you were stupid, and only now he's made you aware of what is important in life."

"Do you have to shout?" he said covering his ear with his hand.

"Ah, this damn dullness of my hearing! It's all because of the explosion," she said. Harameus gave her a searching look.

"This is an old story." The woman unwrapped a small bundle, which she took out of a military blouse. The uncovered photo showed a smiling girl dressed in a sand-colored uniform with sergeant's insignia on the chest. Two soldiers put their arms around her neck on both her sides. The inscription on the reverse read, "Iraq 1991."

"Only I survived, though I should've died together with them," she said in a rueful voice.

"Do you go to church often?" he asked after a while.

"Every day, but only as close as to the stairs. A long time ago, I was suspected of theft I didn't commit. I still feel those stares on me."

Harameus again gave her a surprised look.

"When I was still a beautiful, married young woman, ha ha, I found something precious in this church. The Reverend Dominique, may he rest in peace, saw that thing around my neck. I wore it as a talisman attached to a very thin chain. It brought me luck. He claimed someone had stolen it from him earlier. He received it from a vagrant whom he gave extreme unction to. He didn't believe me, though I swore on the holy cross."

"What exactly was the thing that it triggered off so many bad emotions in the reverend?"

"Soon afterwards, I lost everything: my husband, friends, job. All of them turned their backs on me. This thing really brought me luck earlier, but later on, you see for yourself what it brought me."

"Stick to the point. What was the thing?"

"Oh, young man, I'd never seen the more amazing thing in my dog's life."

"When in the world are you going to tell me? Please."

"A beautiful fountain pen, made of the purest gold. It wrote so smoothly and finely. It was as light as a dove's flight feather."

Harameus felt dizzy. He squinted his eyes and rested his head against the column.

"It's so good you've drunk some water. Like I've said heat dims the senses."

"Did the reverend administer extreme unction to the hobo without a leg, with thick dark hair and beard?"

The woman gave Harameus a surprised look, and, after a while, she asked, "Did you know him? Maybe he was your relative?"

Harameus said nothing. He looked straight ahead, being hardly able to concentrate on anything.

"Take a nap as you look like death warmed up. Can you give me one of your business cards as a souvenir of our encounter?"

"Sure," he answered, not remembering he had showed her his wallet. Perhaps he did not remember this as the heat was unbearable both for the body and for the mind. He spread the wallet and arranged his business and credit cards in a bow on the palm of his hand.

"Choose whichever you like best," he said enthusiastically.

"I like this one," the woman pointed at a chartreuse flourished card.

"Only this one? he asked.

"Yeah."

"What's your name?"

The woman put the card in the bundle and straightened her back.

"God bless you for the water, young man. You have heart of gold, and you aren't disgusted with a beggar-woman."

Harameus tried to clear his head and gather his thoughts; however, it was hard to him to put it all together. The heat was more and more unbearable.

"Thank you for a good word," he said to her after a while, but she and her bundle disappeared without a trace. He thought chat he daydreamed the chat, but the clang of the bells in the cathedral tower made him aware of the realest of all realities. He took off his cell phone and sent a text message to Walter, telling him to arrive at Cathedral Plaza.

CHAPTER THREE

The plane began to descend. In the chink of the clouds, like through a keyhole, loomed into view the glitter of Manhattan. A bright cobweb, woven of perpendicular and meandering streets, dyed the night yellow and orange. A blood flow—driven by millions of small and big hearts, pulsated. Skyscrapers looked like luminous figures, placed on the squares of a chessboard. You could just hold out your hand to move them as pawns. In the distance, in an out-of-the-way nook of the sky shone the moon with its waxing crescent. Like a scythe stuck with its sharp tip in a crystal blackness, it accompanied myriads of shimmering stars. Out of the graphite-gray horizon of the eastern part of the city loomed the outline of the Rockaway Peninsula, encircled by April tranquil waters. Nearby, JFK Airport had its vast seat. The day, embraced less and less tight by the lengthy night, swelled wider and wider, higher and higher. Within sight appeared a strip on whose sides oscillated pinhead-sized red lights. The pilot tilted the aircraft to the right side flying in a semicircle. The wind swayed the plane.

Walter closed his eyes and inwardly muttered, "God Almighty, let me land safely." Harameus turned off his cellphone. The clock indicated that it was still early.

"In a minute it's gonna be over," Harameus said to Walter, who, terrified, looked at him. "I meant to say, we'll soon land safely," he chose his words more carefully.

"I rarely fly, Mr. Lehm. I feel much better in cars."

"From the airport, we'll go straight to the hotel."

"To the hotel?" Walter repeated in disbelief, glancing at his disheveled jacket and shirt. Harameus smiled mysteriously.

The cab drove up to the Pogoria Plaza Hotel. Harameus had not yet paid the fare when he noticed a hotel doorman, with a look of growing impatience and anger on his face, approach them. With an ordering gesture, he told them to leave the driveway right away. Harameus got out of the car, followed by Walter. Unshaven, with disordered hair, he did not look like a Sister of Mercy. The doorman, seeing a taller and unfriendly individual, spread his arms and smiled amicably.

"Welcome to New York. First time in our hotel?" he shouted out enthusiastically. After a while, he stood by Harameus, attempting to take off his bag from the shoulder.

"Thank you for your help, I can manage," said Harameus.

The smile on the doorman's face disappeared faster than it appeared. He pulled down his livery jacket and went back to the entrance. Walter wanted to take the bag from Harameus, but he protested.

"Starting today, I'll carry my stuff all by myself."

"You don't need me anymore, boss?"

"It's not about that, but it won't be the way it was. I'll need a trusted adviser now, not a helper." Walter's face brightened instantly. He opened the entrance door vigorously and followed Harameus.

"Could you reveal the purpose of our visit?"

"Be patient," Harameus replied and turned to the doormen standing right outside the entrance.

"Is the jewelry and souvenir store still there?"

"Silver is on the top floor," the one standing closer to the door replied casually, looking at their unshaven faces and crumpled clothes. "To the right, behind the maintenance room and the ice machine." Harameus nodded and smiled.

"Gold and diamonds, on the second," the other one added with some derision.

Harameus took a bill from his wallet and pushed it into the hand of the doorman who answered first.

"Oh, no need," he said with an innocent tone, eyeing the denomination and slipped the banknote into his pocket. After a while he said in a nice voice, "Do you have any special wishes?"

"Please do me a small favor," said Harameus.

"Whatever you command, sir."

"When we were in the cab, we saw a few homeless people on the church's stairs. Could you come up with something to eat for them. Of course, I'll cover the expense."

"Over there, around the corner, sir, it is a synagogue," the doorman corrected him.

"What difference does it make? There, too, I'm sure, they have needy people."

"Oh, yes, and many," he nodded. "But a few blocks away is the cathedral. There are more homeless folks there."

"In that case, please take the meals to both."

"As you wish, sir," he replied without leaving the place he stood in. Harameus took out his wallet again and pressed a few bills into the doorman's hand. The doorman as if on the wings of the wind, faded away in the abyss of the hall. He stopped, however, behind the philodendron's big pot, looked at the bill against the light and, with a satisfied face, moved on.

"Let's go, Walter, it's about time to eat something," said Harameus, and they headed for the stairs.

"Excuse me, sir . . . aren't you . . . Is suite 816 . . . you look much like someone . . ." The other doorman stammered out fairly aloud.

"No, no, it might not be me," Harameus answered over his shoulder and went on. The doorman muttered something and returned to the door.

"Walter, to new, better times. To a new beginning!" Harameus proposed the toast and dipped his lips in cool white wine.

"Yes, to a new beginning, boss," said Walter, and poured wine into his throat as if it was compote. The tartness of the wine made him wince, but he nodded in acknowledgment, and after a while, the crystal piece of art stood empty on the table. "Walter, it's not appropriate to drink wine in one gulp."

"Excuse me, boss, but I was thirsty," he said cheerfully and shook off the last drops on his tongue.

"I was kidding, Walter. Drink to your heart's content. Today is a great day. Starting from today, each and every day will be great."

"In that case, I think I'm going to drink more, as I have a strange feeling," he said, and filled the glass once more. Harameus also drank it to the bottom.

"You have a good hunch, Walter," said Harameus, and, holding his glass in his hand, looked at the crystal chandelier, which looked like an inverted water-sprinkling fountain hung from the ceiling.

"Not everyone has this rare opportunity to drink wine under such illumination, but I'm going to change this," he said in a raised voice, which caught the attention of two elderly distinguished-looking ladies, seated a few tables away. He wiped dew off the cold glass with his finger and put it noisily on the table. The ladies again looked at him.

"Mr. Lehm, I guess the manager is coming with his retinue," said Walter.

At the entrance to the restaurant room, there was the same doorman who had previously asked Harameus about apartment 816. Pointing discretely to their table, he whispered something in the ear of a small, skinny man, who adjusted a little bow tie on his neck, and walked without faltering towards them, followed by his two assistants with ready-to-be-used notebooks in their hands. They strode evenly as if they had they exercised this kind of walking before. A guy in the advance guard goose-stepped resolutely, but the rears, judging by their faces and slightly stiff movements, were struck by performance anxiety.

"That must be the manager," Walter said without a shade of doubt, and ensconced himself in a leather armchair.

"Walter, you've turned to me that way for the last time. Don't address me as 'Mr. Lehm,' 'sir,' or 'boss.' Call me by name. After all, we've drunk to new life."

"Sure, ss . . . yes, Harameus, as you wish," he said.

"By the way, this wine is real heady. How could it be that a twenty-year-old liquor has such power."

"Yeah, it's hot as hell." Walter barely had time to fill goblets as three marching guys approached their table. A properly dressed man in the advance guard bowed slightly, however, seeing that they were both toasting, waited a moment, giving them time to taste the wine. In the meantime, he smoothed down his starched, impeccably ironed shirt, then buttoned up and tugged his jacket. He looked at the cuffs on which, in the light of the chandelier, sparkled cat-eye cuff links, under which the wrist was adorned with a bracelet in a similar style, shimmering with bottle green and brown. The razor-sharp edges on the pants rested with a slight fold on the polished patent leather shoes. Seeing that the glasses had been emptied and put on the table, he took a deep breath. "Good morning, gentlemen. I am the manager of this hotel. Can I help you?" he asked courteously. Assistants, in unison, at the same instant, raised notebooks, pressing sharp-tempered pencils against paper. However, after the manager's dismissive look, they quickly returned to their basic standing position.

"I apologize to you, sir for not recognizing you, but I've been working here for a short time and I haven't had enough time to meet all the most distinguished guests yet," he said, slightly embarrassed. "What's worse, I have a poor memory for faces."

"Ah, you are in the three percent of the society that do not recognize previously encountered people. Especially those presented in various, insignificant circumstances by a third man and not previously agreed." Harameus hiccupped imperceptibly. "The eyes protect our bodily stronghold from such unwanted acquaintances. I'd even say it's a social rape." Harameus looked at Walter with a slight rebuke until he poured wine again up to the very rim of the glass. Walter, pretending to have not noticed it, shrugged his shoulders a bit embarrassed. Harameus took a long sip and nibbled on the tortilla, previously digging out a large amount of guacamole from the stone mortar.

"The eyes are the first defensive stronghold of our body, fortified artillery," he continued. "They can attack unexpectedly, but also successfully dodge. They protect us against such unwanted acquaintances and transmit an impulse to the brain to command the legs to carry the rest of the body to the other side of the street, or head South as long as it is a safe place." Walter yawned, closed his eyes and rested his hands on the table. His tired head drooped slightly. Harameus hiccupped again, making Walter flinch again and sit upright. Heavy eyelids, however, did not give up, but he kept up his spirit trying to listen with interest to Harameus's disquisition, as he now wagged his finger to tell him not to pour him any more wine. Walter almost welcomed it, not because he would be finishing the bottle alone—after all, the bottom was already visible—but because he was disturbed by Harameus' momentary slight indisposition. However, he was not in a better position himself—he also felt a slight ripple in his head. He even thought to order something satiating to eat, in order to be in better fettle; for example, the goat in herbs, which the waiter had just recited along with other specialties from the kitchen to the noble ladies sitting at the table by the window. But he departed from this intention, knowing that Harameus preferred a more modest cuisine. He filled a clean glass pouring the remnants from the bottle and offered refreshments to the manager. The latter nodded politely but firmly. "What was I talking about?" Harameus asked Walter.

"Something about rape."

"Ah, yes, about the rape." He smiled under his breath, then looked at the manager. "How are things going?" he asked. The latter, however, was silent politely by the book.

"This chandelier, that great cow, is heavy like an elephant. It will fall on our heads." The manager assured Harameus with a negative soft nod that it was impossible. After a while, however, he looked at the hook in the ceiling from the corner of his eye. Harameus hiccupped again, covered his head with his hands and laughed softly. "I need to eat a pinch of sugar," he said to himself, "otherwise, this hiccup won't go away. Do you have sugar in this joint? Ah, hell with sugar," he muttered, "it's un-healthy." He reached into his pocket and pulled out a chewing gum. "I don't know if it will bring you any consolation," he turned to the manager again, unwinding the gum from the paper, "but with this amnesia I have the same thing. I'm fairly a facial forgetter. As if at call. I want to, I recognize it, I don't want to, I don't give two hoots about those new acquaintances and the accompanying rituals. And who would've thought it that not so long ago—," Harameus lacked a word and was silent for a moment. "That not so long ago—" He again searched for words. "I'm not interested in other people's opinions about me. I'm not bothered by this. Oh, I'm better now," he said, chewing the gum. The manager exhaled with relief. "He's one of us," he thought, and immediately relaxed.

"It is by no means blameworthy," Harameus continued, "indeed, a positive trait, provided there is no debt of honor involved. In contrast to it, as if to sweeten, God rewards people with a very good sense of hearing. Although there are also those who both remember and hear better than others. Except for those jerks who want to forget about their loan as soon as possible. Besides, too much familiarity is not of value today." Harameus shifted his glass towards Walter, asking him to finish his wine. Walter quickly read his request and took the glass. The manager smiled shyly and broke the silence, emboldened by Harameus's well-being. "I don't avoid people if it's what you mean—even those who I don't like, and, by the way, there are not many of them, although I also have to admit and I often hear this and that, which is not pleasant for my ears, being on duty in the hotel. And as for the jerks that you've kindly mentioned, you're absolutely right, I personally found out when I asked to return a portion of what I lent to one in a fit of sympathy. I still hear the same echo: 'Be patient, be patient, be patient . . . ' In the end, I was no longer recognized on the street."

"Please don't worry so much," said Harameus. "Of course, when the loan is not painfully high. It's a waste of health, and the lesson of life comes to good with time. They deliberately look for decent people to eat on."

"Not that I worry too much," replied the manager, "but—"

He moved his head towards the table to conceal his confession "Recently, I did not recognize even my wife on the street." Harameus put on a sympathetic look. "Did she notice you?"

"Not really. She didn't pay the slightest attention to me." He took a deep breath again and sighed. "You two got to make a perfect match," said Walter.

"This is what it is like to work too much," said Harameus, "We have to know when to stop. The happiness that life offers us every day won't wait for us forever. After all, every train leaves at some point."

"You're one hundred percent right," said Walter again. "Only that many who want to travel on this train are stowaways, not wanting to give anything to their loved ones."

"Parasite and miser, I mean," the shorter, more vivacious apprentice interjected from behind the manager's back. The latter, twisting his head, scolded him with his look.

"You speak well, son," said Harameus.

"Once again, please accept my apologies for not recognizing you."

"There is nothing to talk about. Besides, I'm not a frequent patron of this place," said Harameus. "To tell the truth, I don't remember when I was here last time."

"I was informed that your family rented suite 816 for many years. It is a great honor for us to have you staying in our hotel. Your late father gave us his portrait in enamel as a keepsake. It still hanging in the spot of honor of the hunting chamber." Harameus neither confirmed nor denied. The Manager discreetly looked with a piercing gaze at the doorman standing at the end of the room, who shrugged slightly and left the room.

"816 is our best suite," the manager continued, "but frankly— He cautiously looked around, subduing his voice.

"Please excuse my presumptuousness," he hesitated for a moment, "it's not worth the price," he said, and looked away towards the floor under the table.

"I am surprised by your honesty," said Harameus. "And even more by your loyalty."

"Patron's satisfaction is the most important thing for me," he responded immediately. "Production is second." He looked at the assistants and gave them a sign to take notes. The pencils were set in motion. The sheets of paper with the hotel logo, scraped with sharp pencil lead, made a sound of gentle shuffling, and when turned over—a pleasant rustle could be heard.

"In that case, you must be prepared for surprises," said Harameus.

"What do you mean, sir?" Harameus looked at the assistants.

"I'm quite easy about them," he said, "They're my cousins. If you have no wishes, sir, let me go away, but if anything, please call me." At the end of the restaurant room, the doorman's head again peeked from behind the door frame. Stealthily, he watched the situation with one eye. After a while, he hid again and reappeared.

"Thank you for your attention. I wish you a quiet job," said Harameus to the manager.

"I wish you nice stay, sir." Harameus rose from his chair and walked to the chaise longue standing by the wall to rest for a moment. Dressed in a dark suit and gray sneakers, an elderly man, sitting at the end of the sofa, bowed politely and said, "Good morning. How are you?"

"I'm fine. Thank you. And you?" replied Harameus. He recognized the British accent immediately.

"As I see you are tired," said the old man, "please, don't be embarrassed, and rest. I also wanted to take a nap before then, but I was a little ashamed," he said.

"Are you an Englishman? asked Harameus.

"A Welshman," he replied in a low voice.

"Are you all right, Richard?" From the depths of the room came a velvet, dignified voice, nothing like the common, human twaddle.

"Yes, honey, all's absolutely fine," the man replied, and smiled at Harameus.

"My wife, Rebecca," he said proudly.

"Ah, what a beautiful name," Harameus sincerely expressed his admiration.

"Let me introduce myself. Harameus Lehm."

"Richard, Bertrand, Philip . . . I am very pleased to meet you," said the old man, "Your name is quite original, young man."

"My father was passionate about ancient history, hence the name," said Harameus.

"I can't say I didn't have problems with it at school, but somehow everyone got used to it, including myself."

"Are you going to stay here for a long time? How about a little game of rummy or baccarat this evening?"

"I'm sorry, but I'm only going to stay here for a very short time—for lunch and shopping."

"Real estate?"

Harameus took a small oblong box from a plastic bag and put it on the table and nodded.

"May I?" The man gently opened the box and unwrapped a neckerchief. His eyes glittered.

"What a dandy thing," he said, enthused. "Is this a gift?"

"Yes."

"I've never seen anything like this before."

"If you want to rest, while keeping your eyes on your honorable wife, lie down here comfortably," Harameus suggested. "I'll move to the other sofa."

"Oh, now I really feel fine," the old man said louder, putting a pillow under his head.

"Richard, how could you!" Rebecca cried, opening her face much to her indignation.

"It's all right, darling," he said joyfully. "I'm not touching the sofa with my shoes."

CHAPTER FOUR

"A walk will do us good, Walter. We'll get some air," said Harameus. With his hand, numb from a nap, he shook the down off his shoulders, bits of straw off his pants, and rubbed the nape. Out of the clouds emerged the sun. A streak of light, which fell through the windows, was filled with the dust, and the next ones followed it—together they projected an image of a tree swayed by the wind on the wall. Under the overhead fan dangled a flypaper full of trapped flies. The blades milled the air, and the flies danced their last dance of life to a serenade. From the loudspeakers came Mozart's "Eine Kleine Nachtmusik." A draft in the garret rocked the wooden shutter; the creaks annoyed some guests. From the portrait hung over the fireplace, a man past his prime with his hair in disarray and unjustly high forehead sternly glanced. His screwed-up lips, fleshy sideburns, and nineteenth-century flair overawed even more. His head, rested on a high collar, watched fixedly like a hawk, in unseemly fashion from the welcoming hall. Regardless of from which vantage point you got a glimpse of the oldish Werther, he drew a bead on anyone who crossed the threshold of the massive door leading to the banqueting hall, or the border of the wall on which the portrait hung from a nail. A member of the Royal Society of a Lost Cause, the creator of the most outstanding works—precious cimelia—before whose image, in the days of yore, no one had ever dared to pass by without giving a bow; he watched the newcomers in the same way as a doctor watches the residents in the isolation hospital on the other side of the window—attentively, piercingly with a searching look.

"Is he this famous pessimist?" one of the ladies asked. The other waved her hand. "You're not a good judge of people," she replied with a wry face.

A waiter entered the hall with a tray in his hands and announced that the entertainment portion would take place in twenty minutes. He was quickly surrounded by a wreath of guests. Ladies, whose backs had been killing them and who had barely risen from chairs only the day before, at the thought of the approaching dances, straightened up like herons, ready for preying. Gentlemen threw out their chests, tidied up their hair and surveyed the site. They pontificated about painting, music, numerology and stuck steadfastly to their own opinions. The garret from which—except for creaks and squeaks other suspicious carnal sounds came—was the sanctum and the favorite place of the founder's father and, in accordance with his last will, written in the presence of two notaries representing the renowned notary public's offices, and the four most professional assessors (two of them for each party), retained its former function, excluding the alcove. Until then, it had served as a resting chamber for auxiliary personnel, as well as a cubbyhole. It contained sacks of flour, an anthracite box, dried sausages, and in the neighboring room (the former parlor)—palliasses, eiderdowns, pillows, and blankets. Upstairs in the attic, where the stairs end, and shy liberties begin, where lingered the smell of sausages, dried mushrooms, garlic, and cologne—time stopped more than a hundred years ago. Although coal had not burned in furnaces for a long time, everyone became so accustomed that no one could imagine the garret without boxes, shovels, and pokers. The last preparations for the "Musical Soirée" were in progress to have everything in perfect trim. The hall was decorated with portraits of great composers. Wrought iron candlesticks were carried into the parlor, and, by the main window, a smorgasbord was brought into prominence so that it could be seen from the outside. A porter in livery stood at the entrance door. People standing outside looked at the table with envy, bit their lips, and badmouthed those inside. When they cast covetous eyes on the dishes licking their lips, the porter immediately took out a wooden ruler from his pocket and angrily threatened them through the window. They then jumped back from the large window and timorously watched him; as soon as he turned aside, pestered by the guests, they clung to the fogged-up window plane. Although a wide variety of delicacies was not too rich, there was nothing bad to say about the table. On it there were predominantly appetizers (camembert cheese pieces squeezed by cucumber slices on both sides), omelets rolled up like salami, crushed garlic bread crumbled by hungry guests, and olive oil spilt from plastic thimbles (thankfully not from all of them). Lumps of cucumber, zucchini, and avocado on cocktail sticks, as well as tofu and miso soup for vegetarians. For executives, cheese fare (reblochon), potatoes au gratin on wine, chowder soup, and the king of the Roquefort cheeses in combination with a tomato slice. Each appetizer was pierced on a toothpick, and, from a fly's-eye view, it looked like a sailboat, where an olive was fastened in the place of the preventer backstay. Next to the platter, sushi and sashimi in five flavors were served. The space by the main window—both inside and outside—came alive even more, making it too dark inside and candles had to be lit. After a few minutes the candles emanated a pleasant, cinnamon-smelling mist. In the corner of the hall, a rehearsal of a six-member choir from a nearby music school took place, and, on the opposite side, a slim girl practiced an iambic pentameter. The table, before the proper sounds could be heard, became empty. Everyone was already in a good mood and impatiently waited for the culminating point. Suddenly, a loud groan came from the northern wing. Silence fell in the hall. In the background, there were only murmurs of a trickle spurting from the mouth of a stone nymph holding a lute in her hand that stood in the middle of the small fountain. Shortly afterwards, there was heard a cry of pain, muffled by a hand, a blanket, or a pillow. Children ran around the jet d'eau, dipping briefly their fingers in the water. As soon as the eyes of their chaperones relinquished supervision, they took water in their hands and spattered on the walls. Those nimbler rolled up their sleeves and picked up the coins. When they got bored, they started moving and spacing widely the chairs that stood by the wall. When the screams and groans stopped, everyone returned to chats and courses.

"A good hotel," said Walter. "Everywhere—feather quilts, straw mattresses, blankets, and sheets of music, and, what's more, good cuisine," he added approvingly.

"The feathers are also everywhere," said Harameus.

"But these are goose feathers, not duck ones," said Walter.

"So you're an expert in the subject of feathers—so to say, a 'featherologist,' aren't you?" Walter, in response, quacked, then he threw out his chest and crowed.

"I'm a countryman," he said proudly. Harameus cast a glance at him with an understanding smile. The guests in the hall looked at their watches.

"Check-out is in an hour," the stoker calmed them down, making a cigarette in a roller. The guests breathed a sigh of relief.

"We have a leak in the basement," the receptionist exclaimed to the receiver.

"In that case, those from downstairs should take a lie detector test," she heard in response on the phone with the speaker on.

"Water! No denunciations!" she explained emphatically. "I've being saying for a long time that the gaskets have to be replaced and the windows closed during a storm!"

"Don't yell like that," he talked back.

"Since it's like wasting my breath," she said.

"It's stuffy," the stoker chimed in, putting his head in the door.

"The air's so dense it can be cut with a knife," he complained.

"And the mattresses were flooded?" he inquired on the phone.

"No," she answered, now more calmly.

"Don't you remember? We keep them in the garret."

"And the stoker, where is he?"

"He went out for a cigarette," she replied. "He said not to worry. He's going to to fix it after the weekend.."

"Okay, you've really calmed me down," he said with a sigh of relief, and hung up. After a moment, he called back.

"Next time, don't bother me about such trifles." He put the receiver back firmly—this time, with a clatter. Harameus and Walter ran down the stairs and, content, went outside. Harameus hummed to himself. It was more of a rap style than composing verse with a refrain, and it went like this:

Ink dripped from a designer's quill
As did black blood from the fiend's chest,
And when old Clootie's heart had stilled,
Without demur, the draftsman said:
The Antichrist is laid to rest;
So many people have arrived,
So many fans the devil had
That Satan's bursting out with pride.

Harameus' hands marked arches in the air, and his fingers showed points of reference. A warm recollection of the father confessor rekindled in his mind. Walter turned to look at the main window.

"It wasn't there this morning," he said and pointed to the banner hanging above the window. Harameus read aloud, "The hotel different than all the others: single and shared cells, torture rooms. The G-spot of the New York hotel trade. Welcome."

"The chief advertising adviser did a good job," he said.

Behind them, they left a view of the hotel veiled in unexpected mist. The street was strangely empty.

"This silence must be brought about by a cartoon on TV," said Walter. Harameus looked at him carefully.

"When in the world are you going to get rid of the straw on your clothes?" he said.

Walter, with an electrifying look, tidied his torso and shoulders.

"I can't explain it logically," he said, surprised. An elderly distinguished-looking woman behind the window covered her eyes with her hands. From the metal-roofed hotel, one could hear a woodpecker's bursts of rattles like those from a machine gun. An elderly man, standing by that lady, covered his ears and opened his mouth. Above the path near the water reddened the sky. From the wing, this time the eastern one, again, cries, stifled with a blanket or pillow could be heard. A young man, standing by the elderly man, dropped a canary cage on the floor.

"It's good they already have a new owner," he said with a content smile.

"The sparrows live twenty years, but song thrushes only three. It's not fair," he said. He lifted the cage and began to shift his weight from foot to foot.

"Do they have the john here?" He asked, not mincing words. The lady lowered her hands and looked at him reproachfully. The young man grinned with pleasure and proffered the lady the cage. "You're overstepping the line," she warned, raising her hand. "There is a restroom beside the waiting room, but only for guests," she said sternly. Suppliers are not allowed," she added and immediately sneezed. Then again and again, and twice more. The old man reached into the pocket of his jacket for a handkerchief. He even touched it with his fingers, but eventually, he changed his mind and withdrew his hand. He turned away, put his hands behind himself, and, whistling quietly, he came up to the display case with the butterflies.

"If you're caught short, use the bathroom in the basement," the stoker, shod in rubber boots, said to the boy." He stuck his fag end in the sand in the bucket and went down the stairs to the boiler room, rapping under his breath: "I'm a whizz of stoves and chimNEYS, so I like to stoke and I like to smoke, and as you can see, such fate fell on me." He checked the clocks on the boilers and after a while he returned back upstairs. A doorman, passed over by Harameus, joined the group of people gathered by the window. It was the same one whom Harameus omitted while giving tips. He looked abashed. All boards and dishes were cleaned.

"Will there be any seconds?" he asked the waiter, who was walking away. In response, he received a dismissive look. The old man uncovered his ears. He blushed like the sky above the path near the water.

"Please, whistle. It helps," he advised the young man.

"Excuse me, have you seen Michael here?" a woman, passing by, asked shyly. Her shoulders were covered with a thin sweater. Everyone looked at her. They shook their heads in denial. The doorman did the same, and the 'stoker-smoker,' who did so with his nicotine-yellowed claw-like forefinger.

"He always came here in spring," she said with sadness in her eyes. "If he appears, anyway, please tell him I'm waiting for him."

"Ever since the swarm of stars over the village and over his head started to whirl, he's never been seen here," said the cleaning man standing behind him.

"And the keys? Who did he leave the keys to?"

"They took them away," he replied, "and him, too."

"Who did?"

"Officers."

"Michael is so sickly. Did they yank him?" she asked with a spark of curiosity in her eyes.

"He went with them of his own free will, but he didn't give away the banner," he said. The cleaning man lowered his eyes and began to mop the baseboard.

"In that case, I'm going to come here next year," the woman said resignedly.

"He likes sunflowers so much. What will I do with them now."

"Put them, ma'am, in a bottle on the game table," the stoker advised.

"Maybe they'll let him out," she said hopefully and walked away.

"They will definitely let him out," said the cleaning man. "They always let them out." The woman did not hear these comforting words. The girl standing at the mirror, who held an ermine in her arms, listened attentively to the conversation. In the corner of the room at the rectangular table covered with a red cloth, two men played cards. One was dressed in a long jacket, the other in an even longer coat. The former had a hat with a turned-down brim, the latter—with a brim turned up, boat-shaped. There was a pipe hanging on the former's teeth, and he looked like a traveling judge, the latter was a skipper, carter, or blacksmith. Leaning their hands on the table, they sat facing each other and raptly looked at the cards. On the opposite side of the hall, in a modest dress, with long dark hair covered with a mist-woven scarf falling on her shoulders, a young woman watched the situation. She rested her folded hands on the half-round armrest, which the porters use at night. She smiled mysteriously. Whistling, a young man pushed the door and ran to the basement. A splash came to the ears of the people gathered there. A grand piano on a giant, albeit quite adequate, wheeled platform was pulled into the hall by a commander of the north wing for a rope, and pushed by the manager and porters. The pianist in the worn-out coat followed them. He had a can of cucumbers in one of his hands; in the other, the score sheet.

Under his arm, he had a poker. He walked slowly, playing for time, munching on his interrupted meal. He stopped near the girl holding the ermine in her arms, with the purpose of stroking the pet. The ermine showed its teeth. The pianist went swiftly under the spotlight. After a while, he spread the score sheets on the keyboard cover. On the floor, next to the piano's leg, he put a half-open can and gave the poker to the stoker, asking him with his eyes to take good care of it. Then he interlaced his fingers, stretching his arms straight in front of him, so hard that, amplified by the room's acoustics, the clicks of the eight digital joints traveled like the cracks of dry twigs. The pianist lowered his head and dug his digits into the keyboard. The sounds started to float in the air. After a while, they fell on the listeners like a squadron of dandelion parachutes. The piano wizard caressed the keys, and the most beautiful-sounding music circled the hall, peeking into its every nook and cranny. It seemed for a moment that the grumpy old man in the blackened portrait slightly raised his labial commissures. As the pianist was about to play the last chord, he looked at the frozen audience. All the cares of the day were gone from their faces. After a short break, the mellifluous tones of Chopin's "Spring Waltz" floated into the ears and hearts of the listeners. The lady at the mirror seated the ermine on a chair, smoothed her hair with hands, and approached the woman with a mysterious smile. Then she bowed gracefully and asked her to dance. The woman adjusted the mist-woven scarf, took the girl by the hand, laying the other hand on the young lady's shoulders. Cuddled up to each other, they drifted into the middle of the room. Others followed them. Ladies with ladies, gentlemen with gentlemen, and ladies with gentlemen. Reciprocally, with their arms intertwined, they whirled among the sounds like wind-blown, fresh-lucked water lilies—free and happy. When the pianist finished playing, the dancers bowed to each other, exchanging partners. After a short break between the piano pieces, the musician reached for the can and drank some juice. He wiped his mouth with the sleeve and changed the score sheet. At the instigation of the hotel emcee, the dancers formed a line. Those more bashful as well as those somewhat aurally challenged—all of them eagerly formed the procession. The pianist, however, did not want to play anything lively and the dancers' train uncoupled after a while. The guests and the emcee, dissatisfied with this turn of events, returned to their chairs and some of them, inveterate wallflowers, to their walls. The next stop in the musical journey was Beethoven's "Moonlight Sonata." The pianist nodded to the reciter to start reciting the iambic pentameter, which she had previously practiced in front of the mirror. The girl resolutely came to the bridge, took the hem of her skirt in hand, and hiked it vigorously, stepping onto the platform. She bowed and took air. The musician switched from mezzo forte to mezzo piano. Staring at an unspecified point, she did perfectly what she was supposed to do. When they both finished, the audience clapped their hands with all their strength. Flowers fell on the piano and before the girl's feet. The pianist picked all of them and handed them to her. She raised them and sniffed. Then she kissed them. The wizards' afternoon was coming to an end. The audience requested an encore, but there were no encores. The essential employees were relentless. A wire-walker's performance and a speech by a professional liar with a university degree were still on the schedule. As the farewell performance, the wizard of the piano played an old Ray Charles hit. The audience relaxed. Clock chimes woke them up from that mesmeric state. When the clock struck a full hour, the master of the northern wing with the manager re-entered the lobby, and they both pushed the wheeled platform with the piano on it back to the banquet room. Then they hung a long custom-made piano string on the hooks between the walls, at whose ends there was a mooring eye. In the depths of the room, in the curtained recess, they set up a cardboard lectern with the name of an orator who was in the process of making his way towards the hotel. Harameus and Walter headed south.

"They must've been looking for something," Walter whispered. "Hence these feathers and the bits of straw."

"But what, exactly?" said Harameus.

From the synagogue, they heard a quarrel. They accelerated their pace, and eventually came up to the temple's gate. A passing droshky's wheel fell into a hole. Its other wheel went by the edge. The coachman jumped on his box seat. A couple sitting in the back fell out of their arms. The Percheron whined, angry. The driver cracked the whip. A police officer in long leather boots, with dark mirror glasses on the nose, flashed by on his motorcycle and shook his fist. The horse calmed down. The couple embraced again, holding each other tightly. The dandy stroked his chosen one's knee. In an ogival window of the tower appeared a bugler. His trumpet started to sound. The driver settled himself comfortably on the seat and waved at that one on the motorcycle, which left behind a draft. The coachman urged the horse. On the other side of the street, the organs fell silent. The portal opened wide. Paraclete—or at least that one took such a pose—waved back at the coachman and sent a sign. Behind his back, a curious organ blower stood on his toes. The bells thundered. In retaliation, on the other bank, a cantor's tenor exploded. In the Palace of Justice, behind the closed doors, but by the open windows, fierce philippics flared up. The culprits, as well as those not burdened with guilt stones, trembled with fear. In the nearby building, where important world decisions were made, a lot of water was drunk. There were complaints between the gulps. In the Third World countries, but not only, salvos of firing squads still reverberate and resound. The stocks of coal are low, albeit more and more of those willing to keep the shovels arrived there. It was difficult to understand what was going on, which was why those inquisitive were elucidated behind the scenes in the back room. Then the subject was changed to a lighter one. In the corridors, there were chases and races, and slides down handrails. At the check-in counter, there was no commotion—only quiescence. In the inner courtyard, a factory light shone on the crowd until late hours. "Explorer's Spurs" were again awarded to the medical corporation. The comforter told about reincarnation. The gainsayer opposed. Paraclete told about lemon groves and eternal happiness. Some believed in those tales. They left smiling. Those who listened to the voice of reason were put to sleep with ether. From under the stairs of the temple, a hullabaloo could be audible again.

"Let's not disturb them," said Harameus.

"Yes, let's wait," Walter agreed, and they discreetly retreated and stopped behind the monumental sculpture of the seal of justice—or injustice, as others saw it—from which flattened tor torsos stuck out. On the stairs, a shaggy-haired young man shook down pieces of jelly and cheesecake off his jacket.

"Son of a gun!" he said under his breath, looking at the food left on the ground. From under his densely matted long hair and bushy beard, a young, hardly perceptible, yet human face emerged. Next to him, a fellow, whose skin color was the opposite of the white matte complexion of the bearded hermit, who picked chicken wings and pieces of baked potatoes from the ground. In spite of looking offended, it was obvious that the white and black duo was connected by an invisible thread of brotherhood—the one that draws the sympathetic souls together. When it cleared between them, they sat down again on the concrete stairs, and the story being told by the black companion reached the ears. Harameus and Walter sat down on the plinth of the seal.

"I was roused from sleep by a cannonade of metallic sounds. They came from a distance. It seemed I'd already heard them somewhere else in the past. I opened my eyes and, it may sound silly, but I saw darkness. It was thick like pitch and heavy like a block of rock, impenetrable like a lump of amber with a bumblebee immured in it forever. I felt that I was lying in a coffin, carried on the shoulders of people walking in a funeral cortège, that my body was swaying to the rhythm of a slow march, and I was the central figure of the obsequies, and it was me who was given the disgraceful honor of participating in that ceremony. 'But why?' asked every cell of my body. 'It must be some mistake, which will be cleared up, a misunderstanding.' But nothing like that happened, and the cortège was moving on uninterrupted. The bells of the graveyard chapel were tolling louder and louder. I wanted to move, say something, but my body rebelled. Only my thoughts were whirling, unnaturally lifeful . . . vivacious. I wanted to get out of that trap and to take my heels and flee from that nightmare as far as possible, but my body still continued rebelling against my attempts. Then it occurred to me what was going to happen to me in a minute: As soon as I felt that the cortège stop, I, wrapped up in a cocoon of darkness, would begin to descend . . . the only sound I'd be able to hear would be the one of a wet, heavy earth striking against the lid. The very thought of that choked me stronger and stronger and pressed me into the white pall. I didn't sleep anymore, or at least, so it seemed to me. I couldn't, however, move my fingertips at all, swallow my saliva, or move my tongue to express my opposition, to say I was alive, after all, that I wasn't the right person to be buried. Cold sweat ran down my back, and panic pushed a cry like a plug from my throat—the cry that stuck in it like a spigot. In the end, it got outside. It was so loud that birds from the surrounding rocks took flight. The echo of my despair and terror circled around for a long time. I could hear metallic sounds more and more clearly. All the graveyard and church bells, which were in the area, pealed more and more loudly. The heavy sounds echoed like the blows of a blacksmith's hammer, getting out of the depths of the earth. I was sure my self was alive, but the body . . . well, I wasn't sure of that at all. I closed my eyes again, and when I opened them again, I asked myself if my mind failed somehow. But the figure standing above me seemed to be a flesh and blood person. Sharp stones stuck in the back. My bed was a stony soil and my cover, an animal hide. I shivered with the cold. I pulled the hide up under my nose. With my eyes left outside, I watched the figure, persistently keeping tabs on me. Above me stood an old man leaning on a whangee. Every now and then, he poked me with this dry stick, as one pokes a snake to see if it's alive. Once he hit me on the hip, then pricked my side, and afterwards, he hit harder my ribs. His hoary hair stuck out from under his cloth hood, and his long, also hoary, beard fell on his chest. He stared at me with his almond eyes—at me, a lying, defenseless intruder, who occupied a patch of his land without permission. I asked myself how I got there and what power made me not know who I was and why there were more and more birds circling over me. I tried to remember where I came from, but my memory was like a blank page, like the face of that pseudo human being standing above me. The old man was still staring at me, and his thoughts persistently permeated mine.

'Do not be afraid,' I heard by way of greeting, not seeing him open his mouth. I took my hand out from under the cover and rubbed my eyes. 'Where am I?' I asked. In response, the old man touched my hand and lifted it so easily as if it was an infant's. We walked slowly forward.

'Where are we going?' I asked again, worried. He smiled it off. From a distance, sounds of talking people could be audible. I saw some silhouettes. They were illuminated by rays forcing their way through the branches of trees. Then I saw a woman separate from the group. Her feet were shrouded in mist. I turned around wanting to ask my companion for an explanation, but he was no longer with me. The woman was slowly approaching me. She raised her hand and greeted me. Joy filled my heart. We were walking towards each other. Yes, I recognized her. She was my mother. It's been so many years since her departure. I wanted to come up to her and embrace her, but my companion again appeared beside me and held my arm. I knelt down before her. I wanted to tell her how much I loved her and missed her, and how sorry I was. But she put a finger on her lips asking me not to say anything, not to blame myself. She watched me as if she wanted to enjoy the sight of me to the fullest. I asked her not to leave me alone, but she looked at me with understanding. After a moment she left. I cried again, but she was already far away. She joined others. The old man took my hand again and helped me stand up. I pushed his hand away and ran after my mother. I ran until I was out of breath. Suddenly, I felt a knock and weight on my back. A big black bird perched on my shoulder. When I wanted to free myself, it covered my eyes with its wings and whispered that it wasn't fair, that every fiber of its being was the very justice, and that it was going to take me wherever I would want. I wasn't sure what to do. Suddenly, a loud rumbling thunder nailed the heavens to the earth. A powerful explosion filled the air, as if the world had collapsed. Everything got shrouded in the dark. Then an impenetrable blackness descended—dense and violent. It lasted some time, but it's hard to say how long. In an instant, from that deepest blackness, a flash of lightning burst out again and kindled a cold flame. Out of the flash, an incredibly loud thunderclap got out of the flash. Its tone was lower than the lowest bass. After a while, it fell into the abyss, like a stony mountain pushed down by an earthquake. The bird fell down following the thunderbolt. Right behind them, still in the bass register, all the water of the world, trapped in the oceans, rose up and hit the earth with an enormous bang. When the sounds became smoother, they went far away behind the dusk and then the night, it was dawning again.

The old man said, 'It is difficult to defend those who attempt to escape.'

'And those in pursuit?' I asked.

'It depends on in pursuit of what,' he answered cleverly. 'Can you hear these groans in the depths?'

'Something like murmurs,' I said. 'Is it the wind rambling?'

'Clutch at my arm tightly and do not let go, even if you doubt my words. We will ascend high so that you can have a bird's-eye view of this,' he said.

'Oh, how wonderful it is down there. Amazing lands are down there,' I shouted with delight.

'Hold on.'

'Where are these moans coming from? Whose silhouettes are there? What a strange chill and smell surround us.'

'Clutch me tightly.'

'Don't fly too low 'cause I feel terribly bad,' I said, frightened.

'Just a little longer until you see yourself.'

'I don't wanna approach that place. These noises are getting louder and louder. Very loud cries.'

'Those who have betrayed come here.'

'Don't shout like this, master, please. My head is splitting. Everything's shaking around, falling apart.'

'Let it fall apart. It is always the end of this.'

'And that stronghold in the middle of the water? Is it surrounded by the Ligurian Sea? What is there on that island?'

'There, where cannons stick out of the sockets in the stone walls? There, hatreds pile up like billows; there rot the most dexterous executioners.'

'Let's run away from here. I've had enough of this,' I said. and covered my eyes.

'You must see this.'

'I don't wanna see this anymore, master, that's enough.'

'There are the very sights . . . and languages from other worlds. Polyglot angels guard them. They speak to them by means of a whip. Oh, did you hear that crash?'

'Something like a crack of a stick being broken and a hiss of someone's burning skin being poured over with water,' I said, terrified.

'Listen carefully.' (Swish! Swoosh! And, and more swooshes were heard again after a while)

'The scourge sounds in the walls, like the crack of a pine being broken. You have to admit it, my dear, this sound is joyful.'

'Let's go back now. I feel dizzy.'

'Okay, I will spare you the bother of watching this wicked flock. However, those who hurt a child will be given the heaviest lashes upon their backs. Over there, behind the mountain. Can you see those fumes? Only there fair mills are milling."

'Please, no!'

'I will show you the golden valley.'

'That sounds much better.'

'Look, can you see that chest?'

'Yes, it's wonderful.'

'Turpentine wood. Can you smell this aroma?'

'Hardly. But not exactly—'

'The chest is filled with gold to the brim. Behind the valley, there is a green meadow.'

'Are you checking up on me, master? You're deviously smiling.'

'I can give you all this. Gold and gems, tobacco-infused air, or—"

"What's there on the other side?' I asked for the sake of appearances.

'Over there is the oasis of love. Over there are happiness and the woman of your dreams. And here is wealth and life full of thrills. Make a choice.'

'And . . . a horse that can carry all this, will I get it too?'

'Even the horse and cart.'

'All right. So, I'm taking the chest and tobacco,' I said, overjoyed. All of a sudden, the horizon darkened and blurred its contours. A sudden gale lifted the golden sand and blew the chest higher and higher. It exposed the peninsula surrounded by the emerald depths. In the depths, a man and woman were taking a bath. Around, citrus trees were bending under the load of fruit and birds of paradise.

'Can you recognize yourself?'

'That happy young man, is he me?' I asked.

'You could have had that love.' After those words, I started to lose consciousness."

"You said you were not addicted," said the boy.

"Because I wasn't." The boy yawned and stroked the beard.

"Maybe you've got a second chance."

"It's possible, but I don't remember most of the events in my life," said Jonah.

"Maybe it's better so," said the boy. The smell of food spread around.

"Sprinkle these thickets with water, or else there'll be no meal."

"If you did it differently, you would've had the chest and the oasis."

"You don't get it, Mophead." The boy nodded silently. Then he poured a handful of water from his bottle and squashed his beard like pouring rain squashes cornfields—hard, but harmlessly, and did so until the next morning. He threw his mustache sideways and, perked-up, got down to eating. He put boiled vegetables into his mouth, followed by roasted shrimps bathed in butter, sucking meat to the last fiber.

"Hey, Mophead! Move a little bit, you're blocking the vent . . . you're taking up all the heat." Harameus and Walter went towards them.

"I wouldn't like to disturb you, but may I ask you something?" Harameus politely turned to them. Raven-black-haired Jonah slowly stood up and with his forefinger stabbed Harameus in the lapel of his jacket. After a while, he repeated the stab, this time, stronger. Harameus slightly leaned back. Seeing the newcomer cleverly dodging between the vertical position and the deviation, Jonah's face beamed with a smile. The apparition, one of hundreds indifferently passing by, which he touched with his finger, turned out to be a human being.

"We want to help you," said Harameus.

Jonah looked at him from above and said, "You look at me mercifully, as at a caged bird, but are you sure that it is me in the cage?"

"I'm a street angel," he added and smoothed his shoulders. "Don't be misled by my black feathers."

"Jonah, let the man ask a question," said the boy. "Any help is always useful."

Jonah bent slowly and reached under the cardboard box. Music floated from the radio. The raven-black angel threw the blanket over his shoulders and began to dance. When the tide of sounds carried him, he spun—once to the right, once to the left; he extemporized forwards and backwards, a step to the side, two steps all the way backwards, and then a turn. The music and strong beats intertwined with unbelievably authentic birds' sounds. Once he squawked like a jay, once he hooted like an owl, another time he howled like a hungry eagle. Undoubtedly, he was the best at corvine cries. Hunched, with a blanket on his back, he spun faster and faster in the middle of the pavement. The music floating from the loudspeaker and the raven's caws provided sensations not even felt at the Metropolitan Opera House. Gazing at the unearthly looking, albeit realest human being, born in pain and joy, the passers-by slowed down their pace, treasuring this moment in their memory and on their cellphones. Smelling of wind and empty pockets, the black angel-raven was the master of sounds, and the sounds were his servants. Finally, panting, he stopped dancing and turned off the radio.

"Do you have a cigarette? he asked.

"Unfortunately, I don't smoke, but later I'll come up with something," said Harameus.

"I've never become addicted to tobacco, either," Jonah said and again smiled with jubilation.

"Can I ask you something?"

"Fire away, we have no secrets," said the boy.

"Are you enjoying your food? And, maybe we could do something more for you. Do you have any wishes?" The conversation took on a cordial tone.

"Don't they have pizzas or burgers there?" asked the boy. "This roe and worms are a bit bland."

"Don't grumble, Mophead," the black raven said over his shoulder, and began to eat a salmon sandwich and a lemon slice.

"You said 'wishes,' sir," repeated the boy. "I have one." He tidied himself up on the stairs and grabbed the leftovers into a paper bag. He looked down at Harameus and fixed his eyes on him.

"Speak, Peter Pan, the golden Fish is listening," said Jonah.

"When I was a child," continued the boy with looking like a hermit. "In London and Philadelphia, at the same time, two Live Aid concerts were held. I regret I wasn't born earlier. I always wanted to see my idols live. To see David Bowie, Bruce Springsteen, Guns & Roses, and Red-Hot Chili Peppers, would be like kissing the queen."

"Halle Berry would be better," said Jonah, "As for me, my benefactor, I would like to . . . I would like to see once again Chuck Berry and Smokey Robinson."

"That's it?" Harameus said, surprised. Jonah and Mophead looked at him with triumph.

"Gotcha, friend," they thought to themselves, convinced that they caught him in a trap, from which there was no way out.

"He's quite a fibster," they came to the conclusion, exchanging looks. In their opinion, he was already up the creek.

"Well, what are you gonna do now, Golden Fish? You shouldn't waste words," said Jonah. Harameus turned Walter aside and checked something on his cellphone. Then he wrote in a notebook and said quietly, "Please take care of it."

"But—," Walter mumbled, surprised. Harameus pushed the card into Walter's hand.

From the inside of the synagogue, a singing cantor was audible.

"Let's go in," said Harameus. Jonah and the Mophead looked at each other.

After a moment, all four of them were sitting in the pews. Harameus spoke in a low voice, "He's singing about a young man who strayed from the straight and narrow."

"That's about me," whispered the Mophead.

"Be serious." Jonah nudged him with his elbow, taking him to task.

"How do you know?" Walter asked.

"My father was a Jew." Apart from them, in the synagogue, there was an old woman in a wheelchair and a girl that looked more than ten, maybe eleven years old. She came up to them and put a finger on her lips asking for silence. Mophead watched her carefully and lowered his eyes. The girl's head was covered with a headscarf, under which he could not see hair. Her delicate face was pink, eyebrows and eyelashes were painted with a black crayon.

"Ezra!" said the old lady, quietly sitting in the wheelchair.

"I have to go, now, my grandma is calling me."

"You have a nice name," said the Mophead. The girl smiled. Outside it already cleared up. The sun showed through the clouds. Harameus approached the taxi driver, exchanged a few words with him and returned with a pack of cigarettes. He pushed it into the Mophead's hand.

"Recently, I heard the old woman talk to the cantor," said Jonah. "She said that the girl was waiting for a bone marrow transplant. It was her last resort."

"I would give a lot so that the little girl can recover," Mophead said sadly.

On the wall of the corridor hung an oil painting of sunflowers. Next to the shelf there was a vase with a yellow floral bouquet in it. The door of a doctor's office opened, and a female doctor stood in the doorway.

"I have good news for you," she said to Mophead.

"You're the perfect donor, a genetic twin. It's a miracle," she said rejoicing.

"Thank you, God, my prayers have been answered," said Mophead, raising his eyes. The doctor smiled.

"How's Ezra feeling?"

"The little girl asked about you. I think you'll soon be able to visit her."

"Please, tell her everything will be fine," Mophead's face was beaming.

"May God be with her," he said, and headed for the elevator. Jonah waited on the street. Mophead took the pack of cigarettes out of his jacket pocket, but after a while he crushed the pack and threw it into the garbage can. They walked along the wide sidewalk, talking animatedly.

"Mr. Lehm, London's on the line," said the secretary.

"Who? Can you repeat?"

"I couldn't hear the name exactly."

"Thank you, please connect the call to my office." Harameus accelerated his pace.

"Good evening, or rather, good morning, because it's still breakfast time there," a voice sounded on the phone. "Robert speaking. I'm sorry I didn't call you back at once yesterday, but I only listened to the message today."

"I am glad, Mr.—"

"Call me Bob."

"Sure. My name's Har . . . call me Harm," Harameus cleared his throat, covering his mouth.

"I haven't heard you well. Is your nickname 'ham'?"

"No, Bob, my name is Harameus, but 'Harm' is shorter and simpler."

"I apologize for that. An interesting first name, but I'm going to address you 'Harameus,' if you don't mind."

"Of course, Bob, as you wish."

"You said yesterday you wanted to organize a small-scale concert venue at the Yankee Stadium."

"This is how I can define it in short, if we assume that sixty thousand spectators are not enough."

"Hm, it sounds interesting, but—"

"Yes, Bob, I'm listening."

"You know, those who played in the 80s don't want to play completely gratis anymore. Well—how to say this—their halcyon days are gone. Some of them lost property somewhere. I don't have to tell you how it is, you know for yourself. People make mistakes."

"I know it better than anyone else," said Harameus.

"Besides, the younger generation listens to different music now. I don't know about boy bands or the hip-hop world. I'm sorry, but I've heard about one loaded guy from New York, maybe he could help. He flings money around. He financially supports shelters and distributes food in churches and synagogues. You know, people are constantly stung by their worms of conscience."

"I've heard about him too. People talk about this in London?"

"Yes indeed. But I wonder when his battery discharges. I know a few similar cases, but when you have to put out for poor children in Africa, they washed their hands of this."

"Do you know what his name is?"

"I don't remember, but he had such a funny, embarrassing name. Har . . . or something like . . . fuck, no . . . ," Harameus heard in the phone a sequence of expletives.

"Yes, Bob, my name is Lehm. Harameus Lehm. You've heard right that the guy went nuts. I think about myself this way. I'm a whole lot of a crackpot. I do confirm this, but I can do nothing with it."

"I'm sorry, I did not mean to offend you. I don't think you're nuts."

"Well, Bob, that's really comforting."

"I thought, only I and a few others are severely loopy, but life as always is full of nice surprises. I'm on your side, regardless of the result of our conversation. Although, as I mentioned, I'm not interested. But you can elucidate the matter. I'll be glad to listen."

"In short, it looks like this: If they rent it to me, or us, I hope, Yankee Stadium for one day, I'd like to organize a great concert for the needy."

"You mean poor young people?"

"Not quite so, but they can't be ruled out. In general, I want to arrange a celebration at Yankee Stadium for all the hobos and homeless of this world. Well, maybe for almost all of them as, rather, there would be not enough stadiums."

"And yet you're a damn freak. I haven't met a nuttier nut in my life, and, believe me, I've seen many of them. I can already see these parks, squares, and gates in the area, the Cathedral at 110th and Broadway."

"Do you know these areas?"

"Not once, at 105th Street, we organized a little shindig at . . . besides, it doesn't matter, it was a long time ago."

"So, what do you think of this, Bob?"

"I haven't heard anything like that in my life. But let me tell you three words."

"You're big, buddy."

"Don't exaggerate," Harameus said modestly.

"And my last words: I'm interested in this. There're already two damn crazy guys."

"I'm gonna pay for everything out of my own pocket," said Harameus. "No nosy TV stations."

"And hairdressers, travel expenses, and accommodation? Are you going also to pay for this?"

"As I've already said."

"A television station will be useful to us. They will propagate this noble idea. There, you can also find some noble people. For starters, I'd have some tips."

"I'm all ears."

"Don't tell people from Yankee Stadium about the social status of our guests. You'll do it later."

"Sure, Bob."

"Not because they'll refuse us, you know, they would be accused of discrimination, but they'll simply put the price sky high."

"I have to tell you I've been in charge of my bank for over a dozen years, but, in this case, I feel like a stripling again."

"Show business is not a loan office. They are people with lives full of twists and turns and different worldviews, but they have one thing in common—I'm talking about artists, in the first place—music counts first, and then money."

"It's good that at least artists are humane. The world of finance is a different kettle of fish," said Harameus.

"Ah, and one more thing," said Bob. "We'll tell the mayor at the very end. Otherwise, the police will still find an excuse not to allow the onslaught of unwelcome guests. You understand, if they decided to stay longer in the city, they would hang us first from the lamp post at Grand Central."

"I'd like, if possible, if you could use your connections to make David Bowie, Guns & Roses, Smokie Robison, and Chuck Berry perform for us."

"You're very demanding, buddy. My name isn't Harry Houdini, but I'll see what I can do."

"So to speak, the originators of this undertaking expressed their wishes of this kind."

"Are there more such crazy millionaires as you? I haven't known till now it's a collective initiative."

"We have people from different social classes here. The street trend prevails, with the predominance of the ground-level class. But there're others, too."

"I have a last question here, but it's a little awkward to talk about."

"Shoot, buddy," said Harameus, resting his legs on the desk.

"I want to ask how much you can allot to this event. Though I can tell you, I feel it, people from the industry won't take too much cash. Maybe with a few exceptions, but they won't be large amounts."

"Bob, listen, I'll say it in capital letters: MONEY DOES NOT MATTER AT ALL."

"You're such a crazy creature. Now I know it's worth living for such moments. And one more sentence at the end:"

"I'm all ears, Bob."

"Don't allot even a penny for me. That's it on this matter. Call me when you know the decision of the Yankee people."

"Thank you. God bless you."

"Come on, Harm, but that's nice of you."

"I'll call you soon."

CHAPTER FIVE

"I haven't traveled by subway for a good few years now," said Harameus, "It used to look completely different, much better." Pressed by human torsos, he looked along the subway car and saw a breathtaking view: people everywhere, leaning against each other, tightly squeezed together. Just one big can packed with sardines.

"We should've entered the car with hammocks and Adirondack chairs," said Walter. "It would be good to give our feet some rest. They walked so many miles recently."

"First, I didn't take my ID badge with me. Second, in large measure, that car is only for VIPs and influential figures of this city. I couldn't hold a candle to them. Besides, I feel ill at ease there." The people glued to them nodded appreciatively.

"I don't think the conductors would refuse some kind of gratification?" Walter said in a low voice. An announcement by the MTA's robotic voice reached the straphangers' ears. The train driver braked hard. Harameus and Walter breathed a sigh of relief. Between them and a few workers standing nearby emerged a narrow clearance. In the next car for VIPs, the hammocks swayed from side to side. The ceiling fans fluttered. Brought out of their slumber, the notables began to look for the conductor. They found him staring at a globe. He spun it and stopped it with his finger and dreamily squinted his eyes. His face showed that his thoughts flowed freely far away. A shooting star lit up the sky over the savannah. From leeward some murmurs could be heard. Above the tops of the grasses, he noticed glistening eyes. They were approaching on bent paws. Suddenly, he heard a roar behind his back: "Yoo-hoo, conductor! What's going on with the train?" The conductor, terrified to the core, straightened up abruptly, then turned away and turned pale. The hungry eyes, which had previously glistened in the grass, at that moment, watched him from under the blankets and plaids, ready to jump. Total silence reigned over the car. The conductor took off his cap, pressed it to his chest, and apologetically bowed. Then he went toward the intercom. After a short conversation with the train driver, he assured that a similar situation would not happen again, and that the car would not sway anymore, nervously biting his chapped lips. The nobles, satisfied with that assurance, turned back to their sides. The conductor dimmed the light and tiptoed away to the car's corner. Suddenly and unexpectedly, a ship, enveloped in the fog of the bay, blew a low horn signal from its typhons. In response, coastal nautophones resonated from the direction of the neighboring islands. The sound spread faster than light. The wall of basses pushed aside the noise of the city and rolled into the tunnel. The windows and the air trembled. The train driver did not want to feel inferior and also let off a load of heavy tones. The locomotive's heaviest caliber cannon was pounding and pounding. The horns honked to the fullest. Beads of sweat broke out on the conductor's brow. He pulled a bunch of keys, on quite a large ring, out of his pocket, and locked himself in the train cabin. Walter moved his face closer to the window plane, barred the beams of light with his hands, peeping into the car for VIPs.

"I can't believe they braked so hard!" he said, outraged. "This can't be tolerated!" Listening to the conversation, a youngish man in a woolen tiger-striped cardigan ran his eye over Walter's pockets. Finally, he stuck his hip to Walter's hip, who vigorously shoved him against the wall with his shoulder. At that moment, the pick-pocket mumbled a half-swallowed swearword under his breath.

"This chapter of my life is closed," Harameus said firmly. "There will be no gratification, no bribery."

"Ah, I'd love to swing a little bit," Walter teased.

"Okay, I don't mind at all, go ahead, walk inside. Maybe the bouncer will take pity and will let you in," he said flippantly.

The subway employee, standing next to him, with flashlights rattling on his belt, pricked up his ears. His pupils shifted toward his inner eye corners. The lights in the car began to choke. The employee slid his hand over his belt and moved the switch of the largest flashlight. A sharp sheaf of light stabbed Walter's eye.

"What the hell!" he swore under his breath. "For the last time, I'm riding with these people! Get me out of here!" he said, upset. He rubbed his eyelids with his hands and opened his eyes. To his great surprise, he was surrounded by the depths of darkness. He got scared. He asked Harameus about something, but he did not get the answer. The train stopped. The sliding door grated and opened. The platform was also bathed in darkness.

"What the hell," he said, irritated. Slowly and cautiously, he went outside. Through the windows of the neighboring car, with his face by it, phantoms of dim light forced their way and lured like a candle attracts moths. At the last moment, before the door had closed, Walter jumped inside that car and stood by the very door. The train started moving again.

"You look worried," he heard from the depths. "Have you brought your stone with you?" Walter stood frozen.

"I know it is heavy. Do not worry, I shall help you out to carry it." Walter lowered his eyes and looked at his hands.

"You are here standing and trembling alone," the voice said drily.

"Where am I?"

"Sit down and take a rest. You wanted to get here. However, one can manage to get here only for committing a wicked deed." Walter narrowed his eyes and strained his eyes. Between the sides of the car, he could see swinging hammocks. In them, sleeping figures huddled against pillows.

"Where's my friend? Where're all these people?" Walter asked, worried.

"Hey, do you indeed fathom nothing? Do you have no knowledge of where you have found yourself?" The black photo-negatives and red photo-positives of the car's interior began to roll around in slow motion.

"Your God is dead," he heard.

"What balderdash!" Walter said, indignant. "I want to get out of here. Immediately!"

"You shall not decide upon this. Sit down!"
The interior brightened up enough so that Walter could see the matter surrounding him. The kaleidoscopic planes of the black negatives and red positives vanished, as did the billets and hammocks. Behind his back, there was a wall made of planks and a wooden bench, or rather two logs and a solid piece of board. On the opposite side, a fireplace was barely burning. Everything resembled a peasant's chamber of yore, similar to the one in which he was born. In the middle stood a Biedermeier table on which there was a block of printing paper and a fountain pen.

"It will be the most enjoyable moment of your life," he heard in his self, more and more vaguely. Walter was losing his strength. He started moving toward the window, behind which a dark green lake of nothingness was waving. He was lumbering, like in a slow-motion movie.

"Do not fight. Sign, and everything you dream of will come true," the voice sounded firm. "They all have signed."

"Am I . . . am I in hell?"
In response, he heard a deep laugh.
"If that's true . . . if God died, where then did the devils go?" he asked in a disdainful tone. "Maybe you're the one." The echo of laughter reverberated.

"Damn you," said Walter, in subdued voice. Outside, the wind began to blow. Walter sat down on the bench and leaned against the wall. The echo of laughter faded away. The wind began to blow. Walter sat down on the bench and leaned against the wall.

"Devil, I want to get myself out of this place! Come back!" he shouted. There was silence all around. The last embers in the fireplace were burning out, throwing reddish stains on wooden beams embracing the ceiling. A revolver appeared on the table next to the block of paper and the fountain pen. Walter closed his eyes from tiredness. After having relaxed for a very short moment, he felt as an icy arrow braided of the air pierced him through. A gust of wind rushed into the room. He felt as if he were in an inn full of screaming guests. At uninvited newcomers looked at the world through his eyes. A mixture of these glances and thoughts swirled in his head. This image was no longer his image. He felt as if someone lived in his body. But whoever it was and how long he was going to stay in it, he had no idea. He heard clearly the call: "Come on, coward, sign it or shoot yourself in the head!" From the other side of his self, he heard: "Do not be stupid! No one needs your light yet."

Between the entities, which had invaded his body, a battle took place. He began to feel drowsy. A crack of sparks jumping over the hearth somewhat dampened the sounds of the altercation. In a momentary lapse of relaxation, his head dropped to his chest. His breath was longer. He was awoken from this state by the sound of an object that fell on the floor. Looking up, he did not notice anything suspicious. He only saw the reflection of a red beard jumping on the wall. All of a sudden, some numbness came over him. He noticed that the one whose name he took in vain came in through the window. He slid in slowly and stood on the other side of the table. They were a few steps apart, but he could recognize him by the smell of a rock soaked in rain and early spring escaping from February's thaws. He saw what he really did not want to see. The newcomer was angry and looked at him with contempt. His gaze was cold and piercing. In his dark red glowing eyes was annoyance, but also vacillation. He wondered what to do with him. He stared at a massive rifle butt, the block of paper and the fountain pen, turning his eyes to Walter. He clenched his bony jaws and made a shrill hiss out of the dark throat. When he raised his head—or rather head-like outgrowth—and drew himself up, he almost reached the wooden ceiling beams. Seemingly, his shape was real, but he was waving, as if he were filled with smoke, as if he were within arm's reach and, at the same time, out of reach. After a while, he vanished into thin air. When Walter's numbness was over, something hammered at the door. The dust of the wooden walls fell on the floor. The sound of huge hooves got out of the night's depths. The doorframe and walls shook in the foundations. The broken staple swayed on the nail. Chill rushed inside again. Walter was filled with anger. He got to the door and slammed it shut. The hooves were still pounding, and the chamber trembled even more. After a moment, the door opened again. Walter pushed it hard, but it requited with force twice as strong, as if it played with him. Shadows and patches began to dance over his head. After a while, they surrounded him tightly, clamping their powers on him, they pushed him from corner to corner around the shadowy rim of the room. Then they grabbed his arms and pulled them toward the window. They took him outside while holding above a dark green void. Walter looked down and the thought pierced his mind that it was all over now. All of a sudden, unexpectedly, an invisible force pulled him back inside, released him from the grip and threw him on the floor. He rose with difficulty and hobbled to the bench. Out of the corner of his eye, he saw the dark outline of the figure escape through the window. When Walter was right behind him, he took the form of a beautiful angel, similar to a woman. By the time he vanished for good, he had spoken to Walter in an unknown language—however, somehow, Walter understood him: "I'll come back for you again." Moments later, the bright light dazzled Walter again. When he covered his eyes with his hands once more, he heard the noise of the crowded car. He looked through his fingers with fear.

"What were you pondering on?" asked Harameus, "You had a nap?"

"I sleep badly these days," said Walter, "besides it's so stuffy here."

"Hum, it occurred to me you might expect a raise, but you are ashamed to ask." A smile flashed on Walter's lips. "It would be good to get one," he said without thinking. "Look at my old worn-out shoes."

The men standing next to them had a look at their footwear. The worker with flashlights, holding a bag of tools under his belly, bent his head and cast a glance at the blackened tips of his shoes. Behind him, two sewermen in muddy rubber boots giggled.

"Appearances often can be deceptive," said Harameus. The guys in the rubber boots nodded their heads. Standing in the corner, leaning against the metal wall, a twenty-several-year-old man yawned lengthily. He must have come from a foreign land because he did not understand the announcement given by the robotic voice. A pregnant woman's face flushed. She barely stood. Other women lowered their heads. The men also pretended that they heard nothing. Heat pumps pressed steam into the radiators. Hissing white threads came from beneath the seats. People began to fidget nervously. When the typhons went silent, tenors began to sing their nightingale-like trills:

Sewermen don't put out fire,
But they work in mud and mire
When they have time off at last,
They decide as one, en masse,
To sneak in the saloon car
As if in some dismal bar.
They don't care, they don't ask,
Each of them has his own flask,
And they take a plush chaise-longue
The conductor says it's wrong,
Then the foreman slaps his face,
Risking to fall in disgrace.

The ladies sitting comfortably brightened up. They looked nostalgically at the swinging hammocks. In the center of the car for the VIPs, parallel to each other, four feet apart, the hammocks were mounted on solid bronze handles. Under them, at a safe distance, were spaced out wooden Adirondack chairs, attached to the floor with bolts. Almost all the notable occupants of them had a postprandial nap. Only at the end of the car, some two men entered into a dispute. Who of them was eventually right no one could lip-read. Generally, there was a tiresome silence, only being now and then interrupted by the squeak of wheels when the train slid on the rails while braking on the bend.

"I guess we chose the wrong time," said Walter. "Those on day shift are coming back home." 125 Street is a little less packed, but still the crowd could barely fit in. The robotic voice at last announced: "Next stop is at 161 Street—Yankee Stadium." The commuters piled off onto the platform.

"Phew," Walter heaved a sigh of relief. The woman standing nearby cast a pitiful glance at Harameus and said, "Here's hard looking at you, kid . . . tough to accustom yourself to the crowd, ain't it?" Then she accelerated her pace.

"Harameus, do you really think it will work out in the end?"

"If I didn't believe it, Walter, I wouldn't take it upon myself."

CHAPTER SIX

"Please, sit down, the president will see you soon, gentlemen." A woman with the appearance of a warm-hearted aunt, wearing a gray jacket, pointed to the armchairs by the large window overlooking the stadium stands. The green grass, and thousands of empty variegated vacant seats seemed somnolent. Harameus came up to the window and looked at the ocean of perfectly trimmed grass. He closed his eyes and imagined empty chairs vibrant with life. The ovation of thousands of hands and throats, mixed up with the first sounds of the song. David Bowie raised the microphone stand and exclaimed between the lines: "I love you." Sixty thousand throats began to repeat the lyrics of the song. When the first staves fell silent, the audience rose from their seats and began to cheer in his honor. On that day he was singing about them and for them. Young, old, lame, and healthy, they all laughed and cried with joy, happy like little children. God was them and they were Gods. The office door opened.

"Is . . . is it her? I must be dreaming," thought Harameus. In the doorway appeared an elegant woman in an orange skirt and a red jacket covering her shoulders.

"What an imperious look. A jacket like Caesar's coat," he enthused inwardly. "Is she soon going to charge at me like Caesar at Vercingetorix?" The pennants fluttered in the wind. The cold swords shimmered in the sun. The brown eyes followed his every move. Harameus was gripped with an inhibition. It seemed that the president read his mind and knew exactly what he wanted to tell her. She appeared to be two steps ahead of him in that skirmish of thoughts. The frame of her shapely spectacles emphasized the shape of her dark eyebrows, and the very lenses extended her eyelashes, quite long anyway.

"I guess, Mr. Lehm, you used public transportation, and, to be honest, only this fact justifies your late arrival." (The first century moved forward.) Monica Keller looked at him reproachfully. "I hate when someone comes late. If truth be told, I barely put up with such people." (The former followed the latter.)

"Come in, please," she said, and, once again, her eyes swept Harameus, focusing her attention on his busy hands. (Two fighting, sweaty spiders spun their limbs like swift sabers winding moulinets, and then played in vibrant vibrato or lively tremolo.)

"Don't be nervous," she said in a slightly softer voice. Her full and velvety cherry-colored lips looked like a small boat dancing on the waves over which a fine mole was flying.

"Excuse me, but it's a little bit hot here," Harameus said, stood up and went to the window. He got lost in thoughts looking at the soccer pitch and the stand. Monica looked at him attentively. After a while he sat down again.

"Oh, I do apologize for that. I should've turned on the air conditioning earlier. How about some water?" (The Legions turned back to the camp.)

"Yes, please. I'll gladly drink," he replied. "Oh! This is my favorite, Manhattan Spring." He reached out to pour himself, but Monica quickly forestalled him.

"Let me take care of you." She filled the glass and put the bottle back on the table. Harameus followed the bottle, then his gaze slid down the skirt. Quickly, however, he took himself to task and looked at the bottle again. He saw on the label a similar handprint to the one he once had seen in Charleston. He hastily drank water, leaned on the chair and closed his eyes.

"Are you better now?"

"Oh yes, a lot," he replied. "May I touch your hand?" he asked hesitantly.

"Will you give me, in return, a check again?" she said playfully. Harameus loosened his tie. Monica Keller stood up and opened the window. The fresh air burst into the room, as did the joy of children walking to the playground. "What did you want to read from my hand?"

"I'd like to make sure that you're the woman who can work miracles."

"Miracles?" she asked, surprised.

"Yes, miracles."

"Ah, that's exactly what you mean." Harameus looked at her questioningly. Monica came up to Walter.

"Are you Russian?"

"My grandmother was Russian, my grandfather was Polish," he replied. "How did you recognize my family roots?"

"Your phone. Unusual ring. I guess, Stravinsky."

"Yes, 'The Soldier's Tale.'"

"And you, who are you . . . deep in your heart?"

"It depends on who I sit at the table with," he replied with a smile. "First of all, I feel a New Yorker." Monica nodded appreciatively and rose from her chair. Harameus and Walter immediately did the same. She knew she was dealing with gentlemen. "So what did you see through that window, Mr. Lehm?" Monica came up to the window and rolled up the blind.

"Sixty thousand people, Ms. Keller."

"We have 50,000 seats, but you can add the ones on the pitch. Last time the stadium was filled to capacity was during the league finals."

"And, these sixty thousand people, what will they be watching?" she continued.

"Can you see that stage in the middle of the pitch?"

"I can't see anything yet," she said, as if out of spite. "Who is standing on that stage?"

"At the moment, everyone is backstage, but I can tell you who is in the stands." Harameus looked at her uncertainly. Her gaze slowly fell on his face.

"You don't have to talk. You have my permission. I'll only have to convince the rest of the board of this madness." Harameus stopped short. Words got stuck in his throat.

"How do you—?"

"Doesn't matter, I just know."

"Thank you very much," he said, surprised. He expected a heated exchange of ideas, some haggling, and here, before even he had started the conversation, it was already over. It came to an end.

"We'll now consult all matters through proxies," she said firmly.

"I'll deal with this myself, Ms. Keller. I'll do my best to redeem … I mean, to make our guests happy," he stammered, and his thoughts sprang out one by one. A little intimidated, he came up to a multicolored list board hung on the wall, where each tinted little square branched out—as in the family tree—joining matching colors. Harameus looked at his pants and shoes and smiled innocently.

"I like your approach, Mr. Lehm. I wouldn't like to share my intuitions, but it won't win you allies."

"I'm not looking for them," he answered sincerely and convincingly.

"Hope for the best," she said, shaking hands goodbye.

"I don't promise anything though. Oh, and one more thing, I hate unreliability more than tardiness." (Caesar put his hand on the sword again.)

"You can be assured."

"Excuse me, gentlemen, but in just a moment I have a few more visitors," she said politely and opened the door. Harameus sighed furtively, unnoticed.

"Oh God, she's one hell of a woman," he thought to himself.

"See you soon, Mr. Lehm. Goodbye, Mr. Wars, it was nice to meet you. I invite you to the match on Sunday. We still have tickets, but probably only the most expensive ones are left." She waved to them and closed the door.

It was one of those fine May days, clad in blue. A rustling breeze was flurrying over a river ribbon. The new asphalt shone with iridescent glass as a harbor mirror next to concrete breakwaters. A strong 500-horsepower engine harnessed to a steel cart, carrying spicy aromas from the Orient. Smoke billowed from the exhaust pipe above the cab. Blended with the air, they roamed through boundless plains, backwoods, deserts, and mountains. Behind the river, embellished with ashen panaches, tall chimneys were panting. The ashes of burnt coal mingled with the ashes of the dead. In distant lands, few garden cities were still breathing, bright and light. In others, winter gardens delighted the eye. Performing penance, boreal deep snow was waiting for an execution of the sentence. Ice kingdoms quickly turned into duchies. The sky above them lit up and went out in red, but the fish already begged for more oxygen. The moon-sailor watched the suffering Earth through the open window of clouds. In the attic of night, the stars disappeared as well. At the fragile table of Mother Earth, the seasons changed their seats. The wrinkles of anger appeared on the face of the mother. The sabers of lightning ripped the sky. The blades of whirlwinds turned even the hardest concrete walls onto their backs. Behind the tall windows of the majestic tenement houses, little monarchies hid. Nearby, on the starfish of the streets, in the winding corridors of the alleys, among the blocks of apartments, children played as they had already once done. Tired and sweaty, they sat on the stairs telling important stories. Older people sought refuge in colder gateways. The tower of the cathedral, aiming with the symbol at the ocean of azure, had them under its care. Below the arcades of the subway, virtuoso skateboarders laughed in the face of the laws of physics.

Jonah slammed the door of the café. "He didn't allow me to take a leak, but I told him I wanted to buy coffee and a donut," he said nervously. "Ain't this guy know now what hygiene is? You can't eat with dirty hands."

"Jonah, don't be upset. You'll fall sick, or something . . . " Mophead linked his arm through Jonah's.

"I understand you perfectly. You'd like to relieve yourself, but there is no place to do it. You have to buy food to be allowed to use the bathroom. Oh, let's take Paris, for example, that's completely different. Toilets are at every intersection: clean, shiny, open to everyone, with fragrant soaps, warm water, and mirrors." Mophead looked through the window at the café's manager, whose sour face spoke for itself.

"Hooray, I defended the bathroom against the invading homeless."

"And you, Mophead, have you ever been to Paris?"

"I haven't, but I believe you," he replied. Then he pulled Jonah closer to him.

"Why did you bring me here?"

"I need your help."

"Did you come on a date?"

"Come with me." Jonah grabbed Mophead's hand and came up with him to the window of the store next to the café. They stood in front of the large display, behind which the walls and shelves were bending under the load of musical instruments.

"It would be enough for two symphonic orchestras." Mophead was delighted. Behind the windowpane, illuminated with halogen lights, there were bells, rattles, cymbals, guitars, violins, clarinets, and trumpets, and all of them scintillated sparks and flashes; next to the long table-counter stood a contrabass and a cello, leaning against each other as if whispering something to each other's ear, followed by drums getting ready for an explosion.

"Look over there, can you see that sax?" Jonah pressed Mophead's nose to the windowpane.

"I can see, dude, five saxophones."

"The one with a large engraving, just above the trumpet?"

Mophead looked hard.

"Well, well, that's a real beaut."

"Custom-made, mate."

"Are you going to learn to play in your old age?"

"Do something for me, please. Enter and ask how much it costs." Jonah almost pushed Mophead inside.

"Your friend is ashamed to come in?" asked the salesclerk. A boy, almost thirty years old, with shoulder-length hair, was adjusting the tuning keys on the guitar. The 1970 Stratocaster. "It still remembers Jimi Hendrix," he said, plucking the strings with the plectrum.

"Well, now, it should sound good," he said, satisfied. He turned up the knobs of the amplifier and ran his fingers over the fret, back and forth, pulling the strings sideways. "I love this leitmotif, it's Slash." He played a few chords more. Then he put the guitar down and turned off the amplifier.

"Can I help you?" he asked, sitting down on the stool.

"That saxophone over the trumpet, can you tell me how much it is?" Mophead asked, pointing with one hand and scratching his cheek with the other.

"This engraved dandy thing?" The boy came up to the instrument leaning against the wall and picked it up. Then he read aloud, "J. T. New Orleans. Grammy . . . the date severely marked-up and illegible . . . illegible . . . this portion is severely scratched and scuffed."

He pondered for a moment and said, "I'm sorry, but it's not for sale." The boy hung the saxophone. "We have others, also good."

"But what's its price?" Mophead did not give up.

"Only the one who pawned it can buy it back. The previous store owner pledged so. Apparently, they were friends. I took over this business recently, but I'm going to keep his promise. I know it was pawned for 300 bucks. I guess it's worth some five grand."

"But how will you recognize the owner?"

"Only he and I know what he'll play when he shows up." The boy smiled and took the guitar again. The sounds of "Blowing in the Wind" hit the windowpanes, drowning out the roars and horns of the street steel beasts. Mophead left the store. A warm wind from the south was coming. Children were flying kites in the nearby park. On the pitch next to it, several teenagers practiced baseball throws, others caught the ball with gloves.

"Jonah, where are you?" Mophead asked, worried. After a while he spotted him on the nearby square on the other side of the street, huddled. He ran toward him. "What happened to you, mate?"

"I'm not well," said Jonah, holding Mophead's hand on his chest. "I feel my end is near."

"Don't worry, it won't happen." Mophead patted Jonah on the back and sighed, "Ah, do y'all there, in that Georgia, have the heart on your right?"

"God forbid!" said Jonah, indignant. After a while, he stood up.

"Every time I walk past this store, my heart gets arrhythmia," he said with a grimace of fear.

"You can always count on me, my friend. I won't leave you in need.

"I'm sure I'll find some job matching my skills."

"Do you have any?"

"Give me this piece of paper." Mophead pulled the nearby snack bar's menu from Jonah's hand and a pencil from the pocket of his jacket. He began skillfully sketching.

Jonah attentively followed his fingers. At the outset, they danced "Swan Lake," then they sped up and tapped out Kozachok.

"I can't! Believe it! Gee-whizz! This is that store!" he exclaimed. "And the guitarist looks like in the photo!"

"Let's get out of here," said Mophead.

They moved forward in the direction of L subway line, singing the song "Under the Boardwalk."

CHAPTER SEVEN

"Ladies and gentlemen, the zero hour will arrive at high noon, on June the first, this year, which was so good for us. There is little time left, but I do hope that you and God can do everything on time."

In the conference room sounded murmurs of an aroused interest in everyone there.

"Seriously? Good, good for whom?" said someone, sitting on a Viennese chair close to a Venetian mirror.

"Silence, please!" Harameus appealed to the bank's employees, who ensconced themselves in the chairs as well as on the floor by the walls.

"I kindly request you to rise to the occasion, spare no effort," he said solemnly.

"How about raises?" someone in the corner of this crowded room shouted in a slapdash manner, having his face smothered by his hand.

"This is always the first thing on your mind, Mr. Barbs," Harameus easily picked out of the crowd a portly man with a chubby face, hiding behind the back of his colleagues.

"Go ahead, please stand up and give us your arguments," he said, a little upset. The noise in the room ceased. A sea of busy heads and busy tongues stopped moving. Complete silence reigned over the room. Only for a short moment, the silence was interrupted by a scrape of a chair. Mr. Barbs rose from squatting.

Dread-ridden, unsecure, he sat down on the chair. The ormolu grandfather clock struck once instead of twelve times as it used to at high noon. From a tiny wooden cabin hanging on the wall emerged a cuckoo, which also announced twelve o'clock with only one call.

"What pay increase do you mean? Twenty, or maybe, thirty percent?" Harameus asked with a flash in his eyes. Several whistles were heard in the room; here and there, stamping sounds. Mr. Barbs was in a troublesome situation, which was not perhaps desperate yet, but certainly unenviable. All attendees fixed their eyes on him. The shafts of glancing beams were burning his ears and forehead. He sweated and flushed. A boy with Caribbean looks, sitting on the floor by the wall, recited a verse from Romeo and Juliet: "The more I give to thee, the more I have."

"That's enough!" thought Harameus. He did not notice the face of the daredevil (only the top of his curly hair), but he remembered his voice. He wanted to identify that brave soul, but when he turned into the alley between the rows of chairs, he lost sight of the youngster for a moment and could not find him anymore among all the heads there that looked alike. So he gave up and returned to the center of the room. The situation began to get out of control. He slowly began to regret convening that meeting. To take control of the chaos, he applied a proven method, which his late father once used in similar quagmire. Knitting his eyebrows to the utmost, showing the ultimate lion's wrinkle, Harameus swept the attendees' eyes with his eyes like with a machine gun, and they all slipped down onto the floor. Finally, he banged the table with his fist. A young woman standing next to him dropped a chocolate bar. All the room lapsed into silence. Everyone was waiting with bated breath for his next move. From the outside, across the entire hall could be heard a lyrical tenor of the janitor: "Out of my sight . . . " maybe not exactly as Chopin wanted it to sound. The cuckoo again looked out of its tiny cabin, but this time it did not give out any utterance.

"It needs to be oiled," Harameus exclaimed towards the janitor. The tenor went quiet. Between the curtains appeared a wide-open eye. After a while, the janitor stood in front of the chairman's table.

"Okay, okay. You can go back to your duties," Harameus said kindly in a balanced voice. The janitor bowed his head as a token of respect, not taking his eyes off Harameus. He withdrew to the hallway. After a few moments, he turned up with a screwdriver in one hand and an oilcan in the other. Harameus raised slightly his hand and halted the janitor halfway. The bird completed the missing cuckoo calls and hid in its tiny cabin. The ormolu grandfather clock also gave out sound. Harameus whistled a short "struck-dumb" melody. Things were back on the right track. Also, some faces had a look of relief, then heaved sighs of respite.

"What did you ask, Mr. Barbs?" Harameus pierced him with a cynical glance. The stars of Mr. Barbs's deep blue eyes fell to the ground. They should've been talking here about the noble project, the rock concert, and some Mr. Barbs, a man from the IT department, a recent intern, who previously had worked as a junior assistant in the Central Office of the Peat Industry, having no reasons to complain, would like to bash with a stick the horn of plenty and to toss the most precious items into his apron. He barely plowed, not even sowed and already he'd like to reap. He jumps before the entire auditorium with a slogan, which no boss is going to discuss in the spotlight, and persistently demands a raise.

"It's sheer impudence! It's the height of impertinence, indeed! How dare he!" said, outraged, one of the senior employees, sitting at the chairman's table, once the cashier, today a consummate negotiator, vice manager of the debt recovery department, extremely proficient in the art of eristic. He wiped his wet forehead with a velvet handkerchief, and then, the tensed-up nape of his short neck. The bank's chief accountant, one of Harameus' most trusted associates, a defender of women's rights and animal lover, beautiful and elegant lady, Ms. Taylor entered the room. There was a customary exchange of bows and smiles, then they approached each other and gently rubbed their cheeks.

"I congratulate you on your grandson," Harameus said cheerfully.

"How is your son?" Ms. Taylor became a little ill at ease, but, almost immediately, she said in a controlled voice,

"Two days ago he went fishing. His cellphone is out range."

Harameus offered his arm to Ms. Taylor and escorted her to the place of honor at the chairman's table. He helped her gallantly take off her cashmere coat and hung it on the armrest of the chair next to him. His gentility revealed itself in all its glory. Ms. Taylor whisked away a few specks of pollen from her jacket and hair and sat down on the chair. At that time, Mr. Barbs tried to bring silence to his mind and arrange his thoughts. There was no shortage of such unruly and unreliable disputants as Mr. Barbs, and there many of them in Harameus' orbit. They usually put forward their arguments vaguely and obscurely and, naturally, did not command respect. On the other hand, however, not defending Mr. Barbs at all, it is necessary to say sincerely that his actions and behavior were quite genuine—he did not try to ingratiate himself, he did not smile stupidly at his superiors, he did not act obsequiously toward anyone. Harameus valued such personality traits, but, at the same time, he could not turn over his everyday thick skin, in fact streaked with decency. Had he agreed to such a precedent then, what consequences would be in the future? Even when he took a liking to someone, he had to put on a mask of a despot that was very different from his real face. Therefore, there could not have been a good solution for both sides. In order to decide to give a salary raise, he had to have a deeper understanding of a particular case, to know a particular employee's both skills and the diligence. Some of them were not able to present their matter in the proper light and justify their claims. In addition, each case had to be verified by managerial personnel, and even if he himself agreed to contribute something to the employee's salary, he always left the final decision to the manager, the direct superior of those requesting the raise. The commonest ruse used by the managers to postpone, or even make the raise impossible, which is still happening, even today, not always with Harameus' knowledge, was to persuade every employee to sign an unfavorable annex—a typical trick used in many trusts and commercial corporations. For example, a junior account executive, wanting to become a senior account executive in the future, or any aspirant, had to sign the annex first, then sit quietly for an undetermined time and patiently wait. Even those employees who were trained in reasoning and were highly professional, they could not count on going shortcuts. What's more, he had to be more careful than others. He had more to lose. The position of account executive in the bank was always strong, and this position provided privileges and perks, including special prerogatives. A flagship example here was special treatment at the bank canteen. A senior account executive, or someone holding an equally prominent position, was always served out of turn. The cook personally poured the soup for that person, taking with the ladle the most solid chunks of meat from the bottom of the pot. It was similar to using the services of craftsmen. Each of them, a tailor, a shoemaker, a barber, and a hairdresser, knew exactly who was crossing their threshold. That is why the candidates for better positions watched their behavior as they could. There could be no question of any indulgence. If the superior caught someone even harmlessly breaking of the bank regulations—for instance, a short nap or browsing the Internet—the merit meter would be reset, the aspirant would be recalibrated, and everything would start anew. Just as in the case of trying to win a woman's favors. You could compliment her for years, be helpful, invite her, go with her, or amuse her with small talk, but it took only one ill-considered sentence such as, "This skirt is already too small for you," and the 'complimenter' would have many reasons to regret it—many years of efforts wasted. An army of the Bar's crafty buggers watched over everything. They prepared the complex annexes in fine print, and whoever went to the conciliation court for justice usually came back empty-handed. The favorite sayings of the managers were, "Be patient," or, "Everything in due time." However, time was ineffectual here, like a comet flying farther and farther away from the sun. You had to be stuck like a stone and wait.

Harameus did not deny any employee's competence and diligence, but it must also be said that his remunerations were rather scarce. For example, Mr. Barbs asked for a raise three times and tried to explain the reasons, but each time he heard the same: "It's not time yet, it is not due time yet, be patient and don't bother us," always said in an openly derisive voice. In the rematch, there were insults, always bringing about offensive phrases in Mr. Barb's mind. That day, however, was special. Everything might happen. Mr. Barbs's request, or rather demand, remained an open matter—a thing of the remote future might become a thing of now and here. Harameus, wanting to nip that dispute in the bud, marked a parabola in the air with his hand and pointed to Mr. Barbs a place close to his leg, in a quite friendly way.

"He calls me like a dog," thought Mr. Barbs. "Who cares. I'm gonna . . . maybe I'm gonna get something." Recently was his twenty-fifth and he thought he just deserved that money. He was working there for a year, and at that time this dripping drop of bitterness broke off the edge. Mr. Barbs's nature, like most people's, liked to hide. For the world, it was modest and slow-moving, at home, a lively spinning top, Tom and Jerry in one, indeed. At work, he did not bear fanfare. When a wise guy began his soliloquy, he would put on the pastor's attire, take a stick in his hands, and instead of goading the sheep to rush, he trove such a know-it-all into a corner with his erudition.

"Mr. Barbs, I'm talking to you!" A pink-faced guy called by name shyly emerged from behind the backs of the chairs. John Lee Barbs, nickname Barabbas, shuffled to the center of the room.

"Walter, we're leaving for Europe." Walter looked at Harameus with worried eyes.

"I know you have a fear of flying, but I'll need your help."

"Why such a sudden decision?"

"A few days ago, Ms. Taylor received an anonymous e-mail. There may be incidents of harassment and mobbing in our Cracow branch office."

"But it's possible they're just groundless accusations," Walter said in a doubtful tone.

"One of the women employed there attempted suicide."

"Yes, it's really a bad thing. Do you want to take care of it personally?"

"Ms. Taylor tried to find something out by phone, but the employees weren't very talkative. Besides, our manager in London, who, incognito, was supposed to investigate the matter, fell ill."

"You wanted to use her as a bait?"

"She's Ms. Taylor's friend. Besides, she volunteered."

"When do you want us to fly?"

"As soon as possible. Maybe even this weekend."

There's a small problem, Harameus."

"What do you mean?"

"On Saturday, the Yankee Stadium will host the Red Sox. I promised my nephew to take him to the match. The kid is a big fan of the Red Sox. Ms. Keller gave us a present, the tickets with box seats for VIPs, so it would be quite awkward to refuse."

"I thought, since you speak Polish, but, okay, no problem, I'll fly with Mr. Barbs, although now the organization of the concert rests on his shoulders."

"Barabbas got a promotion?" Walter asked, surprised.

"He speaks a little too much, but let him show what he can do. His lively language will be very useful now. Relentless, young, angry, exactly someone we need. No bigwig will brush him off with a cheap excuse.

"Don't you believe in the good intentions of the rulers?" Walter asked, astounded. Harameus gave him a telling look. Lost in thought, Walter rose from the couch and walked across the living room. After a while, he said, "No problem, I can take him to the match another time, and I'll send a bouquet of flowers to Ms. Keller, as a token of my heartfelt gratitude."

"Thank you, Walter, I knew I could count on you."

"When we're there, I'm gonna visit relatives. I just need to buy something to calm down," Walter said, cheered up.

"Tell your nephew that when we return, we'll all go together to Boston. He'll be able to see his idols on their own field." Harameus came up to the window and looked at the houses in view. He thought about Mophead, Jonah, the lame hobo and the veteran woman from Charleston. He wondered if they had a roof over their heads and a warm meal on that day. Behind the tinted windows of the President Tower flickered kaleidoscopic spots of TV sets. Here and there, a silhouette, an indistinct vertical line, emerged to at once vanish in the spacious interiors. The lamps seemed to stay out of the way, in the corners. Their amber and yellow lights cleared the way for a garish riot of colors pouring out of the screens. Here and there, in the slits of the slightly open windows glowed dots of lit cigarettes. A few blocks away rose up the luminous Chrysler Building. An outline of the Manhattan Bridge pierced through the crepuscular haze. Behind the pylons of the dark green bridge, the ribbon of the East River vanished in twilight. Distant street lamps, as if squinting their eyes from the drizzling rain, illuminated the city's outskirts with their faint light.

Harameus was standing in front of the flight information board in the departure hall of the seventh terminal. There were a few more minutes left to check in, so he could have a snack and cup of coffee. He was waiting impatiently for Walter, who, at any minute, might come with an aromatic espresso, when he thought he was hallucinating. Beaming, Walter was coming closer and closer, talking vividly with a person whom Harameus would never have expected to meet here.

"Good morning, Mr. Lehm. I'm glad we're flying together," he heard by way of greeting. Harameus looked as if he saw a ghost.

"I see that you're also glad to see me," she said in a friendly way. She gave him coffee and a croissant. "Let's go and sit down," she said. Dumbfounded, he swallowed hard. From the lower level of the terminal, a lively melody was reaching their ears. Monica Keller pointed to an empty table by the glass balustrade. As soon as she did it, at the top of the escalator appeared a corpulent man with a backpack and an accordion hanging on his chest. Having seen the unoccupied table, he quickened his pace. Monica looked at Harameus, then looked at the table. Harameus deciphered her message quickly, and, without hesitation, walked forward. The stout man, in a rather clever way, bypassed Walter balancing his body, and soon the path to the table was open to him. Harameus extended his step, and after a second he sat on the chair at that table.

"How resourceful," Monica said quietly to Walter. The accordionist came up to the table.

"You haven't sat here earlier," He said in a rather impolite tone. "Earlier, not indeed, but now I'm sitting," Harameus retorted.

"And you, were you sitting here?"

"Ask at the counter," he said.

"Don't be so upset, there're enough chairs for everyone," said Walter.

"Sir, I'm a singing accordionist, and I'm going to Vienna."

"In that case, play something Viennese for us."

Walter placed a chair next to him and pointed at the chair for him. The accordionist pushed it aside, parted his legs, unfolded the bellows laughter and pressed the keys. In the window with the inscription "Lost Baggage," a hairy hand opened the curtain and wagged his finger. Then it pointed to the infographic sign showing a crossed-out note.

"Why do they keep musicians from playing," he muttered under his breath, discontented. Then he fastened the accordion and went in the direction of the smoking room. Being in a safe distance, where the eyesight of the man from the window does not reach, he looked around again and began to play a waltz. Monica hurriedly got to the table.

"Can we be on a first-name basis?" she asked Harameus.

"I will be more than honored, madam," he replied without hesitation, however, with some fear. Somewhere in the back of his head he heard the voice of reason that warned against being on too familiar terms. Quickly, however, he silenced the murmurs of grumbling and slowly began to warm up.

"She doesn't look like the lioness of a few days ago," he thought. In Harameus's head, only one persistent question "How does she know?" kept whirling.

In the early afternoon, the clouds dispersed, letting out the long-awaited rays of the sun. The streets, roofs, trees and ground glistened after the morning drizzle, but with each passing moment their steaming breaths were getting shorter and shorter.

"I slept amazingly well today," Harameus said with genuine satisfaction. "And you?"

"On the contrary," Walter replied, patting his yawning mouth.

"Every now and then, nightmares tortured me really brutally."

"Look at Monica, how lithe her gait is," Harameus said with admiration, seeing her leaving the hotel. "As if she doesn't have jet lag at all."

"You sacrificed yourself by giving her your place. She slept snugly throughout the whole flight."

"Not a big deal, just a human thing," Harameus said modestly.

"I'd never risk sitting at the back of a plane, especially by the toilet."

"She fell asleep, as if on cue," said Harameus. "She probably uses some relaxation techniques." Walter looked at him.

"Like in the army?"

"Something more effective. She closed her eyes and almost immediately was in the arms of Morpheus."

"I wish I could do it too," Walter said. "Last night, I hardly slept a wink."

"Are you saying about the nightmare?"

"Yes, I dreamed about a war, but, frankly, it looked more of a hunt: me, alone, and them, many. They were hunting me down like an animal."

"Everyone, once in a while, dreams about a shootout, Walter. It's nothing new."

"When I got hit in the leg, I woke up scared stiff, and the car in the parking lot continued to fire from the exhaust pipe. In the dream I saw rifles pointed at me before I heard the shot bangs on the parking lot. How can it be explained?"

"For centuries, people have been racking their brains over this question," said Harameus. "Dreams work in mysterious ways. Apropos of hunting, I wonder when Monica will turn into a lioness again."

"I guess she likes you, and that's why she's so kind."

"Oh, Walter, you always put the cart before the horse."

"In my family, it's women that rule, so I know something about this."

"Let's leave it alone. Where do your relatives live?"

"In the south of Poland, in a small village near Dukla."

"Do you keep in touch with each other?"

"Since they moved out of the city, it's been difficult to do that," said Walter. "They live in the very middle of nowhere: mountains, forests, and marshes."

"What are you discussing, gentlemen?" Monica asked with the utmost interest, handing them coffee through the car window.

"About techniques of falling asleep," replied Harameus.

"The best one is just getting tired, really tired," she said and sat down on the seat next to the driver.

"We have some 200 miles to drive," said Walter. "I think we'll be there before sunset."

"It's Saturday, so we don't have to be in a hurry," she said quite naturally and spread the roadmap on her knees.

"Would you like to visit your family on the way?"

"It would be great," he replied.

"Why not do it? Let's scram," she said enthusiastically. Walter put the route data into the GPS device, started the engine, and slowly left the parking lot.

"Warsaw is a nice city," said Harameus. "At last a peaceful place. Leaving, now and then, New York, is pure pleasure." He looked around admiring fine and well-kept houses.

They had a good hundred miles behind them when Harameus, seeing Walter's tired face, offered to change with him behind the wheel. Walter stopped the car and moved to the rear seat. He put his head against the rest and fell asleep immediately. Monica was browsing a tourist guide, familiarizing herself with the Bieszczady region and the royal city of Cracow. A quiet music was coming from the radio. After about an hour, daily news was broadcast. Walter woke up and again took the wheel. An announcer on the radio read the latest weather forecast.

"Walter, do you speak Polish?" she asked.

"Expect slight frost and snow tonight," the announcer said.

"It's already growing dusk" said Harameus, looking at the sun hiding behind the trees.

"It would be good if we could find a restroom."

"That can be a problem. We have about 50 miles to go, so there's little chance of reaching a gas station or a restaurant on the way. GPS has led us into the wilderness. No signposts or information boards," remarked Monica.

"Yes, that's something of a puzzle," said Walter and checked the GPS unit again.

"It's strange," he said with an utterly confounded face. "It's showing a completely different topography of the site than just a few minutes ago." On the dark green screen, the road marking turned into a thin thread, and the moving arrow froze. From the narrow road they were now on, not even the shortest path branched off; however, on the screen some side pathways crossed the forest.

"This GPS gizmo must've gone crazy," said Harameus. After a moment, he took his cellphone out of his pocket.

"There used to be a barracks in this area. Maybe that's why the signal is disturbed," said Walter.

"Like on the Brooklyn Bridge," said Monica.

"I can't reach our branch in Cracow. Out of range," remarked Harameus.

"Let's hope we'll soon be within—"

"Walter, can you stop the car?" Monica asked. Walter pulled off to the side of the road.

"Watch out, the wind's blowing really strong," said Harameus, half in jest, half serious. Monica looked at him indulgently. The day was getting darker and darker. The first stars appeared in the sky. Monica opened the trunk and, after a moment, returned with a shoulder bag. She took out a small leather case. She opened it carefully and after a while they saw a walkie-talkie in her hands.

"I'd expect to see a bottle of brandy in a woman's bag, rather than a walkie-talkie," Harameus said pleasantly surprised. "Do you have night-vision binoculars and a compass in your survival kit as well?"

"I have a compass in my watch," said Walter.

"I see, gentlemen, you're in high spirits. Please, get us out of this situation. Find the right road," she said, surprised by their frivolity. "You can always count on truckers and police, as opposed to carefree companions." Harameus rubbed his hands. From his mouth came out cloudlets of steam.

"It's just jokes," he said.

"A reliable means of communication is always useful, especially in such an area."

The sky was glowing dimmer and dimmer. They saw the road lit up by the headlights transform into a writhing lane. Only narrow paths branched off it. In front of them emerged a forest wall.

The car could not go on. Besides, the gas tank was almost empty. Here and there, snow covered gray meadows at the foot of the hills. The trees were all around. All three of them got out of the car. Chilly wind swathed their bodies. They began to look around. A valley stretched beneath them. Mist over the meadows hung at knee height, mixed with the smoke of the extinguished fires. The bloody shield of the moon emerged from behind the mountain. It was so low that it almost touched the tops of the trees. At the foot of the forest on the other side of the pass came the howling of a wolf, and the barking of dogs from nearby villages. The gusts of wind brushed the tops of the trees, bending them in half. The grass, being kicked around, was lying down on the ground. The forest was roaring on a strong note. Frozen trunks creaked under the weight of the wind. Monica zipped up her leather jacket, put on her cap, and set the walkie-talkie to channel one.

"It's the most-used range," she said.

"I think it isn't the best idea," Harameus chimed in. "Who knows who could hear us." She agreed with him and switched to a different frequency.

"This is the channel drivers use."

"May I?" Walter looked at Monica and held out his hand toward her. Reluctantly, she handed him the walkie-talkie.

"One, two, three, four, can anyone hear me?" He waited a moment, then repeated the call again. Only noises and crackles came from the device.

"I'm at the pass. We got lost and we need help, over." The walkie-talkie remained silent. Walter pressed the button once more and began to speak again,

"In the south you can see pylons. In the north, the moon."

"Let's wait a moment, if no one responds, let's come back," she suggested.

"I'm afraid we won't get far," said Walter. "The gas tank is almost empty."

"You haven't filled it up?" she asked, surprised.

"A rental employee assured me that it was full, but, as you can see, it wasn't true. The gas level sensor didn't alarm us either. The level dropped all of a sudden, a dozen miles ago." Monica put the walkie-talkie away.

"We have to go lower. There must be some buildings since we can hear dogs."

"Wolves too," said Harameus. They looked at the bleak valley.

"If there are no marshes, we'll get there in half an hour," said Walter.

They went down the hill, and after a while Harameus suddenly slipped on the frosted grass. With a thud he fell to the ground. He tried to get up while leaning on his arm, but the pain he felt in his back stopped him. Walter took him by the arm and carefully put him on his feet.

"It's nothing, I'm fine," he said with a sore face.

"It doesn't look good," she said, worried. "At least you cushioned the fall with your hand."

"When I was a kid, I trained Judo. Habits remained," he said with a bit of a smile

"Let's get back to the car. You won't get far in such a state. Besides, it's piercingly cold," she said.

"Why don't we cuddle together to keep out the cold" he suggested shyly.

"Walter, maybe you'll warm him up."

"Last time on the plane, you saved me from oppression," said Walter. "It's time to return the favor." Harameus looked mysteriously at Walter and slowly moved his hand from under his arm.

"I'm better, I can go on my own," he said. Walter took a flask out of the jacket pocket and shook its contents. He unscrewed the cap and handed the flask to Harameus. He smiled and sniffed the liquor and took a large gulp. Then he let out a deep breath and handed the flask to Monica. She dipped her lips and gave it to Walter.

"The driver doesn't drink," he said seriously and put the flask into his pocket. As they reached the car, they heard the sound of a horse galloping. They stopped talking and strained their eyes and ears. The silhouette of a rider on a horse emerged from the blurry dark forest background. Being about 50 yards away, he reigned in the horse; the animal turned its neck to the side and shook his mane, then jerked up its head and neighed threateningly. After a while he began to snort.

"He senses strangers," said Monica in an expert tone.

Harameus took two steps back and asked, "How do you know about horses?"

"Didn't Ms. Taylor tell you?"

Harameus, in surprise, looked at Monica. "Do you know each other?"

"We help at a shelter for abused animals," she said. "You don't even know how cruel people can be."

"I know it very well," he said. "Fortunately, there're fewer and fewer such people." Harameus, still walking with a slight limp, sat down on an old stump and fell into a pensive mood.

He walked along a sandy road holding his old suitcase firmly. The leather strap dug into his work-worn hand, but he felt no pain. He wanted to sit down on the old stone to rest for a while, but he knew that if missed the last scheduled train on that day, he might stay there forever. From behind the forest and by the dry plowed potato field, whistles of engines reminded him of their existence. Hisses and puffs of steam, as well as barely audible announcements, coming from a distant railroad station created a galaxy of pleasant sounds. As he listened to this symphony, weariness disappeared from his eyes, and anxiety turned into curiosity. A shy smile appeared on his face. The sky was decorated with cloud flakes which, carried by high winds, flowed lazily from east to west. The air was filled with joyful cantos of birds, as well as chalky white and golden light. Once gentle, when the clouds covered the sun, once sudden and sharp, when this cover drifted away. Short shadows announced the noon hour. It smelled of ripe forest herbs, resinous pines, and half-dried green-reddish junipers. He entered the very midst of these wonders enjoying the landscape enclosing his space. He stared at the farthest distances, trying to evoke all the memories that sank into oblivion a long time ago. He did not know what language God spoke to him now, but looking up, he felt a pleasant shiver revive every hair on his skin. At first, the clouds looked ordinary and familiar—they were light and airy. Soon they began to pile up randomly forming a face with distinctive features.

Huge and imperious, painted with white and off-white spots and lines. The face with quite a different feature than that one invented by people—male and female at the same time. An oval of inexpressible power occupying a huge chunk of the sky, filled with care, and, simultaneously, it seemed angry, looking at this world with worried eyes. The cloud moved to the zenith, covering the sun, which showed even more the majestic details. Behind this one came another—also huge, like a long-necked bird with wide-spread wings and a diadem on its head and a baleful humanlike look. From behind the bird emerged white-winged, broad-shouldered angels with austere features. For an indefinite period of time—maybe it was half a quarter of day, maybe a blink of an eye—everything beneath the clouds grew calmer. The waves of soft grasses fell softly. When the most colossal face and followers sailed up to the outskirts of the town on the hill, cheers came from the plain. The people chanted someone's name. The last of the angels wielded his sword and spoke to them without emotion. Reverberations spread in all directions.

"Ye people with a thousand faces appoint Kobold the Golden-Tongued as king, this tempting serpent whom a jackal plays the panpipes, who dreams of great power indeed. He bites the backs of those who are safely asleep then entwines around their throats to make them ready for the last sleep—their eternal sleep. He promised to free you from troubles and woes of the world, but he injects the worst possible venoms into your hearts, he sows discord between sister and sister, brother and brother. Ye glorify a cockroach on the legate throne, who is unrivalled in the fine art of lying. Do ye not see that when ye cry 'hosanna,' streams of bile flow from his rusty, devious, and vainglorious lips? Ye bring thankful songs to the worms, willing to share everything evenly, therefore, ye shall not smell flowers outside the window, where a butterfly perches, but ye smell a swamp in which to look for pure water is in vain. To make matters worse, ye do not respect Mother Earth. I say ye shall cry on account of that."

Looking at the ruffled sky, he thought that God punished him with madness. A pleasant shiver turned into numbness. He felt guilty to have once lost faith because of the injustice he had suffered, that he had dishonored the name of the great family, from which he descended. He wanted to fall on his knees and beg for forgiveness, but as soon as he thought about it, a sudden and clear light encircled him. Immediately afterwards, he heard a voice inside himself admonishing him not to pray for the Creator to do something for him, not to implore for forgiveness, that everything is perfectly known, and self-pity is worse than talking back to the Lord. Meanwhile, cursing his life, he proves that he does not know the obligation of being grateful to the Creator. When he wanted to protest again, he heard that God does not look at people from the position of the throne, so he had better talk, shout and demand, and then he will be paid back, sooner than he expects. He also heard that the only one who can get to the Divine Table is he who values and respects the most precious and joyful gift—life itself—both his own and anyone else's. After what he had heard, he stood still, like a pilgrim in front of a holy image. He had an irresistible impression that God put the friendly hand on his shoulder, and that he would soon hear something peculiar again, and that it would not be an illusion. And thus, it happened. He heard once more that the taste of vengeance is a confusing sense, and the pleasure that comes from it is sweet only for a moment, then it becomes bitter and poisonous.

"God, you know who I really am," he said remorsefully. "As my tears flow down, the hidden pain and suffering fade away. But they'll disappear forever when I find justice."

He reached into his pocket and drew out a revolver, given to him by an old friend, with whom he had shared a bad time, and who had waited "there" on that day at the gate. He examined the weapon and along with someone else's life, placed it in his hand. Suddenly, a stream of wind swirled around the field, gathered dust, and threw it in his face.

"You are not here to administer justice," he heard. "Your task is to find your son, a young man these days, who, without his father, is still defenseless like a wolf puppy hidden in a deep pit, at the outlet of which murderous dogs lurk—at which sneaky spiders spun webs. His life has not yet crystallized, and when you do not appear in time, he will fall prey to the howling pack. He still needs you. Let it be your goal, not revenge!"

He wanted to cry, but he bravely stopped his tears. He rubbed his eyes with his sleeve, looked at the revolver, took bullets out of it, and threw them as far as he could into the roadside dense thicket. He smashed weapon against a stone. Finally, he heard that if he understood God's words, he should nod, and so he did. Then he knelt down, put the suitcase next to himself, folded his arms over his chest and lowered his head. Shyly, almost silently, in a whisper, he asked that he could someday look into the eyes of the man who had had given him this fate, so that he could testify to his integrity and restore his honor—the man he used to call "D." The full name could not go out of his mouth. However, he did not receive any answer. He rose from his knees and looked up at the sky. In spite of having felt constriction in his chest, he stood proudly. The overcoming silence was broken by the bangs of railroad hammers against steel wheels. Shortly afterwards, steam burst out of the nostrils of the engine. The steel monster panted and puffed.

"Now I understand why wanderers love summer and freight cars so much," he thought. He once had promised himself that as soon as he met someone who shared the copper and glass with him so that he could buy a ticket, eat, and drink something before the end of the day, he would repay him with gold and diamond in the future.

He knew a lot about metals, especially the noble ones, but he knew little about human nature, which made him pay a very high price, the price for a criminal act he did not commit. Nature of those people he seemed to know well was not like the one they presented to the world. No one was able to explain why this was happening—neither a rabbi nor a priest nor the antiques dealer with whom he shared loneliness. For the times he lived in, he was a rather attractive man, despite the fact that the original hair color began to vanish from his head inevitably, and his face began to be decorated with wrinkles. The body scaffolding, however, was quite solid. It had no bends or curves, and it had three spare holes in the belt. In spite of being in good condition, he crawled to the end of his loneliness at the end of his tether. After a long time on the other side, nothing was the same. Today, nobody was waiting for him and hardly anyone remembered about him. Except for one person he did hope was expecting him. He understood that everyone wanted to live their lives to the fullest. He was no longer worried about the fact that on the day they would carve out the dates of his life in stone, they would quickly cover with moss. He never, however, got used to the thought that he was alone so soon.

"Is the law of indifference, which once prevailed, still in force?" he wondered.

He was born as the youngest son of a banker, a citizen of Gdańsk, Geneva, and New York. His father and the father of his father, who had given up their ghosts a long time ago, made him a successor, but because of "D," everything turned out to be different. Today, another person was the head of the family. He was not even sure if he wanted to fight for the succession. If he regained the ring of power, he would not seek revenge. He dreamed that, the following day, he would be woken up by the chill of a drizzly morning, and at last he would find his beloved son. Even if he had to go from house to house, from door to door for the rest of his days. He sensed that he would hug close this adult man and explain everything to him. He wanted to start all over again, forget, forgive, and reject a burning desire to revenge himself. By an unexpected touch of the Creator, even "D" had already forgiven. He felt remarkably relieved afterwards. He did not want to chase anyone anymore, even if he had the best six Friesian horses at his disposal. In isolation, he learned respect and love for humble people, how to enjoy small pleasures, and knowledge of ancient history, as if he had a full-time job at the Alexandria Library. A cooler breeze came from the north. The heat let up. He sopped, opened the suitcase slowly, and from among the neatly folded clothes, he pulled out a bottle of over a hundred-year-old brandy, which had been once deposited with a watch and a gold fountain pen. The only riches that he had to spare today. He filled his mouth and carefully swallowed a trickle. When burning power caught his throat, he quickly spat the rest into the sand. He smiled, realizing that time could not only heal wounds, but also weaken memory. Soon he noticed a lame elderly man with a leaning figure approaching from the opposite direction. He limped, tilting his right foot outward. He pushed an old bicycle on a sandy rut, to which a metal cart was attached. Quite a large wooden barrel rested on the cart. A burning kerosene lamp and a letterbox were attached to it. This man wading in the sand lunatically followed his thoughts. His hands were soiled with fresh work. He clamped them firmly on the handlebar, trying to keep the bike straight, staring at the ground just in front of the wheel. One part of his face was burning in the sun, the other was in a partial shade. The visor of the faded cap shaded his eyes. The limping wanderer looked honest, but he was in some sort of mental confusion. His lips were trembling. When they passed each other, the man looked up and timidly glanced at the man with the suitcase.

"What do you want from me?" he asked suddenly.

They were separated by a strip of sand between the ruts, but the old man took up more space on the road. He was dressed in a much too large linen shirt and much too voluminous pants. He pressed the bicycle against him as if he was afraid that the man he met would want to steal it from him. His body fitted with a wide margin in his large shirt and pants. Unable to guess intentions of the man with the suitcase, he cringed, being afraid of an unexpected outburst of anger, or, worse, a physical assault. Much to his surprise, the man with the suitcase looked at him in a very friendly manner. He pointed to the road, as if giving way to him. The gesture of his hand spoke a lot, but the old man looked at him still suspiciously.

"I don't make friends with anyone anymore," he said timidly after a while.

The man with the suitcase felt a little uncomfortable, but he stretched out his hands slowly and offered a greeting. After a short mutual inspection, they greeted each other with both hands. The man with the suitcase discreetly looked at the box filled with letters, then looked more boldly inside the barrel. Above the straw bed, in the corner by the bedhead, he noticed a metal locker attached to the solid wood Number 189 was inscribed on it. The old man, noticing Harameus' curious look, slid the canvas separating the barrel from the rest of the world.

"I don't open any letters anymore," he said, more relaxed this time. "And particularly not those official letters." His face brightened up a little.

"What secret does locker 189 hide?" the man with the suit-case pondered.

As far as he could remember, legends and rumors about box 189 were circulating already at his time. But was it the same one? An eagle plummeted from under the celestial dome. From the depths of the field were coming squeals of a hare. It ran in zig-zags. Dust rose from under its paws. The eagle followed it faster and faster. Then the predator rose into the sky. The old man shielding his eyes with his hand looked up. He drew a crust of bread from his pocket and took a bite. Then they both looked at the field again. The hare left a dust trail behind itself again. The eagle soared high. Far from the field furrows, they saw a plow-man. He walked slowly, clutching the rope, and the horse's mane, as it seemed. Behind them, there was a plow left stuck in the ground next to a boulder. The plowman turned away every now and then, as if he felt sorry for the lost day.

"Where are you going?" the man with the suitcase asked the old man. Then he looked at the lighted lamp. "It's a pity to burn the oil."

"I'm looking for a human being," answered the old man. "Thank God sometimes it happens to see one."

The man with the suitcase took out a bottle of brandy and stretched out his hand with the treat. The old man frowned and turned his head away. When his gaze returned, he began to look more closely at his interlocutor.

"God answered my payers," he said and lowered his head. "Forgive me. I beg you," he said quietly.

"I don't know you, wanderer," said the man with the suitcase. "Whatever you did wrong, don't worry about it anymore. Go your way and I'll go my way, he said. Then he looked at the forest, behind which the clatter of wheels could be heard. Clouds of vapor rose from the chimneys of steam engines. Sparks danced in the air. When he wanted to look at the old man again, he disappeared around the corner of the road. He felt sorry for him, but he did not bother about him anymore. Now he worried about where he would live tomorrow, and whether he would get some provisions for the way for-ward. He explained everything to himself that on that day, what had happened to him was caused by hunger and fatigue.

When he was about to move on, he noticed a lying unopened letter on the sand. It had a handwritten note: "Wealth is troublesome. At one point of time it palls, especially that gained by exploitation. That's why I gave it away." He took a match box out of his pocket and lit the envelope.

Harameus rose from the stump.

"What else do I not know about Ms. Taylor?"

"She's a very active campaigner for the rights of animals, said Monica.

"And a rabid feminist," Harameus added carefully.

"I hope you're not a male chauvinist?" Monica looked at him as if he had a minute to confirm the worst.

"At the bank we are employed on the basis of parity—fifty-fifty with only minor deviations, when children are born. Much of the merit of mine!" he said with satisfaction. Monica endowed him with an understanding look.

"I'm just suggesting that—"

"I know what you meant." She smiled.

"Less favorable winds are blowing for women; that's why I admire them so much," he said. "Unequal, unfair treatment causes them a lot of suffering."

"You'd better not go astray and keep going on this path," she said, and took a hairbrush out of her purse and started to comb out her hair, shining in the glow of the night, at the same time, holding the hair clip in between her lips. What he said seemed sincere and brought her genuine joy. From the villages hidden in the darkness, the wind blew warmer air. The blast also brought the scent of burning wood and coal. The moon sailed above the canopy of the forest. Monica stared at a rider sitting on the back of the half-egg-shaped mountain, which shook its thick mane and wagged its tail every now and then. The moist pelage of the powerful stallion, silvered by the glow from the sky, glittered as if it were a reflection of the Universe in the mirror of the lake. The rider lit a cigarette and took a few deep puffs. Coughing and spitting specks of tobacco chafing his lips, he threw the cigarette stub on the ground. He spurred his horse with his calves and slowly moved forward.

"I hope his intentions are friendly," said Walter. When the rider came closer, he again pulled on the reins. Wrapped in a felt cloak, with his face hidden under a thick beard, he looked at them closely.

"Welcome, farmer," Walter said in Polish. "We're lost and need help." Then he made a few steps forward.

"Stop! Don't move!" said the rider, jumping down from the horse. Warningly, he turned the rifle slung across his back, placing it on his chest. "Who are you?" he asked, pointing a strong flashlight beam at Walter.

"We lost our way," said Walter. "We're tourists." The rider removed his rifle from his shoulder. "Tourists don't venture here at night," he said harshly.

"What is he saying?" asked Monica.

"He doesn't believe us," said Walter. Then he reached into his jacket pocket.

"Don't try any tricks!" shouted the man, and he reloaded the gun.

"We're foreigners, farmer." Walter took out his passport and slowly placed it on the ground.

"Who taught you Polish?"

"My family comes from here," said Walter. The bearded rider picked up the passport and thumbed through several pages.

"Hmm." He mumbled something under his breath. "These days, you can forge anything you want," he said mistrustfully, and in the same manner he looked at Walter, shifting his eyes to Monica and then to Harameus. Walter interpreted into English the rider's doubts and objections. Monica came up closer.

"And, is this also a fake?" she asked, handing him the ID of Yankee stadium. The bearded man looked at the picture, then illuminated Monica's face. Being a strapping guy, he leaned a little to be able to look at it more closely, especially as the baseball cap visor obscured Monica's forehead and eyes. His hands were big, almost like bread loaves at the harvest festival. He was taller than Walter. Monica's eyes narrowed, and she shut herself from the light beam with her hand.

"A bear is afraid of a deer," she said aside to Harameus. Across the rider's lips beamed a smile. He switched off the flashlight and gave her ID back.

"Thank you for the compliment," he said in good English. "The deer is an exceptionally beautiful and graceful woman," he added gallantly, and his face brightened up.

"The interrogation's completed?" Monica smiled in a conciliatory manner.

"Different people hang around here, ma'am. No one can be trusted. My name's Szczepan Bernard Krzyżanowski, a.k.a. 'Orphanage Dedicated.'" He took off his Cossack cap and bowed slightly.

"From now on, you're my guests. I won't harm a hair on your heads."

"My grandmother was Russian," Walter chimed in. The rider turned and looked at him attentively and said after a while:

"You can feel safe here even more."

"And my father was Jewish," Harameus said from behind Monica's back.

"Your face is rather Mediterranean," said the rider, scratching his beard. "I'd even say it is the face of Caesar."

"I hope not the one of Tiberius," Harameus said with a slight measure of sarcasm.

"Who knows what blood flows in our veins," said Szczepan.

"I grew up in an orphanage. They called me 'foundling.' They pissed in my shoes. But only until I grew up, of course. Some said that my father was British, and not just anybody."

"Diplomat, dammit!" Szczepan brighten up a little. "But would a diplomat disown his son? He betrayed his wife? Dammit, a titular ambassador. Let him play golf in his county."

"We'd be more than glad to impose on your hospitality," said Monica, willing to change the subject.

"As Poles say: A guest in the house, God in the house—which roughly means: you're very welcome, ma'am. So, you've come here from New York?"

"Yeah," said Walter.

"Where do your relatives live?"

"They used to live near Dukla at one time, but I ain't been in touch with them for a pretty long time." The horse jerked up his head. The rider moved the reins closer.

"Stand still, Gladiator," he said and patted the stallion.

"He senses wolves or bears."

"How far from here to Dukla?" asked Walter. The horse jerked his head again.

"The word 'Dukla' makes me nervous, too. The previous owner didn't treat him well." He patted the horse's side again. Monica came up to the stallion and stroked him on the mouth. Then she stroked his side. The horse moved his nostrils towards her hand, as if he demanded further caresses.

"Never before has he allowed a stranger to touch him," he said, surprised. "Over there, behind the mountain pass is my hut. You can get warm and eat something."

"Is there a chance for a cup of tea?" asked Monica, breathing on her numb hands.

"Of course, ma'am. Even plum brandy will be served." Walter and Harameus received that with undisguised satisfaction.

"You'd better ride on horseback," he turned to Monica and Harameus. "Farther from here are pits and rifts. Now if you permit, I would like you to hold you. Spartacus is quite large, so it's fairly hard to mount him."

"I can do it," said Monica. She put her foot into the stirrup and skillfully moved her leg over the horse.

"The saddle is large enough, so you'll also fit. It was custom-made for me."

Szczepan held the stirrup and lifted Harameus up with his hands and mounted him behind Monica. Spartacus bucked slightly, but when Monica stroked his neck, he immediately calmed down.

"It's unbelievable how meek he became," Szczepan said in Polish to Walter.

"How's your leg?" Monica asked Harameus.

"Quite well. The closer it's to you, the less it's aching." Monica nudged him with her elbow. Harameus moved back a little. They saw a small hut in front of them not far away. A thread of white smoke was coming out of the chimney.

"Here we are," said Szczepan.

"Finally ," Monica said with relief, and she got off the horse. Just after her, Harameus slid down.

Monica poured tea from a cast-iron kettle into the cups. In the kitchen, filled with chopped logs, the fireplace was blazing. On the almost red-hot cooktop, in the battered pot, corn was almost ready to be served. Next to the pan sizzled slices of bacon and onions. At the bottom of the oven hissed jacket potatoes, cut into quarters and halves.

"Unfortunately, that's all I have in the pantry," said Szczepan.

The smell of rosemary and roasted potatoes, bacon and onions floated in the room. Harameus picked up a slice of bacon and onion from the pan and put on the plate. Then he impaled a steaming, slightly roasted potato on the fork. He ate slowly, savoring every morsel.

"I've never eaten anything so delicious," he said appreciatively. He took a cup of cold milk from the table and dipped it in his mouth.

Monica was sitting in the corner of the room on a wooden stool and sipped tea. She signaled Harameus with her hand so that he would take care of her, too. Hastily, he acceded to her request. Walter filled his plate with three corn cobs, which he right away buttered. He crammed also a few halves of potatoes right next to the cobs. Moments later, he poured plum brandy into two glasses. In the room, it got very warm. Their faces glowed. Monica opened the window slightly. After a dozen minutes or so, Szczepan stood in the entrance door, holding sheepskins and blankets under his arms.

"I hope, gentlemen, you'll sleep well," he said, and put everything on the floor.

"For you I have something special," he kindly turned to Monica. From behind the door and pulled out a metal military camp bed and unfolded it right by the kitchen.

"Here you'll be warm and comfortable. Besides, the bathroom is closer." He took a blanket and bed linen from the closet and put it on the bed. Then he raked out the ashes from the hearth into a bucket and took it outside.

"Water in the boiler is hot. The bathtub is scrubbed out. I'll sleep on the hay in the barn."

Outside the window, the sky was brightening. The sun was peeking through the slightly open shutters. Monica stretched and rubbed her eyes. Then she got up from the bed and reached for the phone. The clock showed 8:15 am.

"Harameus, wake up," she said loudly. "You all, get up." Harameus, nestled into the blanket, turned over and opened one eye.

"Move it!" She added.

Harameus groaned, achy.

"Good for us, there is cellphone coverage here!" she said. Turning again towards her, he said, "you have nice pajamas."

Walter could hardly get up, muttering under his breath, "I can't feel my back."

"It's time to hit the road," she said, and went to the bathroom. After her morning routine in cold water, Walter followed her. Harameus tried to nap for a while, but eventually, he also got up. Everyone patiently waited for the host. Through the window came the snorting of the horses. Monica opened the window and pushed open the shutters. On the hillock near the hut, she saw Szczepan bouncing on Spartacus. By the side, he was leading his gray mare, on whose back a double saddle rested. Monica came out to the yard. Walter and Harameus followed her.

"In the village, they know I have guests," Szczepan said solemnly and removed a leather bag from his shoulder. He took a plastic bag with food out of it.

"It's from my neighbors on the other side of the valley," he said. "They're good people. They lent a horse and gave gas. It's already in the tank." Monica's eyes lit up with joy. She came up to Szczepan and kissed him on one cheek, then on the other.

"A guest in the house, God in the house, ma'am," he said. "Ready to go?"

"Just a minute, we'll bring our stuff," she said.

Szczepan put the provisions in the bag and mounted Spartacus. After a short while, Walter with a backpack turned up. A moment later, Monica mounted a slender mare. Harameus joined her with considerable difficulty and clung to her, holding her waist. They moved down the valley.

"Ms. Taylor called me some fifteen minutes ago," said Harameus, entering the dining room. "She previously talked to our trusted employee in Cracow. You have an appointment with the manager." Monica moved the plate aside.

"I'm looking forward to it," she said almost enthusiastically.

"I think we should be nearby, just in case," Walter chimed in. "Maybe we'll need a heavier spear to point at this guy."

"What if it's just rumors? Envy?" she asked.

"Soon we'll find out," said Harameus.

"Excuse me, but I have to rest a little." Monica rose from the table. "Can you ask the front desk for an extra blanket?" Monica turned to Harameus. "I was cold a little last night." Harameus went to the reception desk.

CHAPTER EIGHT

Walter parked the car a block away from the bank. Monica walked diagonally across the street, passed the theater building and, after a while, disappeared behind the grand entrance of the bank. Walking down the hall, walking past the ladies' room, she heard a quiet cry of a woman. She momentarily stopped, pushed the door slightly and went inside. She noticed cream-black shoes under the stall door. She went up to the sink and turned on the water. The crying stopped. In the mirror, she saw a woman move her feet back. Monica tidied her hair, washed her hands, and came out to the hallway. She took a few steps when a male voice came from behind her back.

"Good morning, are you the one I have an appointment with today?"

"Only if your name is Kamil Rapidzki," she answered without turning her head. Dressed in a gray suit, a middle-aged man speaking impeccable English straightened his pocket square and sped up his steps. After a while, he pulled level with Monica.

"I'm honored," he said. "I invite you to my office."

In the air lingered the smell of cigar smoke, cologne fragrance, and Turkish brewed coffee. Colorful kilims depicting the stars of politics obscured the pretty pastel-hued walls. On the first one, a plump woman with a tendency to rattle the opposition's cage, standing on the rostrum, threatened them with her fist. On the next one, a politician in a knight's armor, covered with a sheet of cloth, held the rolled-up Declaration of Human Rights in one hand, and with the other, he greeted the world with a Roman salute. Knitted of first-rate wool, he looked as if he were alive. The vibrant verdancy of plants in small pots was relegated to the very corners. Monica was dripping droplets of water from her hand, injuring the floor with dark spots. Although her eyesight was unwavering, she clearly felt Rapidzki's gaze on herself. She walked lightly and gracefully. He rather strode than walked, lifting himself up springily on his toes, giving himself a little more height. They were silent all the way through the hallway. Rapidzki opened a heavy door, and they both squeezed into the office at the same time. Monica almost tore her elegant white blouse against a hinge, but she pulled a thread in her navy blue skirt.

"Please, sit down, Monica. I'm sure you're tired," he said familiarly, addressing her by first name.

"If you don't mind, I'll stand," she answered. "I spent most of my time behind a desk, recently."

"Yes, I know how it is," he said with understanding. They demand more and more from us. Will you have a drink?" Rapidzki smiled, casting a fleeting glance at Monica's neckline.

"Thank you, but, no," she said.

Rapidzki sat down in his armchair, straightened his tie and unbuttoned his jacket.

"I must also tell you, I'm a demanding boss, very exacting. How long have you worked for our company?"

Monica came up to the wall, on which hung kitschy reproductions of the Brooklyn Bridge and the Empire State Building.

"For a short time," she said after a while. "Previously, I worked for Yankee Stadium."

"Hmm, I haven't heard of it. Is that a financial institution?"

"To a certain extent. With a strong focus on women's rights. My branch deals with public relations." Monica stopped in front of the picture of the Flat Iron Building.

"Nice view. Have you ever been there?"

"Oh yes, many times," he said. I could talk about New York for hours. Let's talk about you, though. Are you married? I mean, do you have a family?"

"I'm single. Does it matter?"

"I'm just asking. I'd like to get to know you better. If you're conscientious and follow my instructions, you'll be promoted quickly."

"I'm still on a probationary period in Haram Bank," she replied. "Besides, I had a serious accident, so I asked to be employed abroad. London still evokes associations of pain and stress."

"Don't worry, you'll soon be back in shape. I'd like to make myself clear at this point; in addition to being a demanding boss I'm gonna also be your friend." Rapidzki rose from his armchair and stood right next to Monica.

"Tomorrow we're having a small picnic outside the city. You'll have the opportunity to meet your future colleagues and, of course, me," Rapidzki said with a smirk. He linked his arm through hers, trying to see her to the door.

"Let's go. I'm gonna show you the bank."

"Thank you, I've already seen it." Monica moved her arm away. Then she took a step back.

"Well, then I'd love to pick you up. You don't mind, do you?

"You know the address of the hotel, I hope."

"I do."

"Just don't be late. I hate unpunctuality."

"You can relax. Punctuality is my obsession. By the way, not the only one." He smiled cynically again.

When she put down her cup, the hotel phone rang. She quickly picked up the receiver.

"How are you feeling?" She heard Harameus's voice on the phone.

"Rapidzki is quite a guy," she said.

"You don't have to go if you have any concerns. We can change the plan," said Harameus. "One of the women broke her silence. She claims Rapidzki made sexually suggestive offers."

"I wanna know him better and see what he's really like."

"As you wish," said Harameus. "If you think things have gone too far, just text me or let me know in any possible way."

"Il be fine, but thank you for worrying about me." It had not been half an hour since that conversation took place when the sound of a horn and the whirr of a motorcycle came out of the window. She looked out discreetly through the blinds. Rapidzki, dressed in a leather jacket, set his six-cylinder beast on the kickstand, took off his helmet and hung it on a handlebar, combed his hair with his fingers, and looked up at the façade of the hotel. Monica watched him closely. He pretended he could not see her. He took a handkerchief out of his pocket and started polishing the fuel tank, glinting in the sun. Then he bent down and rubbed his leather calf-length boots, reached into his pocket and took out mirror glasses and put them on, so they perched evenly on his nose. He walked nervously around the bike, holding his jacket with both hands at shoulder height. Every now and then, he pushed the jacket collar back. After a while, Monica heard the horn again.

"Let him wait," she thought and after she had finished drinking tea, she took a shower. Then she got into her tight-fitting jeans, put on her favorite Doc Martens, rigged herself in a short leather jacket, and put a walkie-talkie in her pocket and her cellphone in her purse. After a while, she came out of the elevator. Rapidzki was standing next to his two-wheeler playing a game on his cellphone. When she got closer, he ran his eye over her silhouette.

"I thought you'd changed your mind. We're late," he said, with a reproach in his voice.

"Patience is not your forte, boss." Monica approached the motorcycle and took the helmet, kept ready for her, off the handlebar.

"I thought you would come by car. Who of us is driving?"

"It looks you know a lot about bikes."

"You can say so," she said. Rapidzki nodded his head with disbelief.

"Do you know how much this baby is worth?" he asked ironically. But soon he changed his tone to more tactful.

"Let's agree that I'll drive now, and if it's possible later, I'll put the handlebars in your hands."

"What do you mean, 'If it's possible later?'" she asked inquisitively.

"You know, sometimes there's alcohol at parties. I'm a teetotaler."

"I may not be as holy as you, but I'll be fine." She put the helmet on her head.

Rapidzki put his leg over the back of the motorcycle and started the engine.

"Aren't you afraid?"

"Come on, we're late," she shouted from behind his back. After a while, the bike started throwing smoke and dust from under the rear wheel. Momentarily, they drove along a narrow road, passing cars and people walking by the side of the road. They soon found themselves on the outskirts of the city. From time to time, the wheels fell into the holes in the road, but the two-wheeled Jabberwock was still in good shape. On quite sharp bends, Rapidzki leaned the machine to the limit, almost wiping his right knee on the surface. Monica felt they were going faster and faster. Far too fast. He constantly sped up. On one side of the road there were meadows, on the other side there were fields woken up from the fallow land. They bordered on young trees, which continued to become forests. A veil of clouds spread over the horizon, darkening from minute to minute. Driving now dangerously fast, the bike started to rock violently. She clearly felt that Rapidzki wanted to scare her. Hidden behind his back, she noticed a tractor with a trailer on the bend of the road.

"He can't be that stupid to risk his own life," she thought. When they passed the tractor, the bike slowed down. Dark spots painted by rain drops started to appear on the gray road. The clouds were becoming denser and denser, taking on navy blue and inky hues. Soon they covered the entire sky. The horizon was illuminated on its entire circumference by pulsating lightning spots. Steamy air hung motionless. On the edge of the forest, near the road, she saw a single cottage.

"Maybe this is where the party is," she thought and calmed down a bit. The bike pulled off the road and turned into a side unpaved road. They reached the very entrance to the untended cottage. Monica got off the bike and started to look discreetly around the courtyard. A quiet chirp of crickets was coming from nearby grasses and trees. Rapidzki put the bike by the ramshackle metal fence.

"How did you like the ride? Weren't you afraid?" he asked a little derisively.

"You could've been more careful with the people on the side of the road."

"It's them who should've watched out," he said overbearingly, but momentarily, he assuaged his tone of voice. "I'm always very careful when I see an obstacle. Besides, I know this way by heart."

"It's people, not an obstacle," she corrected him, and walked away a few steps, looking behind the corner of the cottage. Rapidzki walked around the bike and with his boots' heels, he kicked an object lying on the ground. Then he ran up the stairs to the porch.

"I have a car in the garage," he exclaimed. "In just half an hour, we should be there."

"There?" she repeated, with disbelief, reaching into her purse for her cellphone.

"Not a dash of service," she said, worried.

"A dead zone," he said with a smirk. "Storm is coming, we have to wait."

Monica looked up at the sky. Low clouds were growing more and more. Between them and the canopy of the forest, birds rushed by fear, headed for their hiding places. Above the meadows, graylag geese with long necks were cutting the air. A loud clangor spread around. Increasingly pulsating spots lightened the horizon, silent a while ago. From afar came thundering murmurs. Monica looked through the window into the cottage.

"You chose a very strange place to live."

"I bought this shack some time ago," he replied. "So far, only a sign is hanging, but there will be a real motel here. I can show you if you're not afraid."

"What am I supposed to be afraid of?" she said, surprised. Monica put her hand in the pocket, looking for something in it. Then she checked the other pocket.

"Is that what you're looking for?" Rapidzki pointed at the black pieces of plastic lying next to the bike. She came closer and saw the smashed walkie-talkie.

"It must've fallen right under the wheels when we rode into the courtyard. It's gonna rain, real heavily," he said.

The whirling mass of clouds over the old forest was pierced by two dazzling lightning bolts. After a while, a muffled thunder rolled on the ground. The trees began to murmur, being stroked by rain. Monica hesitated for a moment, but immediately followed

Rapidzki. A rusty wall lamp hung between two columns on which the remains of plaster stuck. There was a blackened bulb oozing incandescent glow. To the wall next to the door, attached were handles with flowerpots, in which any verdure and efflorescence, left unattended and cared for, shriveled in themselves memories of their glory, a long time ago. He took a key from under one of them.

"I have a spare one, just in case you ever need it," he said.

Monica did not answer. She walked cautiously on the rotten planks of the porch. The air had a musty tang. The sky blackened. The wind broke. Nearby, the lightning slivered the clouds again. After a few seconds, the thunder rumbled once more. The rain had not started yet, but single drops were getting heavier and heavier. They hit on the roof and the porch loudly. Dark streams were already hung over the forest. Rapidzki turned the key in the lock, and with his shoulder, he pushed the door whose paint had been flaking off for years. He turned around and looked at Monica piercingly. Suddenly, a blinding flash illuminated the sky and a powerful bang was heard at the same time. The thunderbolt struck right behind the cottage. They heard the crack of a torn tree, and then a large branch fell to the ground.

"It was a whomp like fuck," Rapidzki slipped out under his breath.

"This thundering like herds of stampeding elephants," he momentarily corrected himself. On his face appeared a smirk again. They walked inside. He took the matches out of the drawer of the sideboard and lit the kerosene lamp.

"There must be a camping stove upstairs," he said. "It's high time to have a cup of tea." He lifted the lamp and went up the squeaky stairs to the attic. The downpour hit with all its force. Short flashes illuminated the dark room stroboscopically. The thunderbolts blended with the sound of drops hitting on the roof. After a while, Monica heard the sound of water dripping from the ceiling. She also heard Rapidzki's footsteps. Then there was a moment of silence. Monica was sure she could hear him breathe deeply and even snuffle, as if he had a cold. In the light of several consecutive lightnings, she came up to the sideboard and opened the drawer. Apart from a few pieces of junk, she did not notice anything she could use in case of danger. She pulled another one. It resisted, but eventually she managed to get it out. The storm was on the rise. The rain hit on the roof and windows hard. With subsequent fanfares of lightning, she noticed a flashlight in the drawer and a glass ball for pressing paper. Monica pushed the flashlight switch on and lit the stairs. She moved a beam of light over the furniture. Then she pulled the last drawer with a small padlock on it. She pulled harder, the padlock gave way and fell on the floor. In this drawer, under some newspapers, she saw a few plastic bags with white powder. She switched off the flashlight and put it in one pocket and the glass ball in the other.

"It's just in case," she thought, clearly hearing footsteps in the attic, heading for the stairs. After a while, she saw the light of the lamp flicker on the walls. Rapidzki ran downstairs. He was holding the stove and a small bottle with desaturated alcohol in his hand.

"Weren't you bored?" he asked while discreetly looking around the room. Monica saw a smudged bloodstain under his nose.

"The roof is leaking a little bit," she replied.

"Yes, it needs to be repaired," he said, staring at her with greedy eyes. His pupils were considerably dilated. His face spoke with some indefinite grimace of hunger and desire. The look was simply reptilian.

"Does anybody know there's gonna be a motel here?" she asked, a little bit uneasy.

"I've become the owner only recently," he replied. "I haven't had time to boast yet. You're first." Rapidzki started opening the cupboard cabinets in search of cups, lit the stove burner and turned to Monica's side. A padlock rolled out from under his shoe. He picked it up and put on the drawer again.

"As you can see, more things need to be fixed here," he said, glowering at her. The glow from the lamp was reflected in his glassy eyes.

"It stopped raining," said Monica, and walked towards the door vigorously, grabbed the handle, and pulled it twice, but the door did not move, even an inch.

"When it get moisture, it wedges itself," he said, standing right behind her. She heard his breath. A whistle came out of the kettle. Rapidzki poured boiling water on tea.

"What were you looking for?" he asked.

"Where?" she said, as if she were surprised.

"Please, don't pretend."

"I don't know what you're talking about."

"You all think you're so crafty," he muttered through his teeth angrily. Monica wended her way towards the door.

"It's time to go back," she said decidedly.

"Wait a minute!" Rapidzki barred her way.

"Hot tea is waiting," he said more gently now and smiled unnaturally. She went back to the table with him, though unwillingly. Rapidzki raised the cups and passed one to Monica. She took the other he held for himself.

"You don't trust me," he said, and nodded his head. Monica drank a few sips. After a while, she came up to the window.

"The sky's brightening." She reached out her hand trying to open it, but it did not move either.

"Yeah, it's pretty good," he said, standing right behind her back.

"Let's go back, it's getting late," she said again, with difficulty controlling her voice. Her legs got heavy and rubbery. She came up to the cupboard, trying to get her thoughts together.

"Do you have any salt?" she asked.

Rapidzki in surprise looked at her.

"Why do you need salt?"

"It improves the taste of tea," she replied. Monica felt that she was slowly losing consciousness.

"It's upstairs," he said.

Monica opened the cabinet and took out a little jar. Then she shook off a large amount of salt and added some cold water from the faucet. She quickly drank the contents. After a dozen seconds, she vomited in the sink. He got to her in one leap and grabbed her by the shoulders. She got hold of the kettle and, with all her strength, hit him on the head in a half turn. Rapidzki moaned and grabbed his face. His superciliary arch was bleeding. The blood, mixed with hot water, flowed down his face and hands. For a moment, he stood curled up. Monica realized that she had to run away to the attic. She took wobbly steps up the stairs. Her blurred and whirling vision threw her body to the sides.

She bounced off the railing to the wall. When she was upstairs, she heard his steps right behind her.

"You fucking bitch!" he screamed at her. Monica rushed into the attic, slammed the door and bolted it. She looked up at the ceiling and saw an exit to the roof. She moved the table right beneath the hatchway and, using a chair, she climbed onto the table. Wobbling, she unhasped the hatch and pushed the exit flap, which fell on the roof with a thud. She looked up at the sky. It had almost stopped raining. A cool breeze refreshed her face. She grabbed the exit frame with her hands, trying to pull herself up, but her hands failed. She wanted to jump up, but her legs were still too heavy. She heard the banging on the door. First with the fists, then more vigorous, with the boot. The door was shaking in the frame. Rapidzki was kicking harder and harder. After a while, he ran downstairs. She knelt down on the table and, being at the end of her tether, she drew up the chair standing next to her onto the table. Suddenly, she regained enough strength to stand on it. Rapidzki came back after a while and put some metal object in the door, trying to break it down. Monica straightened out. From the waist down, she was in the room, while her torso was sticking out above the roof. A breeze was fanning her face. She pulled herself up with considerable difficulty and climbed onto the rather steep, still damp roof. On its edge, by the very chimney, she noticed a horizontal, quite wide plank, a bit crooked and cracked, but not so much that she could not stand on it. It cleared up outside. The sun was already low above the horizon. Going carefully on all fours, grabbing the humps of old roofing tiles, she reached the plank and hid behind the chimney. She noticed Rapidzki in the hatch opening. He could see her squatted behind the chimney.

"Don't worry, I'm not gonna hurt you!" he screamed, and started to walk on all fours towards her. He looked down every now and then. His legs trembling. Monica looked from behind the chimney and saw that he was only a few steps away. She took the flashlight out of her jacket pocket and threw it at him. Rapidzki dodged. She missed and got dizzy from the effort. Then she took out the glass ball from the other pocket and threw it at him again. Rapidzki moaned in pain. She saw him retreat towards the hatch. His face looked bad. On one its side, a swollen and cut eyebrow arch, on the other, a large lump.

"Serves you right, you son of a bitch!" she bawled him out under her breath, with anger.

Rapidzki withdrew from the roof and slammed the flap behind him. Monica caught a few deep breaths, trying to concentrate. She reached for her phone, but her jacket pocket was empty. Then smoke started to come out of the chimney. First white from burning wood, then gray, irritating her throat and eyes. Monica looked at the horizontal gutter in the corner of the roof.

"No, it can't work," she thought, hearing Rapidzki start his bike in the yard. Monica started to hear the sound of an impact and the clash of a falling bike. At one point, she felt that the roof was getting warm. She looked at the closed hatch. From the cracks around the flap, smoke started to seep in. After ten seconds or so, she also noticed white streaks coming from behind the edge of the roof, which was getting hotter and hotter. Suddenly, on the other side of the gutter, the first tongue of fire emerged. Her heart started beating harder. She looked down. "It's just one floor," she thought. Holding on to the horizontal wire of the lightning rod, she came to the side edge of the roof. Immediately, scrubbing her knees, going back steeply down, she reached the edge at the corner of the building. She noticed a stone garage in the backyard. The other part of the house by the entrance was already on fire. She could hear glass breaking and falling out of the windows. Kneeling, she took off her jacket and tied it to the wire. Wrapping the sleeve around her hand, she moved her legs over the edge of the roof. She tried to rest them on the vertical lightning conductor, but the rods fastening it to the wall were pulled out. The fire and smoke were coming out of the window. She could hardly take a breath. Holding the jacket, close to exhaustion, she tried to hang her legs as low as possible. Her fingers were getting weaker and weaker. She could not hang on to the jacket sleeve anymore, she relinquished her hold and fell to the ground with her legs bent. Still, she fell on her back and felt stabbing pain in her ankle. She got up immediately and, hobbling, she ran up to the ajar garage door. Monica comprehended her predicament when she saw the car. Rapidzki was taking sachets with white powder from a secret hiding place in the wall and stuffing them into his pockets.

Startled, he ran up to her and, with a hard jerk, he pulled her inside. She fell over, hitting her head against the concrete floor. A trickle of blood flowed from under her hair. Monica's body froze. Rapidzki hopped into the car and drove into the backyard. After a while, he got out of the car, grabbed a gas can and began to pour its content inside the garage. He took matches out of his jacket.

"Damn rain!" he said under his breath, unable to light any of them. A moment later, he grabbed the can again, pouring gas right under the tongue of fire coming out of the window. A long horn beep sounded from the highway. Rapidzki returned to the car and drove out of the property with a squeal of tires. The oncoming car blocked his way. Walter jumped from behind the wheel, followed by Harameus and a young woman in cream-black pumps. Walter ran up to the car, opened the door and threw Rapidzki outside. He fell face down. Harameus picked him up and put him on his feet.

"Where's Monica?" he exclaimed. Rapidzki looked away.

"Talk, bastard!" he repeated, louder this time, shaking him furiously. Rapidzki was still silent.

"Your tongue will loosen right away," he said under his breath, and pulled Rapidzki towards the burning house. Heat was sticking into their bodies. On Rapidzki's face appeared terror. Wet stains of gas were on his clothes. A cry of the woman who arrived with them came from the garage. Harameus pushed Rapidzki up the stairs and ran towards her. Choked by the smoke, coughing, Rapidzki staggered back to the car and immediately drove off. From behind a hillock at the end of the still visible road emerged the flickering lights of fire engines and police cars. Rapidzki drove a bit, but when he saw the approaching motorcade, he stopped the car. He realized that he had nowhere to escape. The road, which was behind him, led to the newly created nature reserve; several hundred yards farther there was a metal barrier. The route was surrounded by wet meadows, behind which was a closely guarded military area, encircled by a steel fence covered with a barbed wire mane. Rapidzki knew what was on the other side, but he had no idea what the land hid. Often, watching this area, he saw guard patrols marching along the metal fence. Mostly they were duos—a person and a dog.

Muscular quadrupeds, seemingly gentle and harmless, not paying attention to anyone, walked evenly by the leg of the sentries, ready to respond to a command. They could catch an intruder within a few seconds. Private media reported that deposits of uranium ore had been discovered in this area; however, the state authorities quickly denied these reports, disinforming the public by stating that rich copper deposits had been discovered there. Rapidzki, seeing no chance of escape, got out of the car, and, taking his gun with him, ran across the field towards the forest. He stumbled over the field grooves several times, but a moment later, the forest closed its gate behind him. The day was fading. Darkness more and more boldly entered the sky. Cool breeze wafted the smell of burning, bearing the sounds of the sirens behind the meadows and the fields. Suddenly, a dreadful roar came from the forest. The birds and animals were silent. Not a single branch moved, not even a single crack of broken brushwood came from there. The glow of the great orange-yellow enraged eyes was piercing through the woods. The pairs of eyes scattered in the darkness went on and out forming an ever-tightening circle. Almost simultaneously, Rapidzki's terrifying scream came out of the darkness. One moment, the sound of a single shot split the air followed by a little delayed in the depths of a flash of the huge beam of blue light. Shredded with a dense thicket of trees and bushes, it flickered with countless bright rays. Soon the lights rose above the tops of the trees and quickly disappeared into space. After some time, when firefighters extinguished the fire, Rapidzki's shivering silhouette emerged from the darkness. With insanity in his eyes, mumbling, gray-haired, he pointed to the forest with one hand, in the other, he still held the gun. Only scraps of his clothing remained. His torso and arms were covered with blood-soiled furrows. He wanted to say something with trembling lips, but he could not say a single word. He glanced at the astonished and shocked people looking at him, then he put the gun to his temple and closed his eyes. A smirk appeared on his face again. After a moment, he opened his eyes again and picked out Monica, whose wounds were dressed by a paramedic, and he slowly lowered the gun. A small, red spot appeared on Rapidzki's forehead. The laser dot of the police gun vibrated as did the officer's sweaty hand. After a while, unmarked helicopters arrived from behind the forest, searching the wooded area with spotlights. One of them landed on the meadow on the other side of the road.

"Not a hair of his head shall be touched," the police officer holding Rapidzki at gunpoint heard in his radio earpiece.

"Why is that?" he asked, not believing what he had just heard. A red spot appeared on his temple, too.

"Just overpower him," he heard again.

"Sure," replied the police officer and the dot from Rapidzki's forehead moved to the hand in which he held the gun.

The last walk, the last look at the river faithful to the city, which, thank God, has not dried up yet, the last culinary whims before the evening departure. Refreshed and satiated, they sipped tea in a familiar-looking restaurant, praised and recommended by the hotel's brochure. It was located in front of a large old city bathhouse by an ancient park, which, with the alley of hornbeams, like an arm, embraced the front wall and the adjacent main line of lamp posts, where impecunious people once practiced the oldest profession. Indeed, from time to time, it happened that poor man was hanged by mistake before the judge had given the sentence; however, it was a long time ago and long since, it has disappeared from human memory. Some time ago, the bathhouse was converted into lofts and commercial premises according to the current fashion. Despite the new character of the building, you could still feel the spirit of the old era. On the red bricks of the walls, where the shower partitions had been once installed, there were important dates, symbols, and even phrases scratched with a skewer, whose authors hid behind the discretion of small initials. Under the ceiling, a stone-pine beam lay along, from which hung chains for physical exercises and partly rusty enameled round lamps with gratings. When someone stared at these water-slick bricks, in their mind appeared images of not so distant times slowly fading away from today's memory, as well as the sounds of contemporary life;

factory sirens reverberated around, allowing workers to return home after hard work; church bells called them for an evening service, after a quick eat of soup and a moment of respite, and joyful singing under streams of water, when all the duties were done. The bath-attendant's voice resounded in the small room by the doorkeeper's lodge, greeting the people who came to avail themselves of the bath, the laundry and the mangle; millers whose eyebrows, eyelashes, and the rest of their faces were covered with a layer of flour dust; stokers of various cauldrons whose smile glowed white like the Milky Way against a black sky; and anyone who did some kind of messy work—lending them towels and soap for a petty fee. At present, everything looked different here. The cauldrons and boilers had long been extinguished, the furnaces were dismantled, and the piping was stolen by night scrap stealers. Only the massive doors and windows remained, impregnated with wood tar, grappled deep in the walls, as well as an elusive ghost that, at night, swayed the chains and walked loudly on the shining floor and smothered the barely glowing lights. Today, in the beautiful halls with a view of the old cemetery, poetry contests by candlelight are organized, and various courses are attended by party activists of all political persuasions, who just began their adventure with lies. From the lofts there was a nice view over the park and the river, behind which, in summer, people could admire the extensive harvest padding. In the lower region, in the company of flower beds, the restaurant gardens were planted, where the shadows of the awnings, unfurled with a crank. Flower stores, a boutiques, a bookstore, and several craft factories were squeezed in the bright faces of the houses between the gardens. In the distance, the old church showed red and spread the sound of heavy bells. In the other quarter of the streets, soaring temple towers rose, from where the signal of the trumpet flowed.

In the less stately place, a bit off the beaten track, almost right under the wing of a small hanging garden, a modest restaurant pulsated with life. The one in which cinnamon and hibiscus tea were now being drunk. From the dining hall, on the street looked two lattice windows covered with curtains, and the bare one with a casement, behind which was the yard at the back of the house, from which sporadic farm noises met the ear: the bark of a dog running loose, crackles and flutters of the wings of flushed chickens, and sounds of a blacksmith's shop somewhere among them. A field kitchen and a kitchen cart stood under the window, in full readiness to leave if there was an urgent need to attend some festivities. The hall housed eight double tables and the two larger round ones for six chairs. By the wall, next to the restroom was a heavily worn tiled stove with cracked enamel, next to which sat a fat woman in an apron tied on her hips, reading a book unfolded on her lap about Frankenstein's vicissitudes, entitled by his name. Right above her head, the attached carbon monoxide sensor formed a small glory. A red thread on her wrist disinfected the aura. A light bulb hung from the ceiling, from a central point, casting quite a strong light on the furniture, but the faint one on the plafond, the description of which will come back here again. It is also worth mentioning the great acoustics of the hall, owing to which the words spoken in a whisper in the one corner of the premises were clearly heard in the opposite one. There an electric piano and a rotary stool stood. A few steps away, in front of the windows hung a portrait of someone's great-grandfather in a professor's gown with a monocle in his eye. A large demonstration took place on the street, which marred the joy of the eating patrons and drowned out a quiet music flowing from the radio. A silver-haired, petite-figured woman wiping the countertops bustled between the tables, humming to herself along with the song coming from the radio. A young man's watchful eye, hidden behind the ajar kitchen door, closely followed her every move. A few details of his garment could be seen in the narrow space between the door frame and the door itself. He was attired in a white tailcoat shirt and black pants. He clamped his hands on the braces by the armpits. To judge by his pose and facial expression, he was a person to be reckoned with here. Paintings in shades of red and ocher flowed from the plaster finish of the plafond to the upper parts of the walls, on which mythological scenes were laid. At the foot of the toothed mountains, muscular warriors with weapons in their hands walked in the wilderness: the one in the foreground bit an enraged panther with the sword, the others behind him aimed their bows at a goat god surrounded by dancing centaurs, half-naked young men and girls rested on the soft grass.

When the woman finished wiping the tables, a foot slipped out of the ajar door, attired in a shiny formal shoe, and it pushed a bucket on wheels, half-filled with water with a mop plunged in it.

From deep inside the hall came clanks of pots, noises of the moving of stove-lids, and women's sighs. However, they were not sounds of anguish, but rather compassion. After them came the sounds of chaotic and quick steps. A moment later, sounds of broken glass and falling down equipment burst hardly could be unheard by the restaurant's guests, and the clatter almost completely ceased on the broad back of the man standing in the ajar door; that is why only cursory glances reached him. Concerned and a little surprised, he closed the door behind him without haste and softly, as if nothing had happened. A moment later, Walter's ear picked out a wild chorus of vituperation in the kitchen backroom. It was not an attack of anger yet, but it did move him a lot. In his head even appeared a thought to cool the enthusiasm with which the young man reprimanded the cooks and take the women's part, but, unwilling to interfere with the local relations, he abandoned this idea. Other patrons also realized that something unpleasant had happened, and the murmur of conversations spread throughout the hall. When the vituperation faded, the young man in the blood-spattered tail-coat shirt, holding an ax in his hand, appeared in the door again and hurried up with an explanation.

"It's just a farm rooster, which didn't want to go under the ax," he said with a slight satisfaction and looked at the petite-figured, silver-haired, butterfly-delicate woman, as if expecting praise from her. Two girls sitting at the table under the great grandfather pushed their plates of broth away with disgust. A moment later, the woman came up to him and put her hand on his cheek.

"You can't do it, son," she said tenderly.

"Mom, soon . . . we'll run out of china," he said.

"That's not the point," she said in a worried voice. "Go back to the back room."

The man, as if disappointed and saddened by this answer, began to scrape off the feathers stuck to the blade. This moment protracted. He must have kept on waiting for a good word or gesture from his mother because he looked up shyly, casting short glances at her.

Impatient with his indecisiveness, she opened her eyes wider, grabbed her side, and stuck her head almost under his face.

"Go and find the cook," she told him. The man, lowering his head, stood still, scratching the ax blade with his forefinger as if checking whether it was sharp or blunt. He did it unknowingly, not knowing what to do with his lively hands, he just looked for some kind of occupation for them, even the most trivial one. Finally, he raised his head, as if to check what was happening around him. He glanced at the eating customers while peeking at his mother. The woman intensified visual pressure on him, while demonstrating severity on her face. With her tenacity, she finally forced him back to the kitchen.

"Tourists are gonna be here in a minute," she said behind his back, shook her head, and walked up to the window, curious about the sounds coming from the outside. A colorful procession marched slowly on the sunlit sidewalk. This kaleidoscopic parade was led by a couple entwined in a dance embrace, dressed in regional costumes, dancing in time with a folk dance. They were followed by a small man on high stilts, holding a puppet with a stiff smile. Right behind him was a feminine mime with a nice waist, followed by twin siblings juggling with fire—as like as two peas or two drops of sea. A young man brought up the rear of the first host. His face was full of health. He rode a felt old dragon bareback. Nearby, a historic streetcar, filled with tourists, glided on the rails. Parallel to it marched a small funeral procession with an open hearse in front. Ironically, across the street, in the opposite direction, a big nuptial procession slowly headed. It seemed that the participants of both ceremonies greeted each other with glimpses. People traveling on the streetcar wondered who the late man was that had died in his prime, after having lived only to the age of 58 years and 20 days, and what predicaments he had been involved in that he had not been able to get out of them. There were many questions: Was his life interesting or ordinary? Was he so unsociable that only a handful of people escorted him to his resting place? He might have fallen in love with a street woman—a sort of harlotdom miracle—entering radiantly fermenting love, like an insect, a candle fire, passing on his life achievements to his chosen one without family consultations. He might have died happy in the midst of a storm, like a great composer, and did not intend to regret his choices. It was also likely that he shared the fate of those whom the medical authorities, seeing them leaning on a beggar stick, treated as representatives of a lesser kind who wanted to live under a white roof, counting on gracious bread.

"Here he is, a fraud himself, a loafer!" they might whisper to each other secretly as he approached them to worship them. He might have replied that he demanded no more for himself but respect. He held their negative answers behind his ear and hoped for a human gesture. But he waited in vain for the faintest ray of light from their hearts. And when he proudly lifted his forehead and returned to his loneliness to wait for the inevitable end, then, as a consolation, the sun showed up. The day became warm, and on the branches perched birds—his friends, singing to cheer him up. Today, he left the city in a funeral carriage and was halfway to heaven. And although the shepherd will carefully choose words over the grave pit under the tall white trees, he will think about him what he wishes. Despite sad faces of the passengers on the streetcar, there were lively conversations here and there. In the orchestra car, the musicians tuned in instruments. The priest's wise eyes asked for solemnity saying that there was cortège marching next to them. At this call, the instruments fell silent one by one, and silence ensued. The curious audience needed some more time. Walter placed a porcelain figurine of a smiling Jew on a table, which he managed to buy today in a small antique store, and as the seller assured him, it was supposed to bring good luck.

"May you bring health, peace, and prosperity for this land," said Walter. Monica smiled.

"It's time to get home," said Harameus. "We have something else important to do there."

He rested his elbows on the table and face on his hands. He looked towards the paintings on the wall in the corner of the restaurant and stopped talking. He stared at the figure of a crippled, young vagrant, leaning on a clutch, looking up sunwards. Dark curls fell on his forehead.

"Astonishing resemblance," Harameus said to himself. Walter also looked at the painted figure.

"Yes, he resembles the homeless tramp you spoke with on the stairs of the temple."

"I often think of him," said Harameus, "I must go back there."

CHAPTER NINE

The wheels of the black Lincoln rolled on the road, injured by cat-erpillar-tracked vehicles. The sun rose higher and higher above the horizon, flooding slantwise the world with its blaze. Around—trees, houses, temples and people. Life. Above them—fast-moving birds and their shadows, moving even faster. All of them shared fairly everything. People had their own shadows and lives. The shadows stretched and shortened. They loomed and unloomed like life. They were not only in the good graces of the clouds. But on that day, there were no clouds. There was a man. There was also a temple that had lost its shadow. The trees had also van-ished somewhere. Hammers, pile-drivers, alarms, and laughter. A saw and racks, fanfares and drums, echoes of echoing echoes as if out of an abyssal well. At no great distance were speechless witnesses of perdition: old, yet strong walls, watching from a vic-tim's position. Waiting. But the human hand was unrelenting. It got rid of everything that stood in its way to profit. A temple by a temple, a house by a house, razed to the ground, reduced to ashes, annihilated. People follow them, in solitude and in a tacit protest. Their hearts cannot bear it. A hurricane of new customs breaks fragile lives. A luster forced out new tablets of values. On the main floor of new buildings: glare, gloss, noise, ad signs. Walter stopped the car.

"It seems that we reached our destination, but something is mis-sing here," he said, surprised. They both started looking around.

"I'd swear this temple was standing right here," said Harameus, astonished.

"Yes, the temple is missing," Walter agreed.

Harameus got out of the car and walked up to the fence. On the construction site, bulldozers leveled the rest of the area. Next to the place, where the excavator was digging out the earth, he noticed the remainders of stairs protruding from the ground. They stuck out as the roots of overturned trees that had failed to resist the wind. There were shattered granite slabs next to them. Harameus closed his eyes and clenched his fists. He saw the view of the Sunday morning under his eyelids. The rays of the sun climbed higher and higher over the temple's walls, bringing out a brick belfry from the shadows. At the top, the hunchback pulled on the rope harder and harder, as if he wanted to break the bells down into atoms. He rang the bells for a mandatory prayer. The rays of the sun pierced the stained-glass windows, spattering behind them into millions of colorful droplets of light. Harameus opened his eyes and looked around. He stood on the highest step of the stairs leading to the temple.

"Am I struck down by exhaustion, or am I starting to hallucinate?" he asked himself, looking at the wooden door reinforced with metal fittings.

He grabbed a massive knocker and knocked. He waited a moment, then banged on the door. After a while, he heard the sound of the key twisting in the lock. The door creaked and slowly opened. A narrow streak of darkness and disquiet came into view from inside.

"Are you looking for someone?" from the darkness came these words, spoken slowly, without emotion.

"Yeah, I'm looking for someone," he answered after a few question marks and strange thoughts had passed. The door opened wide.

"Who are you looking for?" a muffled voice came from behind the door. "No one can be found here anymore."

"I don't know myself," Harameus said indecisively.

After the end of the two chimes in the tower, the voice turned into existence. An entity emerged from behind the door like the winter sun. Low and slow. Harameus shuddered.

"If you're looking for someone or something, you need to be

thoroughly positive about that," a deliberate malice drained from the throat of the entity.

"Why are you looking at me like this? You've never seen—?"

"No, no . . . it isn't the reason," Harameus interrupted the entity.

"So, you don't know who or what you are looking for, and, to boot, you are watching me with unhealthy curiosity," he said suspiciously.

"Don't you really have evil designs on me?" The entity narrowed its right eye, raising its brow above the left one. At the same time, it made a slight forward movement. Harameus cautiously stepped back.

"I've just wanted to pray and find the truth," he answered with a sense of guilt in his voice.

"You don't look like a truth-seeker," replied the entity. "Besides, you mustn't pray here."

"How come? After all—"

"I've said clearly you must not pray here, and it's been so for a long time," the entity repeated, irate. "Who are you? Those uninterested in seeking the truth are not allowed." Now the entity almost shouted.

"But I'm interested, and very much," Harameus replied immediately. "So much that I don't even know who I am, and much less who you are and where we are. I do hope I'll receive a sensible explanation from you. Honestly, I'd like to know everything without restrictions, but I realize it won't be easy to get answers to these questions."

"Here, you won't receive any answers. Here, no one has been providing answers for a long time. And if any, certainly not to the ones who do not know who they are and whom they are looking for," the entity said peremptorily. "I'm confident you contrive a plot. I perfectly know those rogue tricks. You must also acknowledge that there are no inquirers here, either. And even when some appear, it's by mistake. Besides, it's required to have the permission to ask questions, especially about conclusive and definitive matters."

"Is it difficult to obtain this kind of permission? And who grants it?" asked Harameus.

"Oh yes, very difficult, especially when such permissions are not granted at all." The entity sneeringly smiled. "It is not worth building a mill for one grain of corn or putting a beehive for one drone and—"

"And destroying the temple for one zero more," Harameus interjected ironically.

"I don't know what you are talking about. But if I had to know, I would say this: Zeros always want to multiply. And they multiply. Despite the rules of arithmetic. Which doesn't change their holotype at all. They will always be zeros. Those who multiply them—today's proconsuls—are not luminaries of morality. Like blood from our blood, but infected with something. As if containing a Luciferian substance. But don't take these words as the beginning of our close friendship. I just respect people who have a face. That's why I take the liberty of talking like this."

"By the way, has anyone ever issued such permissions?" asked Harameus.

"I cannot tell you this. The only thing I can say is that here there's neither 'sooner' nor 'later,'" said the entity.

"So, why do you refuse to provide me the answer—just like that, by virtue of the office?"

"It's better to get a refusal on the spot 'by virtue of the office' than 'by virtue of a notice,'" said the entity. "As to this, I think we agree."

"You suggest that—"

"I'm not suggesting anything. I do refuse."

"I'll have to report this to your superiors, and, if necessary, to the higher authorities," said Harameus. "They will take the most appropriate measures against you."

"Dear sir, here apply other precepts. Here, no one forces anyone to do anything, nor tells what to do, nor berates. And I can assure you that a raised voice locks all the doors."

"In that case, I have to ask for a defense lawyer, regardless of whether this person will be ex officio or not," Harameus said firmly. "I need to get inside."

"You're not entitled to any defender, to say nothing of a candidate for the office of a minor judge. Also, any assistant or any official in charge of anything are out of the question. And even if you were entitled to a public defender, this practitioner wouldn't help you anyway. Everyone has too much work to help anyone. Too much. They're busy building edifices of wisdom and are earnestly preparing themselves to assume the reins. And when they build up and take over, then maybe they'll take care of your frippery, which no one is interested in anyway."

"So, why do they exist, and for whom, since they can't help anyone?"

"I see that the meanders of justice are too convoluted for you. Each office has its own defenders, in wartime quantities. A well-paid and disciplined army. Everyone is selected in extremely difficult examining contests, and they have more important things to do than take care of trivialities. The dignity of their office completely excludes it. Still, you must not criticize them and fight them. When the ally weakens, then the opponent grows stronger. This is what the eternal Law of War and Peace says. Nobody has ever beaten this army yet. It's impossible to start any diatribe or fight against them. That is why you'd better have it on your side."

"So, my old assumptions have materialized," said Harameus.

"What was on your mind?"

"The fact that elephants, when they grow up, can't be removed so easily."

"You follow the tracks, and you go in the right direction, but this is nothing new. It's always easier to cover something than to uncover it. They always eat a lot. In fact, they devour—just to gain weight. Silently and humbly. Sometimes, they even suck on several mothers. Later on, they can't move, whereas we have to roll our boulder uphill forever."

"With pleasure, I carried the stones. Without pleasure, I managed people," said Harameus.

"Exactly. That's the point, because you were not an elephant. Either way, justice will triumph sooner or later. The only question is what and for whom is fair. On the other hand, an individual, without a patron, always suffers from besieged fortress syndrome. I assume you do not have one. Thus, such an individual, friendly to the world, takes to a street two blocks away, becomes an enemy of this world. Do you also have such a feeling that you are surrounded by hostile beings?"

"For now, I have only you in front of me, and that's why it's a difficult case. But I don't have a grudge against you. Besides, I carry a flame in my soul that no elephant can extinguish."

"I hope that the head of the arrow of these offensive words didn't aim at me."

"It aimed at the elephants," said Harameus. "Honestly, I have to admit that in each of us, there is an archpriest of egoism. Not only in elephants. The intensifying of appetite doesn't appear from nowhere."

"That's why everyone must feel that this defender will always be near at hand, and as the lion will deter the enemies, even made of stone."

"And you, for whose party are you defender? What do you compensate for with this refusal?"

"We'd better talk about your case, and it is on the tip of the pin. The report of your vices is substantial. Please don't forget the fact that it is you who wants to trespass on this doorstep," said the entity.

"You don't know my patrons as I don't know them myself. Just as I don't know yours. Let this balance be preserved. And, since we speak about hands, let's shake our hands as a token of our friendships without winning over to your or my side." Harameus tried to put his hand in the door ajar, but the entity reduced the amount of light in the ajarness.

"For objective reasons, I can't shake hands with you. I do this with no one."

"Why? What harm would this 'no one' do to you?"

"You think that you're funny, but I assure you that in order to be able to shake hands, you have to have your own hand functional. It can't be the dead-fish handshake, accompanied by a lazy look. It must be a firm and generative handshake. Speaking of which, turn your head—peacocks are coming. And they are unprecedently serious. You must arouse curiosity in them."

"Maybe they're hungry? Perhaps the aroma attracted them?

"They're always hungry. Their appetite is gargantuan. As soon as they sense free food, they appear. They forage for savory bonne bouchées. They breathe in the upper wind and sense. You're a competitor to them."

"I'm not hungry. I haven't come here for food."

"They say that too. But, as they're given, they take."

"It's no wonder, everyone would take. It's difficult to sit quietly by a table full of food."

"You all are the same. Only one thing in your head: to live to the fullest and receive everything for free. And all this malevolence of yours. Please, again, acknowledge that there're no tables here. We all eat from the bowls together with our animals. But that doesn't mean—and don't jump to a hasty conclusion here—that it's a ritual habit, and that we can't use cutlery. We knew forks and spoons earlier than many a republic. And this is an undeniable fact."

"Be careful, don't eat up from the animal king's bowl because you might leave the bowl without your limbs and head," said Harameus.

"Here, we have our routines. Here, since the beginning, nothing has changed, so I have no intention of opening the door to you."

"I just wanna take a small step forward, I don't wanna give a jump for humankind. And although I descend by halves from the chosen people, show me a human face of yours and a bit of pity," said Harameus.

"I implore you and supplicate for the sake of Romulus and Remus, Osiris and Isis, of all wolves and tigers. And don't coerce us to unmuzzle them—otherwise, you'll hear no more the chanson of life. There're no noble places on earth—all this is only an illusion and lies. No spa can be made of sumps, as once said, ace of trumps."

"I haven't received anything from you yet, not even the simplest answer. I can't see any peacocks, wolves or other beasts, either."

"Ah, yes, I've forgotten that I'm speaking to a lower, half-fallen soul. Even if you conquered the mountains by force of your own wings, and was promised a place in the field of honor, don't support those who don't respect the constitution of rules—as, after them, only ruins will remain."

"Is there any authority here, which I could appeal to void this absurdity?" asked Harameus.

"Don't make me laugh. Here, there's no court—neither a lower one nor a higher one. No tribunal of appeals, and even more so, no court of cassation, which could render void this absurdity."

"Hmm," Harameus gave some thought to it. "In that case,

If you can't tell me who issues the permits, tell me who doesn't issue them."

"You're much of a sly fox. You'd like to sneak into the henhouse through the back entrance, avoiding the biggest rooster's beak, and not to shed a single drop of blood. You talk to me subliminally, but I can easily pick up this message, and I know what's hidden in it. Surreptitiously, you won't get anything from me. Besides, you don't know who you are, you don't know who I am, and you don't even know what to ask about. You'd better tell me what your name is, which would significantly facilitate our communication."

Harameus looked at the entity for a moment, and, with a cynical smile, drawled through his slightly open lips, "Please, call me Hans. Forty-two-year-old. Okay?"

"Oh no! There is no Hans who can look like that."

"No? So, what should Hans look like? Should he have blond curls and grapelike eyes? If you don't like it, talk to me in the third person. Or, even better, impersonally. Besides, your officialese is highly inappropriate. And, as if that weren't enough, you're entirely covered in a spider's web," said Harameus.

"Don't philosophize like this. It's your fault, yours. You've interrupted my postprandial repose, not giving me time to do my toilet, as if you saw a fire in the tower. Besides, no one kills spiders here. And when an irksome one is keen to enter the ear, we take it outside in a piece of paper. Dear Hans, forty-two years old. A spider is a friend, a useful creature, and it shouldn't be treated as property subject to a duty-free relocation. It departs from this life here. It won't end up as tragically as Princess Antigone. And the fact that it weaves its web wherever it likes, no wonder its gossamer is omnipresent, and not accidental."

The entity brushed the gauze-like patches from his arm and wiped his face.

"Do you remember who you are?" said Harameus

"It's indisputably obvious that I know who I am. For the time being I'm incognito here and I'm not going to explain myself. I am who I am, but I can only guess who you are and all the rest of this conundrum. But this is not about my guesses—they're the least important here. What's important is what you can say in this hysteria."

"I advise you to look at everything through the prism of good-will. And finish with this impersonality. My ears are aching," Harameus retorted.

"As you wish. And I don't need your advice. My mind is clean and clear—used reasonably. You dare to criticize it, however—what maybe you don't know—freedom of speech is here the cardinal inviolable, and inalienable right. Besides, I have to say that your time of disturbing me and this place has come to an end. And the related questions and answers that you're never going to ask and receive, and people or other substances that could hear you or not, and then give you or not the answer, is as much as you don't know and are able to imagine. Those who ask for answers to questions can't ask, that is, have them in their minds but can't render them in any human language. So, they must look for answers elsewhere, or just they won't receive them. At this point, freedom is a boundless value, and the truth is a gateway to this freedom. However, not all of us have access to it. To say the least, as I've already mentioned, some of the truths are dangerous, especially for those who, in their unsatisfied curiosity, are ready to cross the threshold. They're pushing where they're not welcome just as you are doing now. Your journey has come to an end."

"But I'm not on a journey. At most, on a little trip," Harameus said, outraged. "Look behind me, over there, a car with the engine running is waiting for me."

"Yes, I can see it. It's polluting and poisoning. Everywhere around, one can see and sense only fumes, smog, and toxins. For you, people out there, the world ends with your lives. But I'll tell you something: Here, apart from you and them, there is no one here."

"You're joking, I suppose," said Harameus. "I'll prove it right now," he tried to shout out at Walter, but his voice did not get out of his throat.

The entity laughed soundlessly.

"Look at them," it said pointing its nose at the street. "They're going to demolish the next houses. A step, a slap, a spit, a swig, a swear word, a look backward, a lunch break, a step forward. They go slowly, with reluctance."

"You're making fun, and it's absolutely not fair. It's not their fault.

"This kind of work is a dubious pleasure of life," said Harameus.

"You know that bile and virulence are dangerous. While we still have time, we need to mend our ways," said the entity.

"That is to say, not to hurt anyone, not to inflict pain on anyone, not to denigrate anyone. Treat people as you would like them to treat you. Then you won't need any higher authority, and you will save your soul."

"Each human being has the soul enslaved from birth. That's why it breaks down so easily," said Harameus. None of them can carry the halter that is put around the necks. Those moralists who swim in the swamps of their lives on a dry, fragile leaf. They paddle their pine needles looking for clean water. Those jugglers who constantly scare or promise Olympus and Elysium."

"You have to spit on adversities," said the entity. "Those who want to get out of here prematurely make the biggest affront to the Absolute Substance. Pantocrator and Prophets. This is a betrayal that it does not forgive."

"Hah!" Harameus bridled. "How do you know all this?! You don't have any proof of this. These are groundless claims. You look like a decent person, but a bit besotted. You have to respect each and every choice. You yourself have said that these are untouchable rights."

"Not in this case."

"You think I am too stupid to comprehend hell and heaven with my mind?"

"I haven't mentioned anything about hell or heaven. These are pure speculations. But one thing I know for sure: Because once I was in the same oppression in which you are now, not having received the answer, I opened the door, which you're now pushing so impulsively. I undertook a journey that I don't wish on anyone. Although I don't know what the devil and the angel mean, I'll say this: each of them may have a fluffy touch or a lethal one. In my opinion, it's some smoke, some mist filling the human mind."

"Are you not a human being?"

"I am, but not like you."

"Anthropologically, you look more of a devil than an angel," said Harameus.

"Ha, ha, ha!" a loud laughter came out of the throat of the Entity, making four and a half birds from a carillon in the tall tower take flight. Four of them rose suddenly, while the half, not yet full-fledged, staring somewhere else, took off irresolutely and flew in the opposite direction. After a while, it flew in a semicircle and joined the quadruple avian flock, which had perched on the high belfry—at a safe distance—carefully watching their conversation.

"You have amused me to tears," said the entity.

"Well, why don't you at last introduce yourself? I'd like to know who I'm dealing with," said Harameus.

"I'm the guardian of this temple. And, at that, a very respectable one," said the entity. "And now, good bye!"

"But I'm not bidding you farewell," said Harameus.

The guardian tried to close the door, but Harameus sharply slipped—that is to say, thrust—his foot in the streak of darkness, which cast a suspicion that he traveled more often by subway than he admitted.

"Your behavior is full of anarchism. You don't know who you are dealing with. Please, move back your foot! Immediately!" the guardian said indignantly, and began pushing the door back to the frame. Although he had one hand in the orthesis, he was pushing the door really hard. Harameus tried to turn his foot so that he could free the stuck ankle, but the guardian, seeing this, pushed against the door even harder.

"You're here to perform extremely hostile actions. Don't try so hard," said the guardian.

"Ah, you're a stubborn being. A never-forgetter," cried Harameus.

The guardian kicked with all his power against Harameus's foot so that it jumped out and the shoe landed three stairs below. The door slammed shut.

"How dare you! I've just wanted to talk to the priest." After a moment, the door opened again.

"So, why didn't you say that right away?" said the guardian. "You looked at this high belfry with such a strange stare. Today the rabbi is present, the priest will be tomorrow."

"Rabbi?" asked Harameus. "Well, then call the rabbi, I'd like to talk to him."

"Wait here, and don't tell anyone that you tried to break into the temple without my permission. You might lay yourself open to highly disagreeable consequences."

"Consequences?" Harameus repeated in disbelief.

"We have devoted and faithful friends here who wouldn't like the arbitrary trespassing of the threshold, and I could not vouch for them in any way," said the guardian. He breathed a deep gulp of air and whistled three short undulating sounds. After a while, the birds perching on the belfry fluttered away and perched on the pot next to them.

"Well, what do you say?"

"They're hungry. Just like the peacocks," said Harameus.

"Not only they." The guardian banged the door a few times with his fist, and from the center of the temple, leonine roars came. The guardian looked at Harameus and patted him on the shoulder.

"Don't be scared. In my presence, you will not be in danger. However, I am asking you not to push your foot for the second time there where you have not been allowed. Do we understand each other?"

Harameus went down three stairs.

"This, in case they would like to destroy our temple," said the guardian. "Pardon me, I must go now. I have duties to perform. Ah, the rabbi, I've almost forgotten."

"Guardian," said Harameus, "I will come another day, when the priest is present here."

"The rabbi is also a decent man . . . but as you wish," said the guardian. "For now, it seems silent and dark here, but soon there will be a gym and a restaurant. You have to make a living of something."

"God bless you, guardian," Harameus said on parting, "I will come back here for sure."

The guardian slammed the door shut. The sound of horn could be heard behind the back.

"I thought, Harameus, you wouldn't leave this fence at all," Walter said, sipping his coffee.

CHAPTER TEN

In the Great Lawn by Turtle Pond sways the sea of thousands of the righteous. The sky is high and blue; the air smells of spring inflorescence. These who are condemned to a life of wandering continue winding their way along the park's lane as a calm river—along a sleeping plain. Seeing this immense meadow, they speed up. With their smiling childishly happy eyes, they look around in their wanderer's customary manner. Some visages are white and dull, others sunburnt, crimson, coming from somewhere in the south and vast prairies. There are also these that are swarthy, raven-haired—they seem livelier, dancing by a fire. They want to rest on the prostrate shadows of cedars from Lebanon—here in Central Park on Cedar Hill, olfactory sensations are pleasantly surprising. Fear, as usual, looks over the world with big eyes. Trees spread their arms to show their gratitude for the sun and water. The wanderers will be here for a while—maybe for half a day, maybe for a shorter time, to refresh themselves with what good people give them, and relax before the evening musical feast. They are not surrounded by fish ponds or orchards, osiers do not sough, pianos do not play sonatas, gargoyles do not grace gutters of the neighboring houses, there is no stone gazebo nearby, on whose columns they could lean their tired backs. Long-maned horses and carriages also somewhat quieter. However, engines roar in unison with horns, sirens and ice-cream trucks. Sometimes only

a rough tongue of cool air licks the bodies; above the heads of
the wandering people flies the blue banner of the heavenly mon-
archy; sometimes only, a bird flies over it, a plane leaves streak,
a kite or a balloon drift blown away by the wind. Focused, or-
derly young people put up a tent on the islet of sand. At the entrance, a smiling woman writes in a page torn out of a notebook
what the boy says: "Sacred solemnity is compulsory here. No
smoking. No spitting at your brother and sister." Some pray silently to known and unknown gods. Someone presses her whispering lips on her companion's small ear; the latter passes the
news on. The message, originally silent, gains strength and
blows against the sails of ears and straightens the backs. It goes
along the spines causing a stir. The air vibrates with it in res-
onance. The midday sun looks into the clear water of the pond
and the narrowed eyes. Cleopatra's Needle of stone indicates a
quarter past twelve. In nearby Belvedere Castle, a peg madly
strikes the metal gong. At last, mosquitoes stop biting furiously.
The wanderers distribute disturbing news; it is carried at thunderbolt speed. Its rumbles can be heard more and more loudly.
Sounds of disappointment and timid disapproval come from everywhere. Everyone, however, hopes that this bad news will be
only an innocent lie. Nevertheless, the seed of anxiety has been
sown. It is not difficult to see that sadness settled in their hearts.
They have come here from many places—both close and distant,
often from the most remote corners of paradise. Not only to see
their music idols on stage, but also to feel the magical atmosphere of home, family, community that they do not experience in their everyday life. To discover that someone else cares
about them. Although many of them have their wings broken,
they walk bravely along various paths, roadless tracks, until they
reach their destination. All these brave knights of the promised
land. Not everyone is suave and meek—it is undeniable fact—
but there is one language, the language of respect and understanding. And yet there are multi-headed snakes among them
with teeth as sharp as the sharpest human words. There are also
fine and beautiful souls, free like birds ever-seeking safe shelter.
There are adventurers who match the talent of Master Caravaggio,
both in the art of painting and in adventurousness. There are
also these are both well-versed in native and foreign literature.

There is no shortage of half-literates, who have forgotten letters and numbers. There are also these who are the most ordinary unlucky people, who were born under a swarm of the unluckiest stars—they are the vast majority. There are also these whose upbringing was too smooth and soft. In contrast to them, there are born winners from cold farming, whose path should be lit by the brightest suns, who grew up according to old strict discipline under constant pressure for eminence. They drowned their lives in the vortices of youth—in spite of their harsh fathers. And they are mocked most.

FROM BOMBASTIC NOTES FOUND ON THE BENCH
(against which rested an umbrella)

King Herod the Great was not a Jew, for whose real deeds or those made up the world incessantly pinches Jews. A long time ago, someone in the crowd threw a derisive word at an innocent stranger. Another shouted a hostile invective in their face. The rest of them leaned down to pick up stones. The governor was also scared, so he ordered to flog the poor man, and banished him from the country. And, although afterwards, he swore on the Holy Bible, no one believed in his nobility and courage. Stubborn people still insist on being right. They take offense and remain silent for years. Around them, flowers and loved ones wilt and waste away, but the demons are happy dancing at the bedside when these poor souls are about to give up their ghosts. They applaud them for their thoughtless lives. The wise are always ready to serve the wiser. On the other side of the barricade, it is quite the opposite. King David was the father of King Solomon, whose wisdom is celebrated by only a few today. And fools despise the world that is not theirs. That's what they thought up to take revenge. New York lighthouse keepers took away the beautiful dark starry sky from people. An unearthly miracle that none of the seven wonders of the world can match, nor can the most beautiful illumination. Wanderers have undisturbed pure and clear minds when they wake up. However, as soon as they get up and stretch their backs, they forget everything. Vodka and pot are cheap again. Now everyone can smile before they die.

Conscientiousness and reliability are the candidates for wonderful wives; however, a playboy quickly grows old with them. The hotheads complaining that this love they eagerly await will come until tomorrow is not even tactless, but totally insolent. On one occasion, a passerby comforted an old prophetess, who earned a living by telling fortunes so that she wouldn't worry about prophetic impotence, because the future consists only of the unknowns. As an expression of her gratitude, she said that if he didn't buy a magic candle for 80 dollars, he could forget about luck and prosperity. Since then, he has avoided those who are distressed. The art of emotions and Latin were eliminated from schools. The elders are betrayed by the young, the poor by the rich. Everyone fights against everyone. Street shadows get tangled under the feet, stumble over them and fall over. The difference between sleep and wakefulness has blurred. Why adults don't tell children that the emperor has no clothes. Will there not be anyone brave enough in such a populous country? There's a rodent race for an ear of corn. We still live in antiquity. Today we have only beer and wine that are better. Indigo children don't come from nowhere. Birds perch on telephone wires. You can see that they don't care about human matters.

The rain has subsided. The clouds have started to break away. Somewhere among them, a ray of sunshine ha glinted for a moment. I close the umbrella. A dry shadow of it is still on the bench. I rest my back comfortably, and, with joy, I cross my legs and look at the last drops falling to the surface of the pond. The wet and heated lane glistens and gives off steam. A belated runnel squeezes between the cobblestones. After a while it soaks into the ground. A woman walks in my direction. She passes by a flowering jasmine bush and stops near flower beds of yellow tulips. She closes her eyes and takes a deep breath. She looks at me and smiles. I don't know whether at me or at the flowers. I suppose that at the flowers, because when a little boy in a khaki-colored kids' military vehicle was passing me a moment earlier, immediately, after he glimpsed me, he began to cry and buried himself in a blanket. Did he see me as Mephistopheles? Or maybe I reminded him of a scarecrow from a fairytale about an unruly raven. The little boy is far away. He carefully lifted the hatch of his small tank, took out his toy gun and stuck out his tongue at me. What a lack of upbringing, I think to myself. But I justify it the moment I become aware that I wasn't better myself. Besides, my looks, my eyes—black with a shade of being lost, this overgrown dark thicket of eyebrows and eyelashes. It's a plus point, but they also have a drawback—because of them I see print more and more faintly and, what is worse, money as well. To cap it all, every spring, pollen ruthlessly hurts my eyes. They're itchy day and night. Red like carmine, combined with black they show a psychedelic, even demonic expression. The woman moves forward. From now on, I'm gonna call her Daphne. I don't know where this choice of her first name comes from—she might as well be Desdemona or Mary Jane from White Plains. Let's face it, I don't resemble Apollo, and even less the jealous Othello (I don't hurt a fly or a spider). Daphne has glimpsed me again. The eye contact is still out of focus, but with each step it becomes sharper and sharper. Now she stops near the bare wet boulder by the pond. Although the pavement has crevices and cracks, not a single blade of grass or moss lives on its surface. The sun peeks out from behind the clouds more resolutely. A dragonfly perches on a stone. Its colorful wings glitter in the streams of rays. Daphne takes a phone from her coat pocket and takes a picture. Moving towards me again, she still looks at the swan swimming along the reeds. I don't lift my pen from my notebook. I wish to describe this beautiful moment and the thoughts that will come—both the golden and crazy ones. Now I feel her eyes on me. I decide to finish writing later. Certainly, most thoughts will fly away forever, but there's hope that the next ones won't be so melancholic. I think it's because of the rain and my rumbling stomach. I haven't eaten anything since yesterday's dinner. Frankly speaking, I'm afraid of hunger. I stop enjoying the world. I can't tame this fear. Apple trees' blossoms are still in buds. An imitation of a snake entwines around a branch. Under the tree, a female figure, carved out of salt, stretches out her hand. A few more such rainy days, and the sculpture and temptation will disappear. Daphne walks by and attentively watches the sculpture. Softly takes each step and sensually sways her hips. I try to imprint the image of this beautiful bird of paradise in my memory. How wonderful it would be to hold it in my arms and hold tightly, at least for a moment. Enjoy this sight to the fullest before it flies away as the dragonfly flew away towards Lilly Pond. She was all alone, in the midst of all those dangers today with no arm under which she could slip her hand. Oh, if only I could take her under my wings, shield her from the wind and rain, warm her up with the warmth of my body, caress her cheeks with feathers of my lips in greeting. Daphne is clearly interested in what I'm producing in my notebook. She may think that I'm writing a deplorable poem, or maybe sketching her figure, hurrying to finish this piece of art before she disappears behind the curve of the park lane. A coat, floral dress, under which is her hourglass-like tiny waist, long legs (down to the ground)—this is the first thing that catches my male attention—probably the gnawing of hunger is to blame. I'm even a little ashamed of it. A hat, shawl, lace parasol, flat shoes—an incomprehensible choice for this rainy weather. When she is close, I put the notebook away. She is worth bestowing more attention. I'll finish writing later. She stops and looks at me carefully.

"Are you a writer?" she asks curiously.

"No," I answer, surprised. "I know nothing about it."

She discreetly looks at me.

"It's a pity, because you look like a writer," she says with a slight disbelief.

"What does a writer look like?" I ask politely, but also a bit perversely. I smile, which she clearly likes, and I move slightly my foot, in a shoe with a soft sole, swung over the knee. I see that she notices the worn-out heel. By her eyes, I see that she's a little disappointed, but she doesn't stop having a friendly face.

"I believe you," she says after a moment. "Maybe it's good you're not a writer."

I can't believe how quickly she gives up. Frankly, my negative answer is also premature—I could tease her, just for fun, for such an innocent intellectual foreplay. Maybe if she pulled my tongue more . . . after all, she saw the notebook on my lap . . . I would change the answer and reveal a half-truth. As proof,

I'd open the notebook, then show the pages of writing, hidden in my coat's pockets and the old envelope on which I wrote something ridiculous yesterday. I'd tell her what she expected to hear. I'd also praise her intuition. I'd certainly not lie to her; I'd admit to everything later that this was all my literary output I have and that I couldn't even afford to buy a new notebook for a fair copy. I'm surprised by this sudden surrender. In thoughts, I look for some justification of this surrender, but nothing comes to mind. I blame hunger again and this fiendish, conscience-ruining desire. It has come so suddenly and unexpectedly. Whenever I look at her and imagine our first kiss, her parted lips—the valley smelling of linden juice between two hills—the fire of desire starts burning inside me. Now I know how the devil enslaves people. This lust can't be suppressed. He's one hell of a blackmailer, an impure power. He turns up unexpectedly with the most dangerous weapon and breathes it brutally into your soul. And the more you resist the devil, the more alluring temptation will be offered to you by him. Then he blackmails you that if you turn away from him, he won't kindle fire in you anymore. And try to be wise—it's not one thing, it's another. Well, unless I'd follow in the footsteps of Origen, but I'm not so brave and ready to sacrifice. Human powers are so weak.

"My husband is a writer," she said.

Suddenly, I became sad. But I continue keeping my chin up and though less happy, I still smile.

"He's terribly grumpy, and mingy," she added unexpectedly. "He spends all days away from home."

A flame of hope starts burning in my heart again.

"Does he throw socks on the floor by the bed?" I ask playfully, somehow spontaneously, encouraged by her sincerity; however, with a slight fear. I even regretted that I asked such a stupid question, but I did so and couldn't revert it. She looks at me with wide-open eyes.

"Well, you've asked for it," I think with terror. "Why so, man? Now you regret." I become aware of how pathetic I am. My only braggable point here is a sophisticated joke, but in this case, I'd probably exaggerate a little.

"I can tell you more," poised, she says calmly. "He even doesn't wipe a dewdrop off the closet bowl after he finishes."

My lips parted in surprise, I couldn't believe my ears again, and yet I have almost perfect pitch, with all due modesty. Well, maybe with some wishing to boast. How this woman has unbosomed to me. She probably has no soul mate.

"I'll be happy to talk to you again someday," she says in a rather nice tone. Then she looks rather lazily at the apartment building on the other side of the park. She adjusts her airy scarf, followed by her hat and reaches out a gentle hand goodbye. Secretly, I dream of how great it would be to hold this beautiful bird and give it a bouquet of wild kisses. Then, when an amorous starry night falls, I'd light fire in the fireplace and we'd listen to the music woven up from whispers and sighs. Will heaven send me this gift? Daphne smiled as if she heard my thoughts, nodded, and walked away, leaving a delicate floral scent behind her. Now or never! I shyly warm up myself to go into battle, but the flame of courage is barely smoldering in me. Then I hear a hellish giggle, and I can feel a ferocious fire of real courage that starts burning inside me, as if someone cast a handful of black gun powder on embers. I look instinctively at the apple tree. A bifurcated tongue vibrates in the snake's wide-open snout. The reptile sticks its orange eyes in me and pierces me with its eyes through and through. It knows everything about me, I know nothing about it, and it knows my innermost secrets.

"Nobody loves you, nobody likes you, nobody understands you, coward." I can hear its scoffing voice.

"You'll end up on the island of the condemned, and I'm gonna take care of it."

Ah, this hunger, it's kicking me around mercilessly. Even the reptile reviles me. Just in case, I pick up a stone lying under the bench, then Daphne looks at me. I surreptitiously put away the stone, still glancing at the tree. Everything's fine as it was before. The rubber gray toy still softly entwines the branch. Reptilian impertinence turned out to be a delusion. I wish Daphne wouldn't vanish into thin air. So, I shout to her.

"If I might, I'd like to see you off."

She pauses and things it over for a while. For me it's eternity, but I wait patiently.

"Please wait," she says in a barely audible voice. and leans down.

Then the woaman grasps her tights, wrinkled on her ankles, with her fingers and pulls them up slightly. She does the same over her knee, exposing the lower portion of her thigh. Ashamed, I look away. The sun is getting hotter. A wave of heat passes through my body. Daphne sits down on the low wall and takes a phone from her purse. I return to my notes for a while. When she finishes talking, she summons me with a nod. I follow her order. I hear snare drums and a triumphal fanfare in me. I can't write anything more, so I finish not letting her change her mind. Hardly can I believe that women have a fickle nature, but I prefer not to risk. Her eyes glitter with fire of a burning candle, but I can see the sun in front of me. I fly to her, like Icarus, like a night butterfly to perdition, like a swallowtail into the web of a black widow. I also have the title for my next story: "Secret lovers under the cover of an amorous day." Maybe, eventually, I'll earn a few pennies. (I write these words for the future development.) I think I've fallen in love.

The light from the sun comes clean and warm today. The colors around are mostly vivid. Real people spread all over the lawn among the trees and water. Many other people's faults and mistakes went to their account. It is possible to see them from a safe distance from above the book's pages. High priests of faith in human solidarity and honesty. The concert, which they looked forward to—which attracted such a large bevy, not only from New York, but also from many parts of the country—was canceled. They are all unspeakably disappointed. Although unrefined, they were friendly and disciplined, despite all fears. Armed with a good word and amicable gesture. From the side of the Metropolitan Museum come sounds of actuated audio equipment. There are popping sounds, clicks on switches, sound is booming. Curious people gather by the monument to the Polish king Jagiełło. Two crossed swords raised above the crown of the brave ruler give strength and encouragement. The crowd thickens by the minute. Two blocks away, a loud voice comes from the speakers on the van:

"This is the police. Please move on!"

In response, someone from the crowd exclaims, "We, the people!" The echo of hundreds of throats repeats these words with the force of a thunderbolt.

A squeaky voice comes from another van standing behind the park wall: "This is a high-ranking town hall representative. I remind you that the event was canceled. Please do not abuse freedom and split up and move on. Otherwise, the police will adequately respond."

Hardly contained giggles come from under the police helmet shields. However, the cordon tightens its grip. The situation heralds trouble. The cops get serious and adjust their helmets and put their hands on the handle of their batons. Dogs jerk on leashes and push forward. Veins on the temples swell up. Predatory glances appear. They are ready. They slowly move forward. Wanderers retreat deep into the park.

The Landscape After the Battle of Grunwald

"They walked attired like envoys with shields—one with the emblem of the Roman king with a black eagle on a golden background, the other with the shield of Szczecin princes with a griffin on a white background; each of them carried a sword, bare, without a sheath until they said that they were going to the king to bring messages. They were led to the hill where Jagiełło stood. The heralds had had faces full of arrogance, pride, and anger, they walked with some contempt, not very low bowing to the king. The one who carried the shield with the imperial eagle began to say: 'Your Highest Majesty, Grand Master sends these two swords to you and your brother, through us, his heralds, to help you with the upcoming battle so that you could come alive with your people, not lingering in battle, so that you would not hide in these groves and thickets, please come out to the open field . . .'"*

Suddenly, the sounds of a guitar chords flowed from the direction of the museum. They have seemed to come from the roof. Someone else turned the string up. Several-hundred-watt speakers trembled. Pigeons jumped from the ledge to fly. When the chord died down, drumsticks hit the drums, and when they also checked kettledrums and half-kettledrums, a male voice, checking the microphone, sounded in the speakers:

---

*Ryszard Filipski, Krajobraz po Grunwaldzie, published by Aurora, Kraków, 2011, Poland

"One, two, three. Sounds good."

The police cordon stopped. The police officers raised their heads looking for ringleaders on the roof. Then the guitar riff stuck into the wall of air. It was not difficult to recognize that introduction "Sweet Child of God" flowing down the strings. Drums and vocals followed. All winds flock here. Curious, they looked at the matter, consulted, then turned eights over the houses, and, lending of their backs to the sounds, they carried the beat to the city. There was a slight commotion in the park. It was now certain that the upheaval of music was coming from the roof. It was possible to see the blurred figures on it. The loudspeakers' power shook the windows of nearby houses. The vocals beautifully resonated with the phrases of lyrics.

"Hey you!" a high-pitched voice sounded again.

"Stop yelling from that roof!"

A guitar solo resounded in response.

"Hey you, you're disturbing public order."

Suddenly, the music stopped. A triumphant smile appeared on the face of an official. He handed it over to the left and right sides of the accompanying minor officials in a way that only can be done an influential person.

"We're not gonna negotiate," he exclaimed loudly through megaphone.

A moment later a loud laugh flowed from the roof loudspeakers. Then someone shouted:

"Hey, buddy! Leave us alone now!"

Then the guitar solo sounded again.

"I promise we won't harm a hair on your heads."

In response, the sound of an acoustic guitar and Hammond organ flow from the roof.

"Mother, should I trust the government?" A voice sang again. There were whistling and humming reverberating through the park.

A moment later, hip-hop beats hit. The calmest of the winds, the one that remains and circles over the park, speeds up slightly. It does not take away headgear yet, but it blows off some straw and earth dust from oblong potato mounds dug out between labeled trees and a nearby arboretum. People cover their eyes and mouths, and if someone has any food and drink, they cover this as well. A goose plucks the grass next to the pond. It goes wherever it likes. At the edge of the lawn, a little girl strolls in a white sailor suit and a hat with navy blue ribbons that hang to her shoulders. A boy walks beside the girl and picks daisies for her. A dog meanders among the people. It distrustfully approaches outstretched hands and sniffs offered food bites. It is even a little fastidious. It is probably prone to vagrancy, because it does not lie down long with a gnawed bone, and as soon as it rises with it and someone's hand wants to stroke the mutt, it puts a hair on its back and runs on. It feels best when it can run freely. A lilac cat (around fifteen pounds of live weight) strolling through the arboretum—just brought from home to work by a park gardener—escapes to a short, flower-covered self-seeding cherry. Clinging to the branches, it watches a chirping sparrow. The gardener allures the puss with catnip, but it only turns its tail up at it. Only when the dog is out of the cat's sight, the cat jumps down to its feline cradle, which the gardener installed her for his feline convenience. He brings an ax, spade and beer from the car. He spits in his hands and rubs saliva in them. After a while, the cherry tree falls dead. As he chops branches, he pushes the trunk with his foot into a shallow pit and covers it with soil. Then he tramples the ground and sprinkles it with grass seeds.

"No regret," he said under his breath, "it's just a cherry tree." Confused bees hover over the compacted ground. The blues sounds after the hip-hop hit. The police cordon loosens. The commander orders a short break, which officers take for a drink and a snack. A line quickly forms at the pizzeria and cart with hot-dogs. The official tries to snatch the megaphone from the officer's hand, but he hides it behind his back, politely, showing him the way to the limousine. Now an opera baritone sounds from the roof. The public in the park receives this very kindly. Some even tries to take on the singer but they are quickly silenced.

"There must've been a storm in New Jersey," says corpulent, very modestly dressed gentleman with a gray beard, eating a chicken wing.

"The ground's wet," he says, satisfied. The raised visor of his cap aimed at the Lord's window.

"It's a good bang on that roof," said an old man, sitting nearby on the grass, dressed in a worn-out coachman's uniform.

"I'm talking about the turmoil of the atmosphere, Ambrose."

"I know very well what it's about," said Ambrose, a coachman ex officio, as he likes to call his former occupation, today without a pension.

"If you're so wise," continued Ambrose, "tell me how long would a man stuck to a cannonball fly to the moon."

"I wish the field tomatoes were ripe already. When the full-faced Luna stares, chill does kill plums and pears," said the fat guy.

"Well, I'm waiting for an answer."

"It's so bad for you, but I do know the right answer."

"C'mon! Tell me. Judging by your hat, you served in the artillery."

"A bullet isn't a missile and can't match another bullet," the fat guy answers back. "The barrels are of different sizes too."

"Oh, yes, there's no doubt about that," Ambrose says astringently.

"So?"

"Thirteen hours, sir."

Ambrose turned his head with appreciation.

"And the railroad transport? How long does it take for a train to reach the moon?"

"There's not enough money for fries," murmured the fat guy.

"Ha ha!" Ambrose laughed. "I gotcha!"

"Some four hundred days. Do you have more questions?" The fat guy takes a tattered bookbinding masterpiece the size of a prayer book out of his leather shoulder bag.

"I never part from it," he said. "I like to read about the planets and stars when I have nothing better to do."

"I can't believe how small this world is," says Ambrose. He opens his backpack and takes out an identical book, and then a notebook.

"And the indigo children, where do they come from?"

The fat guy shrugged shoulders. Ambrose opens the notebook on the third page.

"Here's the answer."

The fat guy took a butcher's pot.

"I can see only scribble here."

"And let's keep it that way," says Ambrose. "As you can see it wasn't written for you, and you wouldn't read it out anyway."

The powerful hip-hop tunes and lyrics come from the museum's roof:

If you are proud,
Don't let the crowd
Tread on your toe,
They might be foes.
When you are meek
That means you're weak,
Then any lout
Will tune you out,
Any galoot
Will toot at you
As if you were
Some kind of twerp.
Give tit for tat –
Simple like that,
And they will know
You ain't John Doe,
And they will know
You are a bro,
But there's a guy
Who will deny
That blue is blue
'Cause it's his view;
Carroty hair—
His only flair,
And to his mind—
Rather no mind—
He is the ace,
Makes no mistakes,
He's always right to his delight.
He twits a lot,
And plots a lot—
Though he should act
And be exact.
Words should make sense,

Not to offense,
But you don't care,
You are aware
That there is more
That makes the core
Of life itself,
And when you delve
Into it deep,
You're gonna weep,
For all your past's
Gone like a blast,
And only hope
Is like a rope,
So you won't fall
From a tall wall.
Your future's bright
To your delight,
At the last trump
You'll be a trump.
One day with paupers' bible in hand
You're gonna know and understand
That nowhere is the Promised Land,
But here on earth flowered and manned.
"I heard somewhere this piece," says Ambrose and takes a hip
flask with liqueur from his backpack
"Can we drink it to get on friendly terms?"
"Sure," replies the fat guy.
They kiss each other's hands and reciprocate their deep bows.

EPILOGUE

Harameus and Monica set off across the lawn in the direction of the King Jagieło monument, near which the police began to handcuff the paupers. One of those poor
people, who still stood on his feet, bony and barefoot, covered with a faded cloth flung on his shoulders, prophesied and warned:

"A half of the metropolis and the entire South shall burn. Hectic teeming cities shall become empty. The megalopolis shall be left with only ashes and smoldering ruins. Diamonds shall not survive the fire."

The cops laughed at him and did not spare mockery, but, undiscouraged, he continued:

"Beyond the horizon of lands and waters, a destructive element, which no one shall be able to bring under control, is going to break out. There is still time to turn back." When he asked for water, someone threw a half-empty bottle at him, for which he repaid with a smile that emanated from his healing face. And after he had drunk and wiped his mouth, he boomed again:

"The die shall soon be cast!" A moment later, an officer handcuffed him and took him to the police van. The other paupers tried to explain something to those uniformed figures, but they were irreconcilable. A twelve- (thirteen at the most) -year-old teenager with a smooth face, spiral-shaped dark hair, arrested probably by some incomprehensible mistake, moved his manacled hands under his feet with quite an acrobatic skill, and from a sitting position, in which he was supposed to remain, jumped up and ran as fast as he could towards Belvedere Castle, on whose turret a city flag was fluttering. The uniformed figures set off in pursuit of him. He was devilishly artful, a rare crafty bugger. He nimbly avoided boulders and baby prams, lightly jumped over benches, and when he was nudged by a tattooed man's shoulder, who fell over and cast a torrent of coarse abuse at the him with a Caribbean accent. However, the rascal quickly apologized when he saw that a little girl in a stroller, pushed by her nanny staring at the phone, was watching him. To shorten his way, the running-away boy headed straight across the warm ford of the pond. Right on the shore, on the other side, he stepped in a shallow swamp. Jumping out of it, he threw away mud-heavy sneakers; he wanted to keep them, but seeing the approaching cops, he ran barefoot in the direction of the castle, where he hoped for shelter. His wild feline motor skills made him quickly gain advantage. The pursuit, however, did not give in. While he was banging on the door, the uniformed figures caught him and carried straight to the van. He shouted that it hurt him, that they were brutal, and he shouted out a few more words—but his mouth was quickly sealed with a tape. He freed himself again. It is impossible to comprehend how he did so. One of the officers tried to scoop his thin neck with his strong arm, but the wild cat broke free from the grip and, tireless, he ran again as fast as he could—very fast. His run for freedom was amazing, just heroic. He tore off the gag from his mouth and screamed out loud that he was born a free man and that the tyranny would soon be swallowed by hell. Then they released the beast. Like lightning flash, it followed him. Its tongue hung from its mouth. Thick, foamy saliva fell to the ground. Dark, motionless pupils aimed at the boy's back and neck. Its silhouette grew larger with each passing second. The beast had him within a jump. Only one bound to be on the boy's back. He had no fair chance of escape. He fell and cringed like a turtle, pulled his head to his knees, locked his hands on his ears and nape. Moments later, the chasers pulled the hound. The wild cat is theirs again.

The rooftop machinery suddenly fell silent. Monica pointed to the officer standing near Cleopatra's Spire, giving orders over the radio.

"He's the boss here," she said to Harameus, "I know him from the VIP box at the stadium."

They sped up their pace. "They were warned as well."

"This is exactly what happens when you pull a tiger by the tail," said the commander of the operation.

"Are you in charge here?" Harameus asked.

"Indeed, I am. What's your point?"

In the meantime, the door of the limousine parked nearby opened. The high-ranking official, who had previously squealed through a megaphone, put one foot shod in a white and brown shoe on the ground, then the other. He stepped on a cigar butt and blew the last cloud of smoke from his mouth. He scrambled out of the car. His big paunch could barely fit into his pants. Surprisingly, as he moved forward, his legs carried him gracefully and quickly.

"You are to blame for this mess," he said to Harameus, "you did want the concert."

"And you, as usual, turn up at the wrong time. Who do you serve?"

"What kind of question is it? To such people like you."

"You can't treat people like that," Monica interjected. "They're not fourth-class passengers."

"So, tell me which one?" He asked ironically.

Monica gave him a pitying look. "You're not afraid of God.

"Are you from a spiritual department? Ah, I've forgotten who I'm talking to," he said with derision.

Harameus took a step toward him and stood almost face to face.

"So, are you gonna beat me?" he asked, looking straight in Harameus's eyes, with a cocky smile. A revolver holster was distinguishable under the unfastened shiny nut-brown jacket, on which he placed his hand ostentatiously.

"What clownish taste," said Harameus, looking him up and down.

"Enough skirmishes, gentlemen. We don't need any more problems here," an officer said, and took a few steps towards them.

"Please release these people," said Harameus. "I'm begging you."

"It's not up to me. The chain of command is what it is." The officer looked at the official.

"Those who break the law will suffer severe legal implications," said the official with official pride. "They will feel the hand of justice real painfully."

"Whose justice?" Monica asked.

"There's only one justice—the only and right one."

"You represent some hooded court? These people deserve respect and their rights."

"Rights to what? To anarchy? They want hearth and home, and they can't even kindle a spark. Only vagrancy is on their minds."

"Don't make a fool of yourself," said Harameus. "When they kindle a spark, you'll be the first to hide yourself in a shelter. These people need help, not shackles."

"Procrust has turned into Robin Hood!" mocked the official. "I'm not gonna be fooled by the flowers you're festooned with."

"What a stubborn type. No movement of thought in this head can be seen."

"I've already finished the conversation with you, ma'am. And to you, sir, defender of the oppressed, I'm gonna say this . . . and I warn you that it won't be pleasant . . . "

"Don't hold back," said Harameus.

"Such people are a shame for any civilized country, and you are as well. Profanum vulgus ignavum pecus."

"Ecce homo!" Harameus replied immediately, and spat over his shoulder. A smirk flashed from the official's lips again.

"And you, do what you need to do," he said to the officer. "And without leniency."

"You have to somehow remedy this situation, chief," said the commander, stressing the word 'chief,' probably wanting to tickle the ego of the official.

"All the vans are already full."

"I have nothing else to add," the other replied, and walked over to the limo.

"And this is the guy who dreams of a senatorial chair," said Harameus.

"Police brutality is unacceptable."

"There're too many guns on the streets, ma'am."

"We owe this to wise guys like this crony," Harameus pointed at the limo. The commander lifted his cap and rubbed his forehead with his hand. Then he put his hand on the spine near the loins.

"Are you okay?" Monica asked.

"I'm fine, it will pass in a jiffy," he replied with a slight grimace of pain.

"A lead gift sometimes makes itself felt."

"Were you wounded?"

The officer smiled with difficulty. "Grim Reaper spared me once, but he left me a souvenir," he said. "Do you wanna see it?"

Monica looked a little confused. The commander took her hand and placed it on his spine.

"Is that—?"

"Yes ma'am, it's a bullet. The one of all five will stay with me to the end of my days.

"It's very sad. I sincerely feel sorry for you," Harameus interjected. "Believe me, these people are not dangerous. Please release them. I can pledge my word and money for them." The officer looked at the limo.

"It won't be easy, but I'll do my best to get them released." He nodded his farewell and walked away. After a while, Harameus and Monica returned to the Great Lawn. After less than half an hour, all the arrested were released. Shortly afterwards, pre-ordered warm food and provisions for the return journey were catered. Aromas rose from aluminum pans. A gust of wind carried the scent around. Soon the music again resounded on the roof of the museum. Harameus and Monica had a quick bite, and after having said goodbye to those around them, they headed for the Dakota building at 72nd Street. They walked slowly along the lanes, reminiscing about the day they met and their stay in the royal city on the Vistula River. They passed by Strawberry Fields and crossed the empty street. It was late evening.

Time slows down—almost stops. A horse carriage passes by. The silhouette of a huddled-up coachman blends up with the folding top. The horse's disheveled mane bounces along with its dark head and neck. The hoof-clatter echoes through the ravine of the street. The twilight chill fills tightly the air. Monica takes a silk scarf from her bag and drapes it around her shoulders.

They stop in front of the building. Orange flames flicker in gas lamps on both sides of the gate. They look up at the top floor. Through a half-open window flows piano music.

"Sounds beautiful," says Harameus. "Eighty-eight keys— white and black, black and white. Wonderful harmony."

"Yes, the former don't exist without the latter," says Monica.

"You know, I have an overwhelming feeling that someone has been following me for some time. Even now someone's eyes are lying heavy on my back."

Monica looks at him with heartfelt concern. Harameus embraces her and kisses her carefully and lightly.

"I love you," he whispered.

"The game's over!" All of a sudden, they hear behind them.

"Joker?" says Harameus

Birds spring from the trees and soar. The flock circles in the Umbrian sky, and change direction every now and again. The day fades into night. The skies are already dark, but still clear. A light wind sways the treetops. A pianist's fingers stroke the keyboard lightly. A lullaby calls to sleep. Memories fade away. Everything becomes so quiet and peaceful.

Made in the USA
Middletown, DE
26 June 2021